D0511562

Some Veil Did Fall

Some Veil Did Fall

Kirsty Ferry

Copyright © 2014 Kirsty Ferry

Published 2014 by Choc Lit Limited
Penrose House, Crawley Drive, Camberley, Surrey GU15 2AB, UK
www.choc-lit.com

The right of Kirsty Ferry to be identified as the Author of this Work
has been asserted by her in accordance with the Copyright, Designs and
Patents Act 1988

All characters and events in this publication, other than those clearly in
the public domain, are fictitious and any resemblance to actual persons,
living or dead, is purely coincidental

All rights reserved. No part of this publication may be reproduced,
stored in a retrieval system, or transmitted in any form or by any means,
electronic, mechanical, photocopying, recording or otherwise, without the
prior permission of the publisher or a licence permitting restricted copying.
In the UK such licences are issued by the Copyright Licensing Agency,
90 Tottenham Court Road, London, W1P 9HE

A CIP catalogue record for this book is available
from the British Library

ISBN 978-1-78189-161-2

Printed and bound by CPI Group (UK) Ltd, Croydon, CR0 4YY

For Shaun and James, with all my love. SSOS inc.

ROTHERHAM LIBRARY SERVICE	
B53090271	
Bertrams	22/10/2014
AF	£7.99
AST MAL	GEN

Acknowledgements

Thank you to my amazing family who have put up with me talking about writing and who have now learned to simply listen and nod where appropriate. Thanks also to the friends who have read various drafts of this book and who encouraged me to keep going. Huge thanks as well to my wonderful editor who helped me polish the manuscript to within an inch of its life and thanks also to my designer, who designed the most fabulously pink cover I've ever seen! Thanks to the lovely Tasting Panel members – Angela, Anna Maria, Berni, Emma, Julie, Liz, Olivia and Sarah. And the biggest thank you of all has to go to the Choc Lit team, who quietly and efficiently took this story from a manuscript to a novel and made it a dream come true. Thank you to everybody who helped me get this far – it means a lot.

Sudden Light

I have been here before,
But when or how I cannot tell:
I know the grass beyond the door,
The sweet keen smell,
The sighing sound, the lights around the shore.
You have been mine before, –
How long ago I may not know:
But just when at that swallow's soar
Your neck turned so,
Some veil did fall, – I knew it all of yore.
Has this been thus before?
And shall not thus time's eddying flight
Still with our lives our love restore
In death's despite,
And day and night yield one delight once more?

Dante Gabriel Rossetti

Prologue

The dream had been so vivid, so real, that Becky wasn't actually surprised – somehow, it made sense. The residual moments of the dream flashed through her mind and she remembered seeing a room, flooded with light. The windows were large and overlooked parkland. Full-length curtains fluttered out into the room as a summer breeze snaked through the casings. A piano stood in the corner, and she saw her fingers picking out a tune. A piece of paper, ornately decorated and embossed, lay on a desk.

Then she was in a bedroom. A mirror on a dressing table reflected the fireplace and a four-poster bed. In her dream she had picked up a silver-backed hairbrush and hurled it at the mirror. The mirror had shattered, cracks bursting across its surface, obscuring the reflection as a shadow appeared behind her.

Then she ran. She ran out of the bedroom, down the stairs, into the hallway and out of the door. She caught the scent of a storm that was threatening to split the sky open and saw a flash of her blue dress, scrunched up in her hands. She saw her feet steadily pounding across the grass and she prayed that nobody would stop her.

Everybody has secrets. It just depends on how many people discover them. He stood for a while on the edge of the cliff, watching the waves break against the rocks. Then he turned and walked away.

Part One

Becky stared at the crowds milling around the town. She couldn't help smiling at the fact that so many people had come out, braving the freezing cold and overcast weather in the skimpiest of outfits. Whitby's Goth Weekend was the perfect destination for a journalist/photographer/dabbling historian; which is how she would probably describe herself if anyone asked. Girls dressed in black lace thronged the streets and men wearing top hats and frock coats walked sedately next to them. It was the sort of event, Becky thought, which made you feel like the odd one out if you were not actually dressed the same as the others were.

Becky looked around, entranced. Where else, she wondered, would you be able to get so many photographs of fabulous Victorian costumes in the modern world? Bram Stoker had made Whitby scarily famous in his *Dracula* novel; so twice a year, in April and November, thousands upon thousands of vampire-lovers descended on the quaint little harbour town in North Yorkshire, all dressed in suitably vampiric clothes, to celebrate the Gothic, the undead and the idea of Dracula.

Becky herself lived in York, on the third floor of a lovely old converted Georgian house. Out of her kitchen window she could just see the spires of the minster and she had long ago learned to duck to avoid the slanting roof in her bathroom. Her flat existed in a constant state of journalistic disarray, and she didn't even have the excuse of it being a student house-share any more. Those days were long gone and now it was simply her own mess. York wasn't too far away from Whitby – but on a day like today, it was a world away. And, upon reflection, she did feel completely out of place in her usual uniform of jeans, boots and a sweater. But at least she was warm, unlike some of these lace-covered ladies who must have been shivering in their satins.

Becky raised her camera and took a close up of a middle-aged couple posing beside an old-fashioned hearse. She walked up to them smiling and passed the lady her business card. *Becky Jones, Freelance Journalist.* Nothing special there really, but it described her.

'Can I ask you a few questions?' she began. 'For my next article? I'm writing about Goth Weekend for *People's History* magazine. Basically, it's about why you come here, what you do when you're here, where you get your costumes from? That sort of thing. Our readers love to know the details.'

'Of course!' the lady answered. 'Just ask me. I'll tell you whatever you want to know.'

Becky smiled. 'Fantastic,' she replied. If there was one thing she had learnt over these last few hours, it was that these people were really friendly and usually more than willing to chat to her. She already had plenty of notes to work on when she got back to the hotel, safe in the knowledge that one of her most reliable editors would accept her article.

The lady began to tell Becky how her husband hadn't been bothered about such things until she had recommended he read Bram Stoker's *Dracula*. She'd been a librarian; he, a customer. It was the start of their courtship, she told her. Becky loved that word; *courtship*. It was so quaint, and the lady was so polite and talkative, Becky warmed to her immediately. It was difficult to associate such a lovely lady with the white-faced corpse-bride she was portraying, but in this town on this weekend, nothing was surprising any more.

Becky thanked the couple and wandered off into the crowds. The rustle of silk and satin surrounded her and the sombre mock-funeral procession that was parading up the street had more of a carnival atmosphere to it than loss or grief. Becky raised her camera again and snapped the head mourner as he went past. She squeezed herself through a few more people and snapped the trail of mourners at the back.

One girl in particular caught Becky's eye as she walked, silently and gracefully, behind the coffin. The girl's head was bowed and her hands were clasped together. Her golden hair was piled up in an intricate style and her white dress seemed to glide along the ground, a lace train fanning out behind her. Her profile was classically beautiful, the curve of her cheek smooth and pale. Becky raised her camera, trying to frame the girl perfectly in the viewfinder. She pushed the shutter just as someone jostled into her and knocked the camera off kilter. *Dammit!* Becky stumbled and swore under her breath. She pressed a few buttons to review the picture and discovered that the whole shot was blurred. All that was visible was a fair streak – apparently the girl's hair – and a white streak – supposedly her dress. Becky looked back at the procession, but the crowds had closed in and the girl had been swallowed up.

Becky was uncomfortably aware of warm breath on her neck. Her other senses kicked in, prickling at the feeling that someone was standing too close to her. She quickly turned around. A man, somewhere in his early thirties, stood there, his face contrite. He was clasping a paper cup with steam curling out of the top and brown liquid dripping off his fingertips.

'Did I get you?' he asked.

'Well and truly,' said Becky. 'Luckily it was just the photograph that was spoiled.' She looked pointedly at the paper cup. 'It could have been all over my camera.'

'I lost my latte,' he replied.

'And?'

'I need another one.'

'You need a lid,' said Becky. She turned, annoyed at his stupidity and went to follow the crowds up towards St Mary's Church. She was sure the girl would head up there. Photographers lurked around the cliff tops constantly, and that girl would make a stunning photograph, set against the sea.

Becky felt a hand on her shoulder and she swung around. The man was following her.

'Sorry – you know what, I've just realised something. It's Becky, isn't it? Becky Jones?' He frowned. 'If you aren't her, you look an awful lot like her. Your hair's a bit longer now though. But we're going back a few years I suppose. Hair grows.'

Becky stared at the man. He was tall, a good six inches taller than she was at least, and he had dark brown, tousled hair that seemed to have lost any style it was meant to be in. He was slim and had one of those open, friendly faces that instantly made anyone and everyone confide in him. But the telling thing was his eyes – one dark blue and one bright green, just like his sister's.

'Jonathon Nelson!' she said suddenly. 'You're Lissy's brother. Good grief. How long has it been?'

'So you *are* Becky then!' Jonathon smiled at her. 'And if you'll excuse the terrible yet not unexpected answer,' he bowed slightly, 'it's been far too long. And my friends call me Jon, by the way. I'll let you call me Jon too. If you call me Jonathon, I think I'm being told off.'

Becky laughed. 'All right. Jon it is. Actually, I haven't seen Lissy for ages. How is she?'

'She's fine. You know what she's like, she's a devil to keep tabs on. She was in Italy last week I believe. Or was it Cornwall? Maybe London? Who knows. She's around this weekend though, staying somewhere up the coast. She always loves Goth Weekend. I'll let her know I've bumped into you. Do you live in Whitby?'

'No, I'm only here for Goth Weekend but it would be so lovely to see Lissy if she is here,' said Becky. 'I think the last time I had more than a fleeting text conversation with her was when we celebrated our A-level results. You were probably well through university by then, though. You moved away after that, didn't you?'

'Yes, I stayed in Plymouth for a while, then I moved to Sussex. Then I came back here almost two years ago. But I remember when we were kids that you were always at our house. You and Lissy were the world's most annoying girls. Then from what I saw when I came home from uni, you only got worse as teenagers.'

'No we didn't!' said Becky with a laugh. 'But you, on the other hand,' she pointed her forefinger at him accusingly, 'you were just Lissy's horrible older brother that I had to put up with when I visited her.'

It was Jon's turn to laugh. 'I had a tough life, living with her!' he said. He shook his head, as if remembering the past and raked his dry hand through his hair, still smiling; the action made his hair even more tousled. 'Well, anyway, as I clearly need another latte,' he said, 'and we've clearly got a bit of catching up to do, how about I take you to get a coffee? It might be a bit warmer too.' Then he seemed to rein himself in. 'I mean, only if you're not too busy. Or meeting anybody. Or anything like that?' He regarded her hopefully out of those strangely attractive mismatched eyes. 'Are you?'

'It's very tempting,' she responded. 'But to be honest, I really want to find that girl I was trying to photograph before I do anything else.'

She scanned the area again, seeing the funeral procession winding its way up the steps towards the Abbey; but as the procession came fully into view, Becky could tell, annoyingly, that the girl was no longer at the end of it. She tried to look down the surrounding side streets but all she could spot was a seething mass of general humanity. Nobody stood out of the crowd like that girl had done. She cursed under her breath.

'That's my fault, isn't it?' Jon was contrite. 'Please, Becky. Let me get you a coffee. I have to now, to make up for it, or I'll feel bad all day.'

Becky looked at Lissy's annoying older brother properly, remembering him as he had been a few years back. Lissy's father was an Italian millionaire. Jon's was someone they never talked about. Yet as half-siblings they had still been close.

Becky tried to sum the adult Jon up in a word or phrase; a little trick she liked to do, trusting her instinct and seeing how close she was to the truth afterwards. The words *axe-murderer* and *psychopath* didn't spring to mind. *Clumsy*, *obstinate* and *harmless* did. Yep. Jon hadn't changed a great deal after all.

'Okay,' she sighed. 'The girl's disappeared so I might as well come with you. Where shall we go?' She cast a longing glance up to the Abbey and wondered if the girl had somehow clambered up all those steps after all and she had missed her.

'We'll never get in anywhere to sit down,' said Jon. 'The town's a bit busy today.'

'Just a bit,' said Becky, putting her camera back in its case.

'We can get some to go and take it back to my studio. I was heading there anyway when we bumped into each other.'

When you bumped into me, Becky wanted to add, but she refrained. Instead, her interest was piqued at the word 'studio'.

Jon must have seen her perk up as he nodded. 'I'm a photographer,' he said. 'That's what my degree was in and I have a studio just over there.' He pointed down one of the winding closes that led off the street. 'It's not huge, but at least we can sit down in peace and quiet. I just popped out for a breather, to be honest. It's been ridiculously busy today, which is fantastic, don't get me wrong, but when you're a one-man outfit you need a break from time to time. And I desperately wanted a proper coffee that I hadn't made from instant granules myself. I'll make sure the place stays shut for another half an hour or so, and then nobody will disturb us.'

'All right then,' Becky said, finally nodding decisively. 'You win. I'll come with you.' They turned and headed back towards the horde of black-swathed figures in the main street.

'So do you do landscapes or portraits?' Becky asked.

'A bit of both,' Jon replied. 'I make my living out of doing them both, anyway – I couldn't say which one I prefer. I do wedding photography too.' He looked sidelong at her, as if wanting to ask the question.

'I'm not married,' said Becky. 'Not even close.' A frown crossed her face as an image of Seb fluttered into her head. 'I was seeing someone, but he's an idiot, so no; no wedding photos for me, thanks very much.'

She shifted the camera bag further onto her shoulder and shoved her hands in her pockets. The wind was starting to bite. She was actually looking forward to the coffee and a warm place to drink it, but she wasn't going to admit that.

'Just here,' said Jon. He touched her lightly on the arm and she stopped outside a small café. 'They know me here and the coffee's good.'

Becky followed him in and the warmth and steam enveloped her. Her stomach rumbled as she smelled the hot food and Jon ordered two coffees to take away. There was a low hum of conversation around her, but she took no notice of it; rather, she gazed longingly at the cakes in the display cabinet. She opened her mouth to speak, but Jon was there first. 'Two ham sandwiches today, please, Lucy,' he said to the girl on the counter, 'and a slice of Victoria sponge I think. Oh – sorry, Becky. I didn't even ask. Is that okay? You're not vegetarian or anything are you?'

Becky shook her head. ''S'okay,' she said. 'Victoria sponge is fine too.'

'Er – make that two slices of cake, Lucy?' said Jon.

Becky saw him blush and smiled to herself. She considered adding *greedy* to her Jon list, but her thoughts were interrupted as he shoved two paper cups into her hands.

'Can you manage these?' he asked. 'I'll take the food.'

Becky turned to the girl behind the counter. 'Do you have a cup holder?' she asked. The girl smiled and passed one over the counter. Becky pushed the cups into the cardboard holes and looked at Jon. 'Ready?' she asked.

'I think so,' he said. 'Come on, this way.'

They pushed through the door of the café and walked towards Jon's studio, Becky balancing the cup holder and inhaling the warm steam as it drifted out of the lid. Jon turned up a side street and waited for Becky to follow him. Then he walked halfway up and unlocked the door of a small building, tucked between a jeweller's and a sweet shop.

'Welcome to my humble abode,' he said, as Becky walked in past him.

'Wow!' was all she could say. The studio was done up like a Victorian photographers, with a variety of props pushed to the side. A few backdrops were hanging up and there was a cubicle in the corner, with a red velvet curtain hanging across the doorway. Becky looked around and saw a wardrobe against the other wall. Clothes hung on a rail beside it, all of them resembling old-fashioned costumes. She spotted ball gowns and riding habits and frock coats similar to the ones the men were sporting in the town. There were top hats and bowler hats, wigs, bonnets and picture hats hanging on hooks attached to the wall, and a variety of gloves, accessories and even a riding crop lying on a circular table that housed an aspidistra in the centre.

'This place is amazing!' Becky said, setting the coffees down on a counter. 'In all the years I knew you, you never struck me as a person who would pay such attention to detail.' She walked over to the table and fingered the riding crop. She picked it up and weighed it in her hands. An image flashed into her head of it curling against a long, flowing, dark green skirt, then resting against the flank of a black pony.

'Perfect,' she said, more to herself than to Jon. She looked up at him. He was leaning against the counter smiling. 'So you own *this* sort of portrait studio,' she said. 'I've always wanted to get my picture done in one of these places. Just to see what I'd look like as a Victorian.'

'This is the best place to do it,' replied Jon. He took one of the cups and held it out to Becky, who took it from him gratefully. 'I'm usually pretty busy, especially at times like this. People come to Goth Weekend and get totally caught up in the atmosphere of the place. Then some start to regret that they didn't get dressed up. They find me and come in and we get them dressed up to match. Believe me, if I unlocked that door now, there is no way we could drink our coffees in peace. There would be people baying for blood – or at least demanding that they want to look like a corpse. However, for you I'm prepared to cut myself a little slack and have a break. What do you think of this?'

He pulled another curtain away from the wall and Becky laughed. The rack held nothing but black clothing and the selection seemed to include a vast amount of lace and ruffles.

'Hey, I might just try it myself!' she said. 'I've been feeling a bit left out, if I'm honest. Jeans don't seem to cut it here this weekend.'

'Help yourself,' said Jon. 'Have a look at all the clothes first though. The best outfits are in the wardrobe.' He walked across and took hold of the door handle.

'Am I going to end up in Narnia?' asked Becky.

'I don't think so,' said Jon. 'Nobody else has. Mind you, they never came back out to tell me if that's where they'd ended up. I'm joking!' he added hurriedly as Becky's mouth started moving to answer him.

Jon pulled open the door and Becky gasped. If the gowns on the racks had been beautiful, these ones were sublime. She reached in and grasped hold of a rose-pink dress, carefully unhooking it from the hanging rail.

'This is pretty,' she said, spreading the skirt out and holding it against herself. She looked down and poked her foot out from the bottom, giving it a little wiggle. 'But maybe not with my boots.'

'No,' said Jon, shaking his head. 'It's not your colour. Here. Try this one.' He rummaged around and unhooked something. He pulled it from the wardrobe and held out a bundle of pale cream satin, which he had draped over both forearms. Becky took it from him and let the fabric unfurl. The skirt dropped to the floor and revealed not only panels of the cream satin, but ice cream layers of white lace on top of it. There were tulle frills, swansdown trimmings and the twinkle of tiny crystals all over the dress. Becky's eyes widened and she was, for once, lost for words.

'It's gorgeous,' she managed eventually. 'Just beautiful.' She looked up at Jon. 'It's hardly Goth though?'

'Not really Goth, no,' conceded Jon. 'I think it's nicer though, don't you?'

Becky nodded, her eyes drawn back to the soft material. 'Is it genuine?' she asked.

'No, it's not genuine,' said Jon. 'It would be far too fragile to handle if it was, let alone wear. The original is probably in a museum somewhere. This is a copy. I do a lot of research into historical costume for the studio. This dress is from the 1860s. I saw a Landseer portrait of a lady wearing it, and had someone make it up for me. It wasn't cheap and it's not something I do very often. Sometimes an outfit catches my eye and I'll push the boat out. That's why I don't let people into the wardrobe very often. It's only for the special customers, such as the bridal parties and so on that come down here on honeymoon.

'For instance, look at these, the normal stuff.' He tugged on a couple of things from the rail outside the wardrobe and showed Becky the backs of them. The items were all cunningly held together with Velcro – easy to slip on and off. The dress she was holding, however, was sewn up properly; a complete dress.

'How clever!' said Becky. 'The Velcro, I mean.'

'One size fits all,' quipped Jon. He dropped his voice. 'You wouldn't believe the size of some of the people who come here and want photos taken. I've got to cater for everyone.'

'I bet you do,' replied Becky. 'You know what I'm going to ask, don't you?' Her eyes slid over to the cubicle. 'Please?'

Jon laughed. 'Well, just because you're Lissy's friend and

as another way to make up for the photo I ruined, I'll let you try it on and I'll even take your photograph. Deal?'

'How much do you charge?' asked Becky.

'I'm in a good mood,' said Jon. 'It's free today for you alone. On one condition, though.'

'What's that?'

'Have your lunch first and wash your hands before I let you wear it, okay?'

'Seems reasonable to me,' said Becky with a wide smile. 'Okay. It's a deal.'

'Oh, and you might need this,' said Jon. He rummaged again and pulled out a bundle of frothy petticoats. 'Otherwise you won't get the full effect.'

'I have to have the full effect,' replied Becky. 'Otherwise, what's the point?'

After they had eaten their sandwiches and cake, Becky shut herself inside the cubicle, pulling the curtain closed. The curtain material was heavy and effectively sound-proofed the tiny room. There was a hook on the wall for her clothes, and another that she carefully hung the dress up on while she changed. She pulled her jersey over her head, kicked her boots into the corner and tugged her jeans off, draping them over a small table. As an afterthought, she took her socks off; she couldn't imagine taking herself seriously as a Victorian lady wearing thick, green socks. She smiled at the thought and tied the petticoats around her waist. There were no half measures here – no child's hula hoop used as a fake crinoline; just layer upon layer of lacy, white petticoat. Becky adopted a new admiration for the Victorian ladies when she felt the weight of the underskirts. It can't have been easy wearing those all day, she thought.

She turned to take the dress off the hanger. Ridiculously excited, she pulled the gossamer-white material over her head and shimmied into the bodice. The skirts fell with a *swish* to the ground and, awkwardly, she managed to fasten up the back, cursing the fact that she didn't have a ladies' maid on hand. Finally she stood and stared at herself in the full-length mirror.

'Oh my,' was all she managed. She didn't recognise herself. Gone was the feisty, twenty-first century career girl. In her place was a girl of indeterminate age, huge eyes searching for some sort of self-recognition in the reflection. Becky lifted her dark chestnut hair up and held it on the top of her head, imagining herself as the owner of the dress in the 1860s. She jumped as a roll of thunder interrupted her thoughts and she remembered how grey and overcast it had been in the town earlier. They had just come in here at the right time. It must have been a loud rumble, she thought, cocooned as she was in the quiet, comforting stillness of the changing room. Devouring the impromptu lunch and bumping into Jon again had put her in a good mood, and she smiled at her reflection.

'Lady Rebecca,' she murmured, curtseying to herself. '*So* pleased to meet you.'

'*Ella*,' came a female voice from somewhere behind her right shoulder.

Becky spun around; no mean feat in a dress that weighed as much as this one did. 'Who was that?' she asked. Nobody answered. Becky was still alone in the changing room and she turned back to the mirror, her heart pounding. *Imagination overload*, she scolded herself but, nevertheless, yanked the curtain back and stood in the entrance to the changing room, face to face with Jon, half-expecting to see someone in the room with him. He was alone.

Jon's jaw dropped, then he stared at her in awe and

finally shook his head. 'Amazing,' he said. 'It looks perfect. You don't look a bit like the girl who was wearing it in the portrait, but you can definitely carry off that style. Lissy couldn't carry it off, even if she tried. She's way too short. But your hair is wrong – their hairstyles tended to reflect their dresses, did you know that? But it doesn't matter, let me take your photograph right now.'

'It would have been a bit freaky, I think, if I'd walked in here and you'd thought I was the reincarnation of the lady in the portrait,' said Becky. 'What did she look like, though?'

'Very freaky,' agreed Jon, with a shiver. 'She was blonde, as I recall. And I'm not entirely sure who she was. I just saw her in a museum catalogue, if I'm honest. Some art gallery had her portrait on loan and it was the dress that caught my eye. Lissy collects all the catalogues for me. She knows what I like and she's got more time than me to go to these places.' He laughed. 'If only, eh?'

'Lissy got the catalogue for you?' asked Becky. 'How did she manage that?'

Jon laughed again. 'Little Elisabetta has her methods. Don't you worry about the "hows". I don't.'

'Ella?' asked Becky suddenly, remembering the name that she had heard spoken in the cubicle. 'Does she ever get called Ella now? Or is she still Lissy?'

'No. It's always Lissy or Elisabetta. Why do you ask?'

'No reason,' said Becky. She took an apprehensive step forward and then picked up the skirts of her dress. 'I really don't want to trip over this thing,' she said, changing the subject. 'I don't know how Victorian ladies managed.'

'I don't suppose they had a choice,' he said. 'Can you walk over here? Then we can arrange you properly and sit you down.'

Becky walked slowly over to Jon, enjoying the swaying feel of the skirts hanging off her hips. 'I'd love to see the portrait of the girl,' she said. 'I think it helps to put names to faces, doesn't it? In fact, it's just given me an idea.'

'Oh?' asked Jon. 'I hope it's legal.'

'Of course it is!' said Becky. 'I was always a good girl, remember? I just think it would be an interesting project to research her. To see if we can find out more information; maybe about where she lived and if she has any descendants. Then you can get the descendants down here, put a female one in that dress and do a "then and now" thing.'

Becky's mind, always on the hunt for a new article idea, began to swarm with possibilities. 'I really think it would work,' she said, half to herself. She made a mental note to pitch it to the editor of *Victorian World* magazine as soon as possible.

'That sounds great,' said Jon. 'You say "we" and I assume it is the royal we. Then you said I could get her down here, so are you involving me then?' he asked with a hint of a smile on his face.

She rolled her eyes. 'I suppose I am, yes,' she said. 'Sorry. I have a habit of getting carried away, you know what I'm like. Just tell me where to get off, that's fine. You wouldn't be the first one.'

Becky sat carefully in a chair that Jon had pulled over into the portrait area and he helped her arrange her skirts, flipping them out and smoothing them down as she settled in position. Jon disappeared behind a big, square, old-fashioned camera on a tripod and began adjusting the lens. Becky stared around the room and her eyes settled on a walnut box that was sat upon a table. It was clearly a prop of some description and she looked at it covetously.

'I want one of those,' she said. The plain old box was, she knew, one of those clever contraptions that unfolded into a writing slope. 'I have one on my wish-list. Is that genuine at all?'

'Hmmm?' Jon ducked back out from behind the camera. 'Oh, the writing slope. Yes, it's original, or so I'm led to believe. Lissy got it for me. I think they used them as portable writing desks or something, didn't they? I don't really know. Lissy told me it was Victorian.'

'She was right. And it's very in character for my costume,' said Becky, still staring at it. 'I think it would be good in this photo, don't you?'

'If you want it, we can bring it over,' said Jon.

Becky watched as he carefully moved the box and table over to her and she knew her eyes must be gleaming with avarice. It was decorated with a coat of arms and embossed with three golden initials: *L.J.C.* Becky ran her hand over the decoration and she couldn't help herself as her fingers slid down and took hold of the little key in the lock. She turned it, and with a tiny click it opened up and she lifted the lid. She breathed in a musty scent of old leather, ink and wood and, carefully, she unfolded the slope. The slope revealed a green, baize surface and two inkwells at the back. A small holder between them was clearly for pens and Becky knew there would be several little compartments for stamps and paper underneath the slope mechanism.

'These things always had secret compartments as well,' Becky murmured, more to herself than to anyone else. She leaned forward, feeling around to see if she could find a lever.

'You won't find it,' said Jon, who had returned to his camera. 'But I just took the most beautiful photograph of you trying.'

Becky looked up, surprised. Jon smiled. 'I'll do another photo. I just wanted to capture that moment – you were so intense. Your hair was kind of falling forward and you looked, well, amazing.' He shrugged. 'Sorry. I'm into art. I see moments and I act on them. That split second was a perfect shot and I couldn't let it go.'

Becky was still staring at him as if she hadn't heard him. 'Won't find it?' she repeated. 'Why ever not? It's here. Look.' She turned back to the inkwells and pulled up one of the dividers. A drawer sprung open beneath the inkwells, revealing a small gap, which reached right to the back of the box. 'And it's still got her things in it,' she whispered.

Becky leaned over and peered into the drawer. Maybe she would find something really exciting. She saw a grey, dried out twist lying inside the compartment. Unlike the fabric in the lid of the slope, the compartment was lined with soft, red velvet. Hidden away for a hundred and fifty years or so, the velvet hadn't worn at all. Becky pulled a face; she had been hoping for something a little more exciting than something grey and decaying. Hesitantly, she poked her fingers inside and drew out the object. Her eyes widened as she saw the tiny bobbled heads and the delicate stalks of the twist.

'Oh!' she breathed. 'Lavender. Dried lavender.' She smiled. Okay, so it was pretty old and dusty now – in fact, it was breaking up as she held it and turned it slowly around in her fingers – but it must have meant something to someone, mustn't it?

An image suddenly appeared to Becky. She smelled the sea and a vision of a fair-haired woman flitted across her mind's eye. The woman was linking arms with a tall, dark-haired man but their faces weren't very clear at all. Becky looked down at the bunch of lavender in surprise. She'd always had a vivid imagination, it was what had driven her towards her career path; this couple was probably the product of it, just how she visualised a loving couple of that era. She smiled at the writing slope and tucked the lavender back inside. How lovely; a keepsake from him to her.

'Is that all there is?' said Jon. His voice broke into her thoughts. 'That's disappointing.'

'No, I think there's other stuff in there as well,' she said. She pushed her fingers inside the compartment and felt around. She could feel thick card and managed to grab a corner of the object, drawing it towards her. It revealed itself to be a small, rectangular invitation of some sort, with gilded letters printed on embossed cream card, which showed the same coat of arms as the one that was on the lid. Becky carefully picked the card up and turned it in her hands.

You are cordially invited to attend
a Celebratory Dinner Party
15th of July, 1863.
Eight o'clock in the evening.

Becky smiled. She began to imagine gorgeous dresses and sumptuous coaches; handsome gentlemen and beautiful ladies. 'I'm getting too carried away with this lot,' she said. 'My imagination is going into overdrive. There's more as well. How come you never found any of these things?' she complained to Jon.

He shrugged his shoulders. 'I never found the secret compartment,' he said. 'It never bothered me enough to keep trying.'

Becky shook her head, and tucked a stray strand of chestnut hair behind her left ear. 'Men,' she muttered. 'Look. What's this?' She pulled out another sheet, folded this time, and just ordinary paper. She began to unfold it carefully, smoothing the creases out. 'Oh my, this is so delicate. It's been in here for years. We're lucky it hasn't rotted or anything.'

She turned the paper over so the printed side faced her. 'What on earth?' she said. 'Oh!' Her eyes widened. She was holding a sheet that showed the hand formations for finger spelling in sign language. She lifted her hands up and spelled out her name. 'I'm slow at this,' she said.

Jon moved away from the camera and came over to have a closer look. 'Well, look at this!' he said, pulling the paper towards him. 'It's not something I would have expected to see in there.' He tried to shape the letters J-O-N and stared at his hands, as if they wouldn't agree to conform.

Becky laughed, watching his attempts. 'Do you have dyslexic fingers?' she asked. 'That was nothing like your name.'

'It's nothing I've ever had cause to use,' he admitted. 'I could learn, I suppose, if I ever needed to.'

'You could,' said Becky, 'but this looks like somebody tried and failed. That's probably why it's been shoved in here.'

'I don't suppose they took too much time to learn it, really,' said Jon. 'In Victorian times they probably thought if people could lip-read that would be enough. Look at Princess Alice of Battenberg. I think I read somewhere that she could lip-read in four different languages.'

'That might have been all right for the privileged classes,' said Becky. 'But what about the ordinary people? They wouldn't be able to do that – and I can't imagine anyone taking the time to learn how to communicate with them in any other way. They'd just be written off. It must have been really lonely for them.' She fingered the piece of paper with the symbols on. 'Someone tried to use it, though.'

'Yes, but this box looks as if it's come from a pretty affluent household, don't you think?' said Jon. 'Perhaps they had no need to use the alphabet after all.'

'If I dig deeper I might find an ear trumpet,' said

Becky with a laugh. 'Perhaps that's why they abandoned the lessons.' As she spoke, she felt around inside the compartment and smiled as her fingertips touched another piece of paper. 'One more thing,' she said. She pulled the paper out and slid it onto the table. 'Sheet music,' she said in surprise. 'Well, I never.'

'Let me see that,' said Jon. He picked it up and studied it. Becky watched his face as he frowned and muttered to himself. He was just as nice as she remembered him. He was six years older than Lissy and Becky and he had usually been quite tolerant of them, apart from when they had really, *really* pushed it. And she had to admit, the years had been pretty good to him and the boy she had known had turned into a very attractive man. She had almost forgotten about the coffee spillage in fact. It was turning out to be an interesting afternoon.

The frown suddenly cleared from Jon's face and he looked at Becky. 'Mozart,' he said. 'It's one of his more romantic pieces, I think. *Là ci darem la mano*. It's from *Don Giovanni*.'

Becky looked at him blankly. 'I don't understand Italian,' she said. 'What does it mean in English?'

'Oh, sorry – it's something like, *there we will join our hands*,' said Jon.

'Opera's not my strong point, which isn't surprising, really,' she said, 'but how do you know all that?'

'Remember that big piano in the hall?' he said. 'That was mine. I had lessons, but I didn't play it as much as I should have done and I still don't bother much now, but some things just stick with you.' He nodded to the sheet music. 'For instance, I can still sight-read this sort of stuff.'

'I'm not musical at all,' said Becky. 'Good job you are here. I could never have fathomed it out.'

'Well, you worked out the other sheet,' said Jon. He

looked at his fingers again and flexed them. 'You'd think I would be able to do that spelling thing after learning piano.'

'Probably different parts of the brain,' said Becky with a smile. 'We've all got our strengths.' She sat back in the chair and fingered the items from the writing slope thoughtfully. 'What an odd collection, though. I need to piece it all together I think.'

'Now it's back to "you" piecing it together. It was "we" before. Remember, when you wanted the portrait lady's details?' said Jon.

Becky realised there was no malice in his voice. She lifted her hands up and shrugged her shoulders. 'You can help,' she said. It was so strange. She hadn't given him more than a passing thought for years, but she felt an affinity with him. Her instincts had been right.

'So you wouldn't mind meeting again? With or without Lissy?' She realised Jon was speaking again as he moved back to the camera. 'That's good to hear, anyway.'

'Yes, I think it would be a good plan,' replied Becky. 'Do you want me to pose properly now? So we can get this picture done?'

'Yes please. I'm so glad I spilled that coffee on you before.'

Becky laughed as Jon clicked the shutter. Then she realised that was the wrong sort of expression. She made her face expressionless and stared at the camera. Jon raised his thumb over the top and clicked the shutter again.

'Perfect,' he said.

Becky took the dress off carefully and hung it back on the hanger, hooking it on the door of the changing room and putting her own clothes back on. She looked at herself in the mirror and half smiled.

'Hello, Becky,' she said to her reflection. 'You're not quite Lady Rebecca any more, are you?' She sighed. 'Never mind.' She pulled open the door and brought the dress reverently out of the changing room. She handed it to Jon and sighed again as she saw it disappear into the Narnia wardrobe.

He shut the door and turned back to face her. 'I'll padlock it later,' he said, 'just to make sure you don't go back in for it.'

'Hardly likely,' she said. 'It's not like I could get in here on my own. I'm assuming you have an alarm system in place? One that needs a certain combination to get in, perhaps?' She put her head on one side. 'Eighteen ninety-seven,' she said suddenly. Jon's face registered surprise and she saw him slide his gaze to the door. She turned, following it and laughed. 'Nice one,' she said, 'that's the combination and the keypad worked out.'

'How did you …?' he asked.

'Hmm? How did I do it? I don't know.' She shrugged her shoulders. 'It just came to me. Oh – it's also the date that *Dracula* was first published so maybe I had an inkling; especially since you have a copy of the book right there, right next to the door. Probably in case you forget – you can just look inside, can't you?'

'Unbelievable,' said Jon. 'Of course, I'm forgetting you're a journalist now. You lot poke around places all the time.'

'I'm not that sort of journalist,' replied Becky, putting her camera inside her bag and zipping it up. 'I have to go. I need to find my hotel. It's been very nice meeting you again, Jon.' She held her hand out to shake his and he took it. He held it, she noticed, for a little too long.

'Where are you staying?' he asked. 'I can probably help you find it.'

'I have satnav, thanks,' she said.

'Oh, come on, surely it's better to have a human direct you sometimes?'

'Maybe it is, but I need to get there quickly. I have a bag full of notes to sort through, photos to download and I have an article on a deadline. I need to find this blasted hotel before it gets any darker and the thunder starts up again.'

'What thunder?' asked Jon.

'The rumble that went on when I was getting changed,' said Becky. 'You must have heard it! I did.'

'I couldn't hear any thunder,' said Jon, shaking his head.

'Oh,' said Becky. 'I was pretty sure I heard some.'

'Nothing I heard,' replied Jon, still shaking his head. 'Which hotel is it, anyway?' He smiled, disarmingly.

Becky narrowed her eyes. 'I don't know if I can tell you,' she replied. 'What if you've changed into some weird stalker type who follows me there instead of that innocent boy from the countryside?' She paused, wondering if her sixth sense would jump in; no, no *stalker*-type phrases came to her mind. *Good company* did, however. She sighed. 'Okay. I'll tell you. Are you going to follow me there, by any chance?'

Jon stared at her, exuding innocence. 'Probably,' he said. 'If they do good evening meals I might just come along and try one. Oh, don't look like that, Becky. I'll go home and get showered and changed first. Then you won't be ashamed of me when we sit together—'

'Enough!' she cried. 'It's Carrick Park. It's a few miles north of here, on the moors. I've never been before; it was the only place I was able to book into with it being Goth Weekend. It looks nice on the website.'

'Carrick Park. Very grand,' replied Jon. He bowed mockingly, doffed an invisible cap, then said something that seemed to involve the words 'reet' and 'crackin'.

'What was that meant to be?' enquired Becky, frowning. 'I didn't understand a word of it.'

'Sorry. That was broad Yorkshire,' replied Jon. 'Come

on, you've lived here long enough. Anyway, I couldn't resist. I said it seems like a nice place.'

Becky shook her head in despair. 'If you say so,' she said. 'Right, I'm going now. No doubt I will see you later.' She turned and walked out of the studio, closing the door smartly behind her. If he was at all sensible, he would see the business card she had left on the table by the *Dracula* book. She smiled to herself as she felt her phone vibrate. She took it out of her pocket and read the text message. I'm changing the key code right now, it said.

'No you're not,' said Becky, putting the phone back in her pocket and hitching her bag over her shoulder. She looked around the darkening streets at the people wandering about, still dressed in deliciously Gothic costumes and she shivered with pleasure.

It was only when she was driving away from the Abbey car park, that she realised she hadn't managed to track the girl from the procession down after all.

Becky's phone vibrated again on the car seat next to her as she followed the satnav's directions to Carrick Park. Driving along a country road, she didn't dare chance looking at it – the night had really 'put in' as Becky's granny used to say, and it was a strangely silent and fogbound road she travelled.

'Middle of nowhere,' she muttered, slowing the car down as she went around yet another bend. Her headlights glinted off a signpost pointing to Carrick Park and she felt her heart rate slow down to that of mild panic as opposed to pure terror, knowing that she couldn't be that far away now. A third of a mile, according to the satnav – and not a yard too soon, she admitted. For a fleeting moment she felt guilty about Jon driving all the way out here, but she quashed the thought as she admitted to herself that it might actually be quite nice to see him again. She smiled as she saw the lights up ahead, by the side of an enormous gateway. Once, she imagined, there would have been huge iron gates between the posts.

Becky drove through the gateway and along a one-time carriage drive studded with brightly lit lamp posts, which led towards the hotel car park. She pulled up into a space and put the handbrake on thankfully. She picked up her phone and saw the text message. Jon again. What's it like? Are you there yet?

Becky quickly typed an answer. It's nice. Stop stalking me. She pressed 'send'. Almost immediately, a smiley face icon came back and she groaned, stuffing the phone into her pocket as she made to leave the car. It vibrated again. See you at 8. She shook her head and went around to the boot to haul her case out.

The hotel had once been an old house, that much she had gathered, and tonight it was lit up rather spectacularly with floodlights outside. Becky stared at the honey-coloured stone and porticoed doors, the roof of the massive porch-like structure over the entrance supported by beautiful classic columns. There was something familiar about it that she couldn't quite place. All of a sudden she shivered as if someone had breathed air onto her neck. She looked around, but there was nothing near her except the darkness. She hurried up the staircase onto the wide, front step as fast as she could, bearing in mind the weight of her luggage, and pushed open the big, panelled front door.

Becky found herself in an entrance hall with a grand staircase leading up the centre. It split into two and she knew without a doubt that her room was on the left hand side, three rooms along the corridor. She felt something brush past her and again she shivered, her eyes seeking out Reception – a small desk to the left of the staircase, guarded by a neat receptionist whose dark hair was almost as shiny as the mahogany staircase.

'Hello, I have a room booked in the name of Rebecca Jones?' she said, putting her case on the floor.

'Certainly, Miss Jones. It's room one hundred and thirteen, it's just—'

'Up the stairs to the left and three doors along?' said Becky mechanically.

The receptionist looked impressed. 'It certainly is, Miss Jones. Have you stayed with us before?'

Becky simply smiled and dropped her head, studying the papers she needed to fill in for her stay. She hoped it would stop the woman asking any more questions. Her tactic appeared to work as the receptionist didn't pursue the point. Becky pushed the paperwork back to the girl and tucked her hair behind her left ear again. *Damn you, nervous habit*, she thought. What was there to be nervous about here, anyway, for God's sake? The place felt familiar. It felt – and she hated that she was even thinking such nonsense – as if she was coming home.

The receptionist handed over her room key and Becky bent to pick her case back up from the floor before setting off up the stairs.

Becky was at the first landing, where the staircase split into two, and it was as she turned to climb the next flight, that she found herself facing a full-length portrait of a woman whose hair rivalled the honey colour of the stones outside.

'Good Lord,' she said. A jolt of pure recognition flooded through her and she stared at the girl. She had sapphire-blue eyes that seemed to drill into your deepest thoughts and a creamy complexion, set off by perfectly red lips. She wasn't exactly smiling. There was a hint of something Becky understood in her eyes, but she couldn't put a word to it; a struggle, perhaps, or a need for acceptance. But the thing that stood out most for Becky was the dress the girl was wearing. It was exactly like the one she had tried on at Jon's studio that afternoon, even down to the tiny crystals that covered it. They seemed to twinkle out from the portrait under the electric lighting and she stood entranced by the girl. Becky, with no thought for her luggage, dumped her case on the landing and ran back down the stairs. She seemed to know exactly where to place her feet and that the third step from the bottom was uneven. *Shut up!* she told herself. *You came up them, you know that from a minute ago.*

'Please, excuse me,' she said to the startled receptionist. 'That portrait on the stairs. Who is she? I've seen something similar in a museum catalogue,' she fibbed.

The receptionist smiled suddenly and nodded as if she was talking to a very stupid child or a slightly mad woman. 'That's right, a museum catalogue,' she said. 'Lady Eleanor has been on loan to the British Museum for a while for the Landseer Portraiture exhibition. She only came back this week.'

'Lady Eleanor?' Becky said. And again, it was as if someone shouted the name in her head. *Ella.* She felt faint and slightly dizzy and stood staring at the receptionist. 'Ella,' she said.

'No, Miss Jones. Eleanor.' The girl enunciated it slowly, giving Becky a queer look that spoke volumes.

'I'm sorry – it's been a long drive here,' Becky said. 'I think I'm ready for some food and a rest. Tell me, can I book a table in the restaurant?'

'You can, Miss Jones. What time?' The receptionist clicked the end of her pen and flicked open the restaurant reservations list.

'Eight o'clock please. For two.' Becky almost choked on the words. Jon had to turn up tonight. For the first time, she desperately hoped he wasn't teasing her and would do his stalker-ish best to come to Carrick Park that night.

'Miss Jones,' said the receptionist, 'your name is already in for that time.'

'What?' said Becky. 'You mean there's a reservation already?'

'Yes,' said the receptionist looking at her oddly again. 'There's a note beside it – we have to tell you that a Mr Jonathon Nelson—'

'Oh, thank God!' said Becky, laughing maniacally. 'He's already done it! Thank you. Thank you so much. Sorry to bother you. I'll go now, shall I?' She backed away from the desk, feeling a strange mixture of elation and embarrassment. *Thank God for my stalker!* she thought. Then she turned and headed up the stairs again. She retrieved her case and practically ran up the second flight of stairs, taking care not to look at Lady Eleanor as she passed. She had the feeling Lady Eleanor was looking back at her though.

Becky found the room just where she had anticipated, unlocked the door and walked in dumping her case and shoulder bag on the floor. She sat down on the bed and stared into the dressing table mirror. In the absence of another human being she spoke to her reflection, feeling slightly ridiculous.

'Ella? Are you Lady Eleanor?' She listened carefully for an answer, but nothing came. 'Ella. I can't hear you. Are you here?' she continued. 'I wore your dress today. Did you see me?' Nothing. Then that odd little draught against her neck again. 'Oh, for goodness sake.' Becky stood up. 'Look, I don't know who you are or what you want, but if you are Lady bloody Eleanor trying to get my attention, then please don't blow on me!'

She headed towards the en suite and turned the bath taps on as far as they would go. She felt her taut muscles begin to relax as the steam rose up and swirled around the room, and she tipped a generous helping of bath salts in for good measure. The hotel management had very kindly left a good selection of toiletries in the bathroom and she made a mental note to kidnap any residual ones at the end of her stay.

She got ready for her bath, stripping down and discarding her working gear in a pile on the floor before easing herself into the water. She closed her eyes and lay back; blessed peace and quiet and nobody to disturb her – the favourite part of her day. If that woman's voice invaded her privacy here she would be *really* annoyed.

Half an hour later, Becky decided it was probably time to re-enter civilisation. She sighed and climbed out of the bath, finding a lovely big towel to dry herself off with and then wrapping herself in a white, fluffy robe, again provided by the hotel. She sat in front of the mirror and blasted her hair with the hairdryer, brushing it out until it hung straight and shiny past her shoulders. She debated putting it up, then decided she might as well. A couple of swift movements and it was in a loose knot at the back of her head. She raked through her case and found her black dress, the only nod to sophistication she owned, and packed for just such an occasion as a meal in the hotel. She finished it off by slipping pearl earrings in, putting a little make-up on and squirting her perfume in a floral haze around her, before she walked through it. The fumes tickled her nose and she coughed. Never mind; it was worth it.

There, she thought eventually, *that'll have to do*. She stared at herself in the mirror, a world away from the girl in the evening gown this afternoon. She shivered as she remembered the portrait on the landing and wished that eight o'clock would hurry up. She was desperate for some earthly company, instead of having this weird feeling that she was entertaining someone else in this room.

Becky could see the door to the corridor in the mirror; she could almost swear the handle was wobbling. She jumped as someone suddenly gave a loud knock. Now that was no ghost. She reached the door in three strides and flung it open.

'For heaven's sake, Jon!' she yelled, as she saw him standing there, hand raised. 'Are you trying to scare me to death here or what?'

'I'm early,' he said unnecessarily. 'I thought I'd come up to your room and see if you wanted a drink first.'

Becky studied him silently. 'Did you ask which room it was?' she asked finally. 'Be truthful.'

Jon dropped his gaze then looked back up at her. 'No,' he said. 'I kind of … knew.'

Again, that draught on her neck; the feeling that someone was standing next to her, welcoming Jon into the room – the idea that he actually had every right to be there. It all flooded over Becky and she had a sudden vision of the two of them standing together in that room, as if they had done the same thing a hundred times before in another life. But then as soon as it came, the image disappeared.

'Yeah. I thought so,' said Becky. Her voice somehow sounded too far away from her, ebbing and flowing in and out of range. She didn't like it. 'Please. Just come in for a second.' She stood back and he walked past her. He stood in the middle of the room and she saw him shiver.

'It's weird in here,' he said, looking around. 'It's like we're intruding on someone. I don't know – it's like it's this hotel room, but it's not this room.'

Becky nodded. 'I know. Did you see her?' she asked. 'On the staircase?'

'A ghost?' asked Jon, his eyes wide. 'You mean you *saw* someone?'

'No, no she wasn't a *ghost*,' replied Becky, picking up her handbag. She was relieved to realise her voice sounded normal to her again. 'She's a portrait. Lady Eleanor. She's wearing that dress from this afternoon, the cream one with the crystals. I think it's the portrait Lissy saw. It's just come back from the British Museum, apparently. Honestly, Jon, it gave me such a fright. And I knew which room I was in as well and where it was – the receptionist didn't have to tell me.'

'I think we both need a drink. Have you got everything? If so, let's go. You look lovely, by the way. You suit your hair like that. You never liked to wear it up before.'

'Thanks.' Becky smiled. 'I still don't particularly like it, but I'll survive – and it's only because I know you. Anyway, I'll show you the picture on the way down. You can't miss her. Well – I couldn't. Obviously you could.'

Jon raised his hands mockingly in a helpless gesture and led the way out of the room.

He waited for Becky on the landing, watching her lock the door. 'Do you know where the restaurant is?' he asked. Becky knew he was only half-joking.

She stood still on the landing, making a big production of looking around her. 'Downstairs?' she said finally.

Jon laughed. 'I expect so. Come on.' He offered her his arm and she shook it off, striding ahead of him.

'Here it is. Lady Eleanor,' Becky said, as they rounded the corner and began to descend down the staircase. She stopped in front of the portrait and tried to read the girl's face again. 'There's something about her,' she said slowly, 'but I just can't get it. It's as if she's trying to tell me something. You know I mentioned Ella earlier – it's like someone said the name to me when I was in your studio. But I don't know if it's her who's saying it or not.' She shook her head. 'I can't get it. And I feel a bit stupid.'

Jon came round and stood by her, looking at the girl. She was aware of him shaking his head, but the fact that he was so close was doing funny things to her …

'You heard someone speak to you? That's bizarre. Not stupid, but bizarre. There was nobody else in the studio. Maybe you were just hearing things? Something from the street outside perhaps?'

His voice brought her back to reality and she felt herself colour a little. God, if he even *imagined* she was thinking that way about him …

'No, it was more than that. She was … in my head,' confessed Becky. She shivered at the thought. Or maybe she was just shivering at Jon's proximity. She wasn't too sure.

'Hmmm. Well, I know what you mean about the portrait,' said Jon. 'I wish she *could* talk to us. She looks a really interesting character. It's good to see her here and, well, you did say you wished you could see the real deal for your project. And here it is. Maybe … Okay. Come on.' He took her by the elbow and gently steered her away from Lady Eleanor. Becky was horribly aware of his warm fingers on her skin.

They headed down the stairs, Jon's face thoughtful. 'I really think we need to bring Lissy into this. She's really good with research. If there's a story to be found here, she'll find it. She's got the time to do stuff like that. Of the two of us, she's the one that got the rich dad after all.'

There was no spite in what he said. He stated it as a fact. 'She doesn't have to work like I do – my stepfather gave her an independent income on her twenty-first. He said she could follow her dreams and not be stuck in a rut like everyone else. She's taking full advantage of it until she decides what she wants to do with her life.'

'Very nice,' said Becky. 'So what exactly does she do with her time now?'

'She visits galleries and museums; she loves art and history. She buys me interesting things like the writing slope and deals with all the costume commissions for me after I see the catalogues. She's a bit like my personal historian, I suppose.' They had reached the bottom of the staircase and they paused.

Becky tugged Jon's arm to the left. 'This way,' she said. 'The restaurant is this way.'

'How did you …?' he began.

She laughed. 'I'm starving. I can smell the food. My nose is highly sensitive when I'm hungry.' She led the way through the corridors to the bar, following the scent of garlic and coffee. Beyond the bar, she saw, as she had guessed, the restaurant. She stood still and stared around her. 'It's not right, though,' she said, half to herself. She suddenly felt dizzy and a wave of complete and utter silence washed over her.

She walked into the room where the piano was and saw it in the corner, the polished wood glowing against the pale walls. She reached her fingers to the keys, picking out the notes from the score on the music holder. She felt the melody; she didn't hear it. A sense of pure rage swept across her, and she suddenly took hold of the piano lid and crashed it down over the keys. It made no noise at all, but the force of it throbbed through her fingertips as she slammed it down.

Becky's eyes widened and she jolted back to reality. Jon was standing in front of her, holding the top of her arms. She stared first at him, then tried to work out where the piano should be, her heart pounding in her chest. What the hell was going on?

'Are you all right, Becky?' Jon asked.

'I need a drink,' she managed. Jon nodded and guided her to a comfy seat in the corner of the bar next to a warm fire. He cast anxious glances back at her as he stood at the bar, apparently ordering her a whisky and soda.

Her mouth twisted into a smile. Well, that had been interesting … *not*. The silence hadn't scared her – it had been the images and the feelings.

Ella. The voice came again, stronger than ever. She put her hands over her ears, squeezing her eyes shut. The voice was in her head, it had to be. She felt someone pull her right hand away and she opened her right eye, squinting at the culprit.

'Drink it,' said Jon, pointing emphatically at the glass in front of her with the forefinger of his other hand. 'Now.'

She let her other hand fall away from her head and curled her fingers around the tumbler. 'There was a piano in the room,' she said. 'It was over there. I – or she – played it. I think. But there was no sound there. She slammed the lid down, but there was nothing. She … we … weren't very

36

happy. Jon, she's definitely trying to communicate.' She dropped her gaze and stared into the tumbler. 'But I don't know if I like it. Her world seems so ... quiet,' she finished flatly. She looked up at Jon for some sort of validation.

'Maybe there's a reason why she's trying to communicate with you,' he suggested carefully.

'I don't know. I don't know what it is. I think I need some food. It's a while since we had lunch. Today has been probably the weirdest day I've ever experienced.' She forced a laugh. 'I'm not usually this excitable. I think Goth Weekend and bumping into you again has gotten to me a bit. I'm imagining way too much. But it was so bloody vivid! I could see her sheet music and I could feel her dress dragging along the floor. I knew exactly how to play the piano ... what?' Jon had raised his hand to stop her.

'You said you saw sheet music?' he said. 'And you were wearing her dress?'

'Yes,' replied Becky, confused. 'What are you trying to say?'

Jon smiled. 'And it was all quiet – too quiet?'

'Yes,' said Becky slowly.

'It's the writing slope stuff,' he said, visibly relaxing. 'It's been going around your mind all afternoon. You're tired, you're thinking about your article and your project and the research ... seeing that dress on the portrait was too much for your poor little brain. It's all muddled up. You do indeed need food.' He checked his watch. 'It's eight o'clock. They can sit us now. Not long, Miss Jones, and you will be fed.' He stood up and offered his hand to her. She took it and he guided her into the restaurant.

Once they were seated and had ordered their meals, Becky

began to calm down. He was right, of course. It was her overactive imagination at work again.

'All I need is that invitation to materialise,' she said, shaking her head. Then she spread her hands out and laughed. 'And, oh look, here we are, having dinner. That's it. The final piece of the puzzle.' Except it wasn't of course, she realised with a churn of her stomach. She stared at Jon. 'Her name, Jon,' she said slowly. 'How did I know her name was Ella? How did I know it was Lady Eleanor's dress? And the lavender? That hasn't happened yet, either. Oh! The initials on the slope, as well; L.J.C. I'm wondering if that was more like a Lady Jane's initials. I suspect it's not Lady Eleanor's.'

Jon paused in his buttering of a dainty slice of bread. 'That, Becky, I don't know,' he said. He looked up and gestured for a waiter to come over. 'The wine list, please,' he asked.

'I hope you aren't driving,' Becky said, watching him open the folder.

'I'll get a taxi, don't worry,' said Jon. 'I think we need the wine list after today though, don't you?' He leaned across the table to her, a mischievous twinkle in his eye. 'Or, instead of a taxi, I could see if they have another room free here tonight?'

Becky burst out laughing. 'Yes; get your own room. You aren't getting back into mine, mate!' She knew deep down she didn't actually *mean* that, but it didn't do to let *him* know that. Her school friend's annoying older brother? Seriously? She wouldn't let herself fall for Jon Nelson, of all people. Not after he had hidden her and Lissy's favourite boy band CD. He said the noise of the singalong and the thumping of the dance routines had interfered with his homework; and Lissy had called him a 'killjoy swot head', which Becky had thought was very inspired and very true at the time.

'Damn!' said Jon. 'It was worth a try.'

'Maybe,' said Becky, 'but I think I'm doing well to even let you entertain me tonight, given our history!' *Yeah, yeah.* She shook the thoughts away and concentrated on Jon's face again. It was rather a nice face, it had to be said. Yes, the years had *definitely* been kind to him. He still had the quirky little smile as well – the one she had found so irritating when he was pulling the 'big brother knows best' routines.

'Glib,' muttered Jon, studying the wine list.

'Glib?' said Becky. 'Well, now. I've never been called that before.'

'You're very glib!' said Jon. 'It's annoying, that's what it is …'

'But it's such an old-fashioned word!' retorted Becky.

'And it suits you,' said Jon. He closed the wine list and laid it down in front of him. 'I wish I'd spent a bit more time with you when we were younger,' he said. 'Although it pains me to say it, you're just about the most interesting person I've met in ages. Who would have thought that?'

'Hmm. I may well be the maddest, though,' she replied. She stared at the front of the wine list and after a moment, tilted her head to one side. 'Let me see that?' she asked, pointing to the folder. Jon handed it over and she turned it around so it was the right way up. She traced her fingers across the golden stamp on the front, which announced the list belonged to Carrick Park Hotel.

'Do you see what I see?' she asked quietly. She looked up at Jon, and knew there was more than a hint of confusion in her eyes. Her heart felt like it was going to leap out of her chest and the dizziness was coming again. Just after the oppressive silence descended, she thought she managed to say the words *coat of arms* out loud.

Through the strange, over layering sensation, she saw Jon take the folder and study it. He frowned and looked at her. She squeezed her eyes shut and opened them again, concentrating on the here and now.

'It's the writing slope again,' Jon was saying. 'That's it, isn't it? The coat of arms.'

'It looks like it,' said Becky. She steadied her breathing, relieved to realise that things were back to normal. 'I wonder if that C in the initials on it means Carrick? Or am I reading too much into it? Maybe all coats of arms look the same.'

'There's only one way to find out,' said Jon. 'Would it be unbearable for you to see me again tomorrow and come back to the studio? I could give Lissy a call, see if she would meet us there?'

Becky nodded. 'That would be great. And yes, if Lissy's able to come that's even better. It would be wonderful to see her again. But if she can't make it, even if I just get to see the coat of arms – just to compare it – it'll be worth it. It can't be the same one. Can it?'

Jon shrugged. 'Who knows?' he said. 'Well, dinner is served. If you can manage anything, that is?' He nodded at the waiter over Becky's shoulder, seeing him heading over with the starters.

'I'll force myself,' said Becky. The words weren't that far from the truth, if she was honest. 'But before that ...' She leaned over and took the wine list back from Jon. She pulled her phone out of her bag and quickly took a photograph of the cover. 'One has to collect the evidence,' she said. 'It'll be easier to compare them tomorrow if we have a decent copy of it today.'

The rest of the evening passed pleasantly enough. Jon was an entertaining companion, as Becky had suspected. Once again, she wondered why she hadn't bothered that much with him when they were younger. It was probably a lot to do with the age gap, she reasoned. He probably hadn't bothered with her, mostly. But tonight they sat there long after they should have left the restaurant, ordering coffees they didn't really want in order to spin the evening out.

Eventually, Becky looked at her watch. 'Oh my!' she said. 'It's after eleven. I was supposed to be working tonight. It's your fault.' She poked him with her fingertips, slightly tipsy by now. 'Your fault. I have a deadline.'

Jon waved his hands expressively in the air. 'No, no work tonight, Miss Jones. Time to relax.' He smiled at her, not quite focused on her and Becky snorted out a laugh.

'You're drunk,' she said. 'Very drunk. We need to go to bed. In our *own* rooms!' she added, seeing his face light up. 'Come on.' She waved the waiter over. 'Mr Nelson has a room here tonight. Please ensure the bill gets added to his account?'

The waiter nodded. 'Very well, madam. Which room is it?'

Becky stared blankly at the waiter. 'I don't know,' she said eventually. She turned to Jon. 'Go and book your room,' she said, frowning. 'The waiter is waiting for your details.' For some reason she found the comment hysterically funny and waved at Jon as he nodded and wandered off, weaving his way through the tables to the Reception desk. After some time he returned and smiled at the waiter, who appeared again next to the table.

'Room one hundred and fourteen,' he said. 'In the west wing. I need to get my luggage from the car, I think.'

'You planned this!' accused Becky. She smacked her hands on the table and sat back. 'Well! You devious man!'

'I just thought I'd come prepared,' said Jon. 'Just in case. I was a Scout, remember?'

'Oh! Yes! I loved your woggle!' cried Becky

'Ahem.' The waiter cleared his throat, professional to a 'T'. 'If that's agreed, then, I shall charge the bill to one hundred and fourteen and bid you a goodnight.' He made Jon sign something and Becky sniggered.

'You'll hate me in the morning,' she said, leaning over to Jon. Then whispered, she thought, quietly. 'Don't try to get into my room. I won't hear you and I won't answer you. I'm going straight to sleep.' She nodded sagely at Jon and stood up, rather unsteadily. 'Thank you for dinner.'

'You're welcome,' said Jon. 'I need my luggage. And I could never hate you. Well, I maybe did hate you when we were kids. But not now, I think. No.' He shook his head decisively. 'Not now. You've grown up, Becky Jones. I like you better like this.'

'So you say,' replied Becky. She picked up her bag and tucked it under her arm. 'Well, goodnight. It's been a lovely catch up.' She clapped her hands awkwardly. 'And I might see the elusive Elisabetta tomorrow. Hurrah!'

'Oh, come with me to the car,' pleaded Jon. 'It's a nice night.'

'It's not a nice night!' said Becky as she led the way out of the restaurant. 'There's a storm brewing. Thunder. Rain. Everything.' She threw her hands into the air, her bag almost slipping to the floor. 'Everything,' she repeated. 'No. I will see you in the morning. Goodnight.' She leaned awkwardly towards him, trying to aim a kiss onto his cheek. Jon was quick, though, and he turned his face at the last moment. Becky's eyes widened as she realised she was kissing his lips. Then she relaxed as she began to enjoy it.

Eventually they pulled away and Jon, it had to be said, was smirking.

'Do not come to my room,' said Becky, waving her forefinger. 'I need to sleep. And, I repeat, I have no intention of hearing you or letting you in. I shall see you at breakfast. Eight o'clock seems reasonable to me.'

'Eight o'clock,' repeated Jon, looking at her wistfully. 'Goodnight.'

'Goodnight,' repeated Becky. They peeled away from one another at the foot of the staircase. Jon disappeared through the door into the car park, and Becky turned and walked slowly up the stairs. She paused at the portrait again. 'Goodnight, Ella,' she said under her breath. Then she turned up the second flight and headed to her room.

It didn't take her long to discard her dress, bag and all the accoutrements of civilisation. Within fifteen minutes she was in bed, drifting off to sleep with part of her wondering exactly what Jon was doing at that point in time …

Then, sometime during that night, she had the dream again.

She was in a room, flooded with light. The windows were large and overlooked parkland. Full-length curtains fluttered out into the room, as a summer breeze snaked through the casings. A piano stood in the corner, and she saw her fingers picking out a tune. A piece of paper, ornately decorated and embossed, lay on a desk.

Now she was in the bedroom. A mirror on a dressing table reflected the fireplace and a four-poster bed. She picked up a silver-backed hairbrush and hurled it at the mirror. The mirror shattered, cracks bursting across its surface, obscuring the reflection as a shadow appeared behind her.

Then she ran. She ran out of the bedroom, down the stairs, into the hallway and out of the door. She caught the scent of a storm that was threatening to split the sky open and saw a flash of her blue dress, scrunched up in her hands. She saw her feet steadily pounding across the grass and she prayed that nobody would stop her.

Becky woke with a start, her heart pounding, disorientated. Looking around her she remembered the hotel bedroom she was sleeping in, the staircase she had ascended only hours ago. She squinted her eyes through the gloom, half-expecting to see she was lying in a four-poster bed, but she was relieved to see only the dark shapes of her clothes draped over the chair where she had left them, looking exactly like a figure sitting on it.

She lay down again, cursing the writing slope, the alcohol and most of all Jon for leading her astray, when she realised that she hadn't actually draped her clothes over the chair. She had dropped them on the floor where she had stripped off. She opened her eyes wide and sat bolt upright. The chair was empty.

Becky didn't wait until Jon came knocking on her door for breakfast. Eight o'clock found her knocking on his door, her article on Goth Weekend all but emailed to *People's History*. After waking up from that dream, she hadn't managed to sleep very well and had been working on the article from about six o'clock. Her head was fuzzy and her concentration lacking by now, but resolutely she banged on his door, something inside her relishing the idea of being the one to wake him up.

She only waited a few moments before Jon opened the door. She was disappointed to realise that he didn't look like the half-asleep, unkempt dormouse she had expected, but was washed, shaved, dressed and smiling. He didn't look half bad, actually.

'Perfect timing,' he said. 'I was just coming to knock for you. Wow, you look rough.' To take the sting out of his words, he kissed her on the cheek. 'Good sleep?'

'No, not really,' she confessed, waiting as he pulled the door shut behind him. 'I hope you have your key.'

He waved it at her and put it in his pocket. 'I do have the key,' he said. 'Thanks for checking. What was wrong? Was the bed uncomfortable?'

'No, not at all,' she said. 'I was fine until I had a really bizarre dream.'

'Not about Lady Eleanor again was it?' he asked, nodding at the portrait as they passed it on their way downstairs.

Becky suppressed a shudder, averting her gaze and trying to avoid the girl in the portrait's eyes. 'It might have been,' she said cagily. 'She might have been in my room. Just saying.'

Jon stopped suddenly. 'What?' he asked, rather too loudly.

'Shhh!' hissed Becky. 'I'm just saying, I thought someone was sitting in a chair in my room last night. I woke up after this weird dream and it was like someone was sitting in the chair.'

'You should have come and got me. You could have bunked up in my room. Don't look at me like that, I would have let you have the bed.'

'I was too frightened to move!' growled Becky. 'I couldn't sleep after that. I put the light on and I wrote my article. Jon, what does she want with me? Am I completely mad or is it real?' She ran her hand through her hair nervously, tucking the stray bits in behind her left ear as an afterthought.

'In the dream there was a lake. She was heading off towards the lake. And she was in the dining room and the bedroom. It's like I'm *her*, like I can see and feel things as *her*. I don't like it.'

She paused as they reached the restaurant again, half-expecting the visions to start up again of the piano. They didn't, although she couldn't help but cast her eyes over to the corner where the piano should have been. The restaurant, she noticed, now that it was daylight, had the big, tall windows of the dream. She watched the curtains, wondering whether they would billow out into the room suddenly. She stood entranced, lost in that other world, until Jon tugged on her arm. She looked at him, dazed, and he pointed to a table.

'Come on,' said Jon. 'Breakfast, then we're out of here. I'll drive us into Whitby. We'll go to the studio. I assume you've got the room for another night?'

Becky nodded. 'Yes, it's mine for a few days, actually. There's nothing waiting for me at home. I might as well be here. I wanted to do some sightseeing.'

Jon snorted; a sound between cynicism and disbelief. 'You seem to have got more than you bargained for on this break,' he said.

'Just a bit,' muttered Becky. She picked up the breakfast menu, a simple list printed on an A5 piece of card. 'The coat of arms is on this as well,' she observed. She sighed and put the menu down. 'The writing slope means more than we think. I can't see how it connects to Ella or Eleanor, if indeed it is her who is trying to speak to me. I don't know who L.J.C. is either. It's their writing slope, I guess. Someone Carrick, I guess, if it is the Carrick Park coat of arms. I'm clutching at straws.'

Jon lifted the lid of the coffee pot, which had appeared on their table thanks to a small, red-haired waitress, and sniffed. 'Mmmm, this is good coffee. I'll ring Lissy before we set off. If there's an L.J.C. to be found, she'll find them, don't worry.' He poured coffee into the cups and set the pot down again. 'I'll ask her to meet us at the studio. She can tell us what she knows. We'll have to work together on this one I think.' He flashed the sort of smile at Becky that was guaranteed to make a girl's heart flip. 'Just like old times. Can you put up with me a little longer?'

'We never worked together. You were too annoying,' said Becky. Then she quickly looked down at her cup and clasped her hands around it so he wouldn't see her blush. 'But I guess I'll have to put up with you for a little longer, as you say it seems like we're in this together, whether we like it or not.'

'I actually quite like it,' said Jon.

Becky looked up quickly, her eyes wide. There was a smile in his voice and he was leaning in towards her.

Honesty, said the little voice within her, adding something else to his attributes. *Just go with it,* continued the voice. *You might just like it yourself.*

It didn't seem to take as long going back towards Whitby in the daylight as it had done driving to the hotel in the darkness. Becky watched, intrigued, as Jon expertly steered the car around the tiny, twisting lanes of the town and pulled up behind the studio. There was room enough for one car in a space marked 'Private'.

Jon switched the engine off and smiled at Becky. 'Perk of the job,' he said. 'Not all the traders have private spaces, though. I was lucky with this one.'

'It's a fascinating old town,' said Becky, undoing her seat belt. She climbed out of the car and stood in the back lane, sniffing deeply as the salty air from the North Sea infiltrated the cobbled street. 'I can see why you came back. Plymouth and Sussex are lovely, but you can't beat the coast up here. Our beaches aren't as pebbly for a start. That's partially why I decided to move to York when I finished my degree. It's got enough about it to be a town, but it's so close to the moors and the seaside as well, it's perfect. I can't see me moving away from Yorkshire, to be honest.'

'I love it here as well,' Jon said, smiling down at her. 'I'm glad you feel the same. Shall we have a coffee first?' he asked, leading her out of the alleyway and towards the coffee shop they had visited yesterday.

'Don't you think of anything else?' asked Becky, falling into step beside him and smiling back up at him.

'I think of many things. But I think better after coffee,' Jon replied.

'I think it's probably my turn to get them,' said Becky, feeling slightly guilty in the cold light of day that she had engineered a free meal last night. 'You phone Lissy, I'll go in and get them. Latte?'

'Please. A large one.'

Becky watched him as she waited in the queue. He was having quite an animated discussion with Lissy on his mobile. The way he was waving his hands around as he tried to make his points amused Becky and she almost missed her turn. By the time she left the shop balancing two cups, he had finished the conversation and was sitting at an outside table, watching the second day of Goth Weekend unfold around him.

Becky sat down opposite and pushed the cup towards him. 'I still feel under-dressed,' she said, as a girl walked past in some sort of short, black, lace prom dress. She wore heavy, studded biker boots and fishnet tights and Becky smiled as the girl pulled an iPhone out of her dolly-bag and began to text someone.

'I think it looks funny, don't you, when you see the modern world clash with the Victorian one.' She realised what she had said and suddenly found her coffee cup really interesting.

'Very funny,' said Jon. 'Is that what's happening to us?'

Becky ignored him and stared past his shoulder at a man dressed as Dracula.

'Don't pretend you didn't hear me,' said Jon. 'You're not that good an actress.'

Becky pulled a face and focused on the man opposite her instead of Dracula. 'I heard you,' she admitted, 'but I don't know what to say. The only thing I can liken it to is having ... her ... impress herself on me. But I don't know why. I don't know why she's picked me of all people. Maybe it was the dress thing ... I don't know.' Her voice tailed off and she shook her head. 'It's something to do with the hotel,' she said eventually. 'And it's something to do with the writing slope, but the things we found in there don't help much. I'm assuming someone liked Mozart. I'm assuming someone liked parties. I'm assuming that, for whatever reason, someone was using or learning finger spelling. I think our Lady Eleanor is this Ella person. I think it was her portrait and her dress Lissy saw, and I think Ella has something to do with Carrick Park. That's as much as I can piece together and I have no idea who L.J.C. was. Anyway,' she shrugged her shoulders and sat back in the seat, 'we don't know for sure if it is the right coat of arms. That's the first thing to check.'

'We can do that straight away,' said Jon. 'Lissy said she'll be about an hour. I'll open the studio in case anyone is interested in coming in while we're waiting, and you can see how it all works with the Velcro dresses. If that's okay with you? You can be my assistant.'

'Of course, you need to make a living,' said Becky lightly. 'It'll be good fun. And then I'll write about a day in the life of a seaside photographer. How does that sound?'

'Sounds ideal,' said Jon. He stood up and aimed his empty cup into the waste bin. He looked through the window and waved at Lucy the barista, and then took Becky's arm. 'Come on,' he said. 'Let's get to work.'

They walked around the corner and Jon unlocked the door of the studio. He disappeared and Becky knew he was putting the alarm code in. She headed straight towards the prop table and picked up the writing slope. She peered at the coat of arms, then put the box down and got her phone out. She pressed a few buttons and got the photograph from the wine list up on the screen. She held the phone out next to the slope. The images went in and out of focus as she felt the blood rush away from her head. She groped for a chair and sat down, still staring at the two items. The silence washed over her again and she knew without a doubt that it was the same coat of arms and that this slope had something to do with Carrick Park. She felt Jon place his hands on her shoulders and she reached up to grasp one of them, trying to ground herself in her own reality.

'It's the same one,' she said. 'I knew it would be.' She turned in the seat, looking up at him. 'That's the first part of the mystery solved anyway. I hope Lissy is as good at this as you say she is.'

Jon nodded. 'She is. You've gone white,' he said. 'Are you okay?'

'I will be in a minute,' she said. She turned back to the slope and leaned over it, feeling around for another secret compartment, another latch that would help her with the mystery; but there was nothing. She shook her head. 'We'll have to wait. I can't do anything else until we have Lissy here.'

Despite her comment, she opened the slope and found the original catch from the day before. She lifted it up and the drawer sprang out again. She carefully took the things out of the slope and laid them all on the table, side by side, trying to work out the connection.

Jon pulled up a chair and took the finger spelling sheet. 'I'm fascinated by this,' he said. He put it down beside him and tried to form his fingers into something.

Becky smiled. 'She's Ella. Not Etta. Look, you have to spread your fingers out on your left hand like this. Then you touch *this* part of your palm with your right forefinger. You've got your fingers all closed up there, like they're stuck with glue; and you've put your finger *here* instead of *there*. Understand? It's quite clear on the diagram.'

Jon sighed lustily. 'Okay, clever clogs. Sing this aria,' he said, thrusting the Mozart sheet towards her.

Becky couldn't help but laugh. 'I wouldn't even try!' she exclaimed.

'Then that's the difference between us,' said Jon. 'I'm trying to learn this, and you won't even give my music a go.'

'Forget it!' said Becky, pushing him good-naturedly. 'Face it, you're useless.'

He opened his mouth to retaliate, but at that moment the bell rung above the shop door and he turned his attention to his potential customer. Becky turned with him and saw a middle-aged lady standing there, with a tall, thin man. The man looked vaguely uncomfortable; the woman excited.

'What a lovely little place!' said the lady, looking around her in delight. 'We're here for Goth Weekend, but you probably know that already. And because we want to feel properly part of it, I think I'd like a photo of me and my husband dressed up.'

'Certainly,' said Jon. 'Come with me and I'll show you some of the clothes we have here. You can really look the part,' he said. 'This is my assistant, Becky. She'll help us choose something, won't you, Becky?'

Becky stood up to follow them towards the clothes and Jon turned, winking at her over his shoulder. Yep, he had really meant she was going to be his assistant today, hadn't he? Before she knew it, she was the receptacle for swathes of black lace as the lady picked and discarded dress after dress after dress, piling them all up in Becky's arms as she rejected them. Becky slowly disappeared under the clothes and before long she couldn't even see above the pile and amused herself by wondering what the woman would eventually choose. At length, someone, probably Jon, lifted the pile of clothes out of her arms and she was faced with the lady, holding up some Goth version of a twee little milkmaid's outfit and smiling.

Becky couldn't help it. She shook her head. 'Oh no. No. I think you'd look much better in something less ... frilly,' she said. 'I'm sure we have something that will look better. I mean, something that's a little more special and a hundred people haven't already worn this weekend.'

She rummaged through the racks of clothes and eventually pulled out a more flattering Victorian-style day dress. She handed it to the lady and watched as she wriggled into it, her husband tugging at the Velcro backing, trying to make the edges meet. Becky was pleased to see that the new dress nipped the lady in where it should nip her in and emphasised more of her hourglass shape. Yes, *much* better than a Goth milkmaid would have been, she thought. The husband himself was dressed as if he was going to the opera, even down to the monocle and the top hat. He looked extremely uncomfortable as they made their way out of the dressing room into the photograph area. Jon moved them around until he was happy with their positions and disappeared behind the camera as he took the shot.

Eventually, he was satisfied, and the couple changed back into modern-day tourists.

Jon fussed at the camera, sorting the plates out and heading over to his workstation in the tiny darkroom to develop the picture. He always tried, he had explained to the couple, to stay faithful to the old traditions – no digital imagery in here. Becky snuck into the darkroom. She peered over Jon's shoulder and then tapped him on the back. He turned, scowling at her for interrupting his work. She held up the finger spelling sheet and indicated he should hold it under the low light. Then she lifted her hands up and very slowly spelled out *Y.O.U. W.O.R.K. M.A.G.I.C.* She grinned at him and slipped out of the darkroom, taking the sheet with her, just in time to see the couple heading back towards the front of the shop. She moved behind the desk and smiled at them, pushing the finger spelling sheet under the counter.

'He won't be long,' she said. 'Do you want to pay now and wait, or pay now and come back later?'

'Oh, we'll wait!' said the lady. 'All the better to see these fabulous photographs. I say, Brian, have you seen this one? No? Well, pay the lady and then come and see it.' She walked over to the wall and studied a photograph that was mounted and framed in the centre. 'Oh my!' she said. She turned to Becky and smiled. 'You are a beautiful model, my dear. How fabulous is that dress? Now, I wish I had seen that one today. I would have liked that one.'

Becky, clutching some notes from Brian, didn't quite understand.

She came out from behind the till and stood by the lady. 'Excuse me? What do you mean?' she asked.

'It's you!' said the lady. 'You look fabulous.' She pointed a beautifully manicured forefinger, heavy with rings, towards the picture.

Becky stared, astonished. It was the photograph of her from yesterday when she had bent over the writing slope. It looked as amazing as Jon had said. She was pleased her hair was falling across the side of her face and not tied up – it was much better, in her opinion.

Nervously, she tucked the accursed hair behind her ear again, then fluffed it back out as she peered closer at the picture. 'It looks really old-fashioned, doesn't it?' she said. 'I truly hadn't seen that on the wall until today.'

'He's a talented man,' said the lady. She smiled at Becky, genuine warmth in her expression. 'You're a lucky girl.'

Becky couldn't help but laugh. She began to shake her head, ready to deny it and give her the 'oh, we're old friends' routine, until she thought better of it. The lady obviously loved the idea that they were together. Why spoil it for her?

Instead, she smiled graciously and pointed randomly to another wall. 'There's some nice ones over there as well,' she said, not knowing if there were or weren't. 'Just have a look around, he won't be long.'

She put the money into Jon's till – the drawer was left

indiscreetly open, it had to be said – retrieved the finger spelling sheet and took up her position beside the writing slope again. She piled the papers up in front of her, placing the music score on the top, as she deemed that the least likely to generate questions. She waited for Jon to come out from the darkroom, and watched the customers enjoy the gallery.

At length, Jon emerged and held out the photograph to the couple.

'Oh my, that's wonderful,' said the lady. 'I look so … vintage! Well, we paid your girl over there – your best model in my opinion – and we just love your studio. We'll be coming back next year, I'm sure. We might even wear our own costumes next time!'

Becky smiled as Jon thanked the couple and escorted them out of the studio, the lady still singing his praises. He bid them farewell at the door and turned to Becky.

He leaned against the door and smiled. 'So long as she's happy, eh? Thanks for taking payment, by the way.'

'My pleasure,' said Becky. 'I didn't know you'd framed that photograph from yesterday.' She stood up and walked over to it again. 'You should have told me.'

'Ah well,' said Jon, flushing slightly. 'I did it after you'd left. It came out really well. I wanted to put it on display.'

'It's nice,' said Becky. 'It doesn't look like me, though.'

'Yes it does,' said Jon. 'You can have it if you want. I can always do a copy for myself. But I've got the other one done as well.' He reached over to the table next to him and picked up another framed portrait. It was the serious one that Becky had sat for yesterday, the one she had posed so carefully for.

She took it from him and studied it. Never in her whole life had she ever thought that she looked like the girl in this photograph. The dress fitted perfectly and her hair fell down past her shoulders. Normally it was straight, but somehow this picture had captured a wave to it that framed a heart-shaped face she didn't think she possessed. But it was her eyes that held her attention. They looked out of the picture, entirely focused on the photographer, a slight frown of concentration behind them. She studied the picture, thinking how unlike her own eyes they seemed to be and yet they looked oddly familiar.

'I have eyes like Lady Eleanor's,' she said suddenly. 'They've got the same expression in them. Look!' She thrust the picture at Jon, pointing at her face. 'I'm not her, but I *look* like her across the eyes.'

'Don't be daft,' said Jon, taking the picture from her. He studied it himself and shook his head. 'No you don't. It's the dress and the lighting. That's what makes it look like the painting, I'm sure.'

'Can't you see it?' she persisted. 'It's her, looking out of that picture. It's not me.'

'Ridiculous!' said Jon. 'No, it's you. It's exactly how you looked yesterday.'

'I might have looked like that, but I *don't* look like that!' said Becky.

'Yes you do!' argued Jon. 'The camera never lies.'

'Yes it bloody does!' said Becky. She was willing to argue more, but the bell above the door dinged again and a small, dainty girl walked in. Her bobbed hair was dyed jet black and she wore leggings and a long, geometrically patterned tunic. Her mismatched blue and green eyes were thickly lined with kohl and framed with hugely long lashes, but her lips were a pale pink and the entire look owed more to Mary Quant and the 1960s than to Whitby in the twenty-first century.

'Jon!' she shrieked, catching sight of him. 'And Becky! My God, what a treat! I've missed you sooooo much!' She threw what looked like a laptop case down on the table, slammed the door shut and quickly flicked the sign on the glass to 'Closed'. She ran over to Jon, hugged him, then threw herself likewise at Becky.

'Hey, Lissy!' said Jon, laughing. 'Good to see you too. Thanks for coming down.'

'No problem,' she replied. 'And Becky! I couldn't *believe* it when Jon told me he'd bumped into you – literally, by all accounts.' She laughed at her own joke. 'I meant to email you or text you but I got a little sidetracked. You know what it's like. You know what *I'm* like.'

'Yes, but what was *he* like?' Becky replied. Lissy had never and apparently would never change. Unlike her brother, she looked exactly the same – only her make-up was more professional now and yes, her fingernails were to die for. Not to mention her clothes.

'God, you know me too well,' said Lissy, 'but I'm not talking about him. He doesn't deserve my time. But anyway, Jon said we've got quite a lot of interesting stuff going on.'

'We have indeed.' Becky grinned. 'Starting with this.' She indicated the writing slope. 'Don't let me down, Lissy.'

'I never let anyone down. It's just I'm useless at keeping in touch. But you know that anyway.'

She looked sidelong at the writing slope and Becky detected a hint of eagerness; Lissy was clearly raring to go. 'So it's definitely something to do with this?' Lissy asked.

'Definitely,' said Becky. 'We found some intriguing stuff inside it, and what we want to know is who owned the slope and what the contents mean. Did Jon tell you about Ella?' she asked, feeling rather silly at even mentioning Ella.

'He did,' Lissy said with a nod, as if it was the most natural thing in the world to be possessed by dead Victorians. 'And you think she's Lady Eleanor at Carrick Park?'

'I'm not sure,' said Becky slowly. 'It seems likely, but I don't know for sure.'

'We'll find out,' said Lissy. 'There are certain things I can do to help us.'

Yes, Lissy had not changed. She was always so confident that she would triumph in whatever she did. And part of Becky marvelled at how easily she just railroaded in there and started chatting as if they'd only spoken yesterday. And seriously, *lots* of things had happened in between times – not all of it for general consumption – so it was probably just as easy to let Lissy talk at her and not ask too many questions about the past.

'Lissy!' Jon interrupted. 'No funny stuff. We want facts.'

'You'll get facts,' said Lissy. 'My methods may be unconventional but they work. Now, let's have a look at the slope. Jon says you managed to find the secret compartment. My brother spent ages looking for it, but he couldn't find it. It's so clever; it reminds me of a CD tray in a laptop.'

'You knew where it was?' asked Jon. 'And you didn't tell me?'

'Of course I knew!' said Lissy. 'It was pretty obvious. But then, I guess I went to London just after that so I haven't had a chance to show you. I did mean to, but then I forgot all about it.' She turned to Becky. 'I went to the V&A. Fantastic. It's the costumes. I love them. But I found that dress in a programme from the British Museum. They had an art exhibition there and I saw the Lady Eleanor portrait and couldn't resist *her* dress, so I sorted out a copy for my brother because he always likes to have unusual things here for special clients ...'

Becky stared at Lissy fascinated, letting her ramble on. She had obviously never learned to stop for breath in the years since they'd last met up. Emails and texts were all very well, but Becky had forgotten what it was like to be with her in person.

'... And then as I say I forgot all about that slope. I got it from an antiques shop, just down the road there. It's a really nice shop, you can have a good old poke around it and they've always got something new. They said the slope had come to them from an auction and it was in really good condition ...'

Becky looked at Jon, trying not to laugh as Lissy bent over the slope and began fiddling with one of the hinges, never ceasing in her monologue. Jon rolled his gaze heavenwards and made a helpless gesture with his hands.

'And they said that some of these pieces are really clever, because you find the compartment by lifting the bit up between the inkwells, but nobody *ever* gets the one from the hinge. They sold it with all the contents intact, they said there was nothing of any value in it, so I managed to get the whole lot for such a bargain price—'

'Hang on!' Jon interrupted. 'There are *two* compartments?'

'Yes, didn't I just say it was like a CD tray?' said Lissy, frowning at him. 'You weren't listening to me. You never listen to me.'

'Lissy, shut *up*,' said Jon. 'Show me the damn CD tray.'

'Okay, don't get annoyed,' said Lissy indignantly. 'Here it is. See? A CD tray.'

She was right; the hinge she had been fiddling with was now standing at right angles to the base of the slope, and a drawer, exactly like a CD tray, had popped out from the side.

'I don't know if there's anything in that bit, though,' said Lissy. 'I didn't get a good chance to look at it.' She hunkered down and peered in. 'Oh yes. Look, there's something. It's all curled up though.' She poked tiny little fingers tipped with bright blue nail varnish into the drawer and coaxed out a curled up piece of paper. There was a scuffle as both

Jon and Becky dived for it at the same time. Jon won, snatching it out of Lissy's hand.

'Hey!' cried Lissy. 'Watch it!'

Jon carefully flattened the paper out. His eyes widened and his mouth formed a silent 'Oh!' as he apparently realised what it was.

'It's a photograph,' he said, when he had recovered the power of speech. 'A genuine photograph.' He swore under his breath and stared at the picture. 'It's not a professional one. It's a bit blurred, not very well preserved and a bit cracked. But nevertheless ...' He laid it down on the table and the girls crowded around him.

Becky looked at the photograph in wonderment; a man and a woman were facing each other in front of a fireplace and it was, clearly, unprofessional. It had been taken at an odd angle whereby it didn't exactly centre the people, and they definitely weren't posing for it. In fact, the more she looked at it, the more Becky thought they hadn't even been aware that it was being taken at all. There must have been a flash involved, as there was a streak of light reflected on the girl's hair, which gave a kind of halo effect and left part of the man's face in shadow. Even so, Becky could see the look of total adoration on the man's face and the girl's face, upturned to his, mirrored his feelings. Becky noticed the girl's hands and arms were blurred – she must have been trying to drive home a point, using them to make herself clear. Whatever it was they were talking about, the man was smiling at her and leaving the conversation to her.

'Beautiful,' said Becky. 'It's such a natural photograph of them. I wonder where ... oh!' She leaned forward and peered at the picture. 'Jon, have you got a magnifying glass. Something I can use ...'

There was that queer feeling again – Becky's reality was slipping away and this time, Lissy seemed to feel it too.

At exactly the same time, they looked at each other and Lissy's face drained of colour. She stared at Becky, and an expression of pure fear came over her.

'I ... can't ...' she managed.

'It's all right,' Becky said slowly, taking the girl's hands in hers. 'It's all right. Look at me. It's all right. It'll pass.'

Within a few seconds, Lissy's colour returned and her face relaxed. 'That was horrible,' she whispered. 'God, that was *horrible*. I've never ...'

'You get used to it,' said Becky. 'It's her. Did you feel her?'

'Yes,' whispered Lissy. She looked all of a sudden very scared. 'Is that what she does?'

Becky nodded. 'Yes. This is part of the reason why I want a magnifying glass. Jon?' She turned and saw Jon looking at them, as white as Lissy had been moments earlier. 'Jon? Are you okay? She didn't get you as well, did she?'

'No,' said Jon, sitting down on the table. He looked at Becky and shook his head in disbelief. 'But Adam did.'

'You're kidding?' exclaimed Lissy. 'There was somebody *else* here with us? Adam?'

'I'm not kidding,' said Jon. 'God, I need a coffee.' He put his head in his hands and shook it. 'It was like he was right in my head. I swear I heard a voice, something like "I'm Adam, I'm with her."' He looked up at the girls; his sister was staring at him with wide, disbelieving eyes and Becky's brow was creased with that little furrow he realised he found so endearing.

'Well, I think this girl is Ella,' said Becky decisively. She picked the photograph up and brought it over to him. 'I need a magnifying glass to check. Ella had a beauty spot on that portrait on her left cheek. The way this girl is turned to the camera, I can see a mark in the same place.'

'How the hell did you spot that?' asked Lissy.

'Oh, I'm quite observant,' said Becky. 'I take a lot in. It comes with the territory.'

'She's a journalist now,' muttered Jon. He closed his eyes. 'God help us all. Worry when she starts doing those exposé things.' He felt a sharp jab to his shoulder and opened his eyes to see Becky glaring at him.

'I hadn't considered that until now. But apart from that, like it or not, I think you are definitely part of it all now,' she said.

'Do I detect a note of complacency in your voice?' Jon sighed. 'I don't want to be *that* involved. Adam. Adam *who*?'

'I think this is Adam in the photograph,' said Becky, 'and judging by the way they are looking at each other, I would imagine Adam is her lover. Lissy, can you find out if there were any Adam Carricks? If she's Lady Eleanor, he might be Sir Adam.' She shrugged her shoulders and stared at the picture again. 'Once more, I'm clutching at straws. But the feeling I get from, well, from Ella, is that this man is Adam.'

Jon watched Becky sidelong as the furrow on her brow eased and a small smile played about her lips. He knew Ella was somehow about again, telling Becky in her own special way that she was right. Adam or no Adam, this was the man she loved. Jon reached out and touched Becky's hand. She jumped and snapped back into the present. What he would give, he thought, for her to let him hold her hand just a little longer.

'Sorry, Jon,' Becky said, looking up at him.

Jon whistled a breath out from between his teeth. Over the last day or so he knew he had actually become quite fond of Becky, all over again. He'd always preferred her to any of Lissy's other friends anyway, but most of the time, they were just kids tearing around the house together and shrieking. He liked this new, improved, grown-up Becky even more. And he wanted Becky with him, not Ella. He briefly wondered what would happen if Ella decided to stay, then pushed the thought away. Becky was a device for communication, nothing else, he told himself. He looked at her again. Yes, he definitely wanted Becky with him. Her hair had the sort of sheen to it that a thousand hair product commercials would promise, but she seemed completely unaware of it. Even as he watched her, she twisted that little tendril around again and, yes, there it went; shoved behind her left ear. Only the left one. The right side of her hair, she left hanging down.

'Adam Carrick is as good a place to start as any,' said Lissy, interrupting his train of thought. 'I'll get my laptop set up.' She slipped away to the table by the door.

Jon stood up and walked over to the writing slope. 'If he is indeed Adam, then it still doesn't explain L.J.C.,' he said, looking at the slope. He peered into it and fished out the sprig of lavender that Becky had left behind. He turned it thoughtfully in his hands. 'Maybe the owner was called Lavender?' he suggested. He heard a snort of laughter behind him and Becky came up to him.

'Now who's clutching at straws?' she asked. She was still holding the picture. 'Do you have a magnifying glass, then? If this is Ella I want to see her properly. I want to see her face when she's not posed. I want to see what she's *saying*. Does that make sense?'

'Sort of,' said Jon. He fumbled around in a drawer and gave Becky a magnifying glass. 'You're lucky. I use it to identify the tiny defects in the photos – I like them to be perfect and if there's a splodge over their face, I like to know what's caused it.'

Becky raised the old photograph up and peered through the glass at it. Jon longed to take hold of her hair as it fell forward and tuck that strand away for her again, but he somehow thought she wouldn't appreciate the gesture. He was so caught up in the idea of touching her hair and maybe seeing where it would lead, that he was brought back to reality with a kind of muffled squeak from Becky.

'It *is* her, I'm almost certain!' she cried. 'And even more exciting – look at the fireplace. See the carving in the middle of the plaster mantelpiece thing. It's the shield from Carrick Park, isn't it?'

Jon took the photograph and the magnifying glass from her and peered at the carving. It wasn't the clearest of details, but he definitely saw a 'C' shape in the middle of it, just like the ones from the hotel depicted. 'It looks like it,' he said guardedly, 'but let's not get ahead of ourselves.' Almost reluctantly, he moved the glass over the faces of the people. He saw the beauty spot on the girl's cheekbone and the soft tendrils that escaped her carefully styled hair. He saw the look on the man's face and shuddered to think that this might indeed have been Adam who had spoken to him moments before. He moved the magnifier over the background, trying to pick out more details and felt his heart beat faster as he settled on a table in the corner. Placed on the table were a decanter and a set of glasses. He could just see the outline of what looked like another person reflected in the decanter. The person appeared to be sitting down and a box-like structure was on the desk next to them. 'Good Lord,' murmured Jon. 'I think we've got the photographer as well. There is a reflection in the decanter.'

'What?' asked Becky. 'Let me see!' He handed the magnifier and the photograph to her and watched her squint into the glass. 'Can you do anything to make it clearer?' she asked, looking up at him.

'I suppose I could have a go,' he said. 'There are ways of enlarging it. It would be easier if I had the plate, of course.'

'Well you haven't,' said Becky. She thrust the photograph at him. 'Go on, see what you can do in that little darkroom of yours. Pretty please?'

'All right,' said Jon. 'How are you doing over there, Lissy?'

'I'm checking a few records,' she replied. 'I'm looking for the usual things – birth, marriage and death records, census returns, that kind of thing. I think I'm way off track though. I'm looking at the 1871 census return and I can't find a record of any Carricks at Carrick Park. I just thought the easiest and quickest way was to check Carrick Park first. At least we know the place we are dealing with, if nothing else.'

'Good plan,' said Becky. 'What year was that? 1871? Wasn't there a return in 1861? Every ten years? I think the date on this invitation here was nearer to that.' She disappeared and moved the pieces of paper around, searching for the invitation. '1865. Are there any Carricks in the 1861 census?'

'Let me check,' said Lissy. She pressed a few keys and stared at the laptop screen. 'Ooh. I've got a hit. There is one person called Carrick at Carrick Park in 1861– she was seventeen then. Oh, these transcriptions are terrible ... wait. I think if I zoom in on here ... got it! Well. Our Miss Carrick is called Lydia Jane—'

'L.J.C!' cried Jon, turning to Becky. 'We found her!' He put the photograph down and ran over to Lissy.

Becky laughed. 'So not Lavender then!' she said. 'That explains why the writing slope has the Carrick coat of arms on it. It was Lydia's. But it doesn't explain the rest of our puzzle. The finger spelling or the invitation, for instance. She would have been twenty-one in 1865. I wonder if it was an engagement or something really special for her?'

'Hmmm,' said Lissy. She moved the mouse and scrolled the page along to one side. She studied the screen for a moment then shook her head. 'And the census doesn't explain the finger spelling sheet either,' she said.

'How would the census tell us that?' asked Jon.

'The final column states whether the person was deaf, dumb or blind,' replied Lissy. 'I just wondered if that was why Lydia had it. But she's not classed as deaf here, so it can't be hers.'

'No further forward on that one, then,' said Becky. She looked at Jon. 'And it doesn't explain Adam either.'

'I'll do a bit more digging,' said Lissy.

She typed away and Jon returned to the table where the photograph was. He wondered if he had time to start working on it now, while the girls were busy and stared towards his darkroom, thinking. Whilst his attention was elsewhere, he felt someone grab hold of his hands and cover them with their own, trying to force his fingers to move. The feeling was so strong, that he looked down sharply, half expecting to see Becky holding them. Instead, he noticed that she was still beside Lissy, eagerly bending over his sister and reading the information she was pulling up on the laptop. Jon shook his hands, thinking he had maybe cut off the circulation somehow, but the feeling intensified. He felt himself grow hot and cold and stared at them, feeling oddly disassociated from them. He concentrated on trying to hold them steadily in front of him and looked around the studio, feeling scared and helpless. This was all new to him, and if it was something ghostly, he really didn't want to know.

Becky looked at him over her shoulder, as if sensing his discomfort. Her eyes flicked down to his hands and back to his face then she turned and walked over to him. She took his wrists in hers.

'Just go with it,' she said quietly. 'Let them talk.'

'No! It's weird,' he hissed under his breath. He tried to pull his hands away, but Becky shook her head.

'Jon. If I have to put up with Ella, you need to let this happen.'

Jon took a deep breath and tried to relax. He closed his eyes and he felt Becky let go of his wrists. As if they didn't belong to him, he felt his hands shape four perfect letters. Then they dropped to his side. He opened his eyes and looked at Becky.

'What did it say?' he asked.

'*Adam*,' replied Becky. 'I think you've definitely got a connection there with him.' She half smiled, but there was no humour in it. 'Tell me, could you still hear what was going on around you?'

Jon nodded. 'I guess so. It was just my hands that felt like they wanted to do … *that*.'

'So Adam knows how to communicate through you. And he knows how to finger spell so he is either deaf or needs to communicate with a deaf person. We know Lydia is not deaf, according to that census, and when Ella has taken me over I realise that there is no sound. So by process of elimination, I think it's Ella. I think she's the deaf one. This could prove interesting; what wonderful conversations we could have in the guise of Adam and Ella—'

'No! I want to be Jon and Becky!' said Jon, panicking. 'I can't understand all the finger stuff.' He shuddered. 'I want to *talk* to you.'

'You said you would be willing to learn,' said Becky.

Jon hoped she was teasing. 'Well, I would, you know that. But I don't want to be Adam—'

'And I don't want to be Ella!' snapped Becky. She clearly hadn't been teasing that much. 'I can't stop thinking about her now,' said Becky. 'It explains a lot.' She picked up the photograph and studied it again, then sighed and laid it down. 'Dear God, the poor girl; fancy being deaf in that day and age. I can't even imagine it. You know something? I think she's talking to him here – really talking to him. Oh, Ella. What are you saying?'

She moved her hands vaguely, apparently trying to copy the blurred movements on the photograph. 'Maybe she's saying something like ... *what's happening*. Yes, we would all like to know that, Ella.' She walked over to the table where the writing slope was. She sat down, staring at it.

Jon debated whether to go over to her or not, then decided she probably wouldn't thank him for it. This was more awkward than he had anticipated. *Damn his thoughtlessness. Would he ever learn?*

For a moment Jon wasn't sure whether that was Jon talking, or indeed Adam. He had a horrible suspicion, though, that it was Jon.

BECKY

'Adam is still rather elusive,' said Lissy, her voice breaking into Becky's thoughts. 'If he was off travelling or on his Grand Tour or something, we wouldn't be able to pin him down in 1861 and we aren't sure of his surname either. We just *think* it's Carrick. Damn and blast!'

Becky stood up and went back over to Lissy. 'Can you find any marriage records on that lovely site of yours?'

'Marriage records?' asked Lissy. She looked up at Becky, curious. 'Why marriage records?'

'For Adam Carrick, if he is indeed a Carrick,' replied Becky. 'I'm just wondering if he actually married our Ella. If we can find his marriage record, it might help.' The way they were looking at each other in the photograph, Becky thought, if they hadn't married, it would have been a crying shame.

'Good idea,' said Lissy. She gave Becky a thumbs-up sign and turned back to the screen. 'I have a few Carricks coming up here over the years ... I'll try and narrow it down a bit. We think it was around 1865, don't we? Okay, I'll do it for, say, two years either side. Oh! How about this one? It's the exact year, as well.' She turned the laptop towards Becky, her face glowing triumphantly.

Becky read the details out loud. 'A.J.E. Carrick. Married third quarter of 1865. Spouse's surname ... E.C. Dunbar. Well, it's a start. You know what I'm going to ask you now, don't you?'

'If we can find an Eleanor Dunbar or an Ella Dunbar somewhere, yes?' asked Lissy. 'Oh! Oh no! Oh damn it. I knew I should have charged this thing up.'

Becky saw the screen turn black and the laptop blinked. Then it stared at her, uncommunicative. 'Out of battery,' Becky said. 'Great. We all know how that feels, don't we?'

'I'm so sorry!' wailed Lissy. She bashed the side of the laptop in vain.

'That won't work,' said Becky. 'Have you got a charger?'

'Not with me,' muttered Lissy flushing scarlet.

'Great,' repeated Becky. 'This day just gets better and better. Lissy, you know I've always loved you and it's wonderful to see you – but I could scream at you right now.'

'I know! I really am *so* sorry!'

'Can I do anything to help?' said Jon, coming over to them.

'I think you've done enough,' replied Becky curtly.

'I didn't mean it before. I wasn't thinking. I meant that I would rather communicate with you as we do now, than have to do what Adam did all the time—'

Becky held her hand up to stop him. 'You don't know it was all the time,' she said. 'We don't know anything about their situation. All we know is that for one moment, the moment of that photograph, they seemed really happy together. Lissy, where's your charger?'

'At home,' she mumbled, talking into the keyboard.

'Pardon?' said Becky. She knew she had sounded sharp.

'At home,' repeated Lissy, more loudly. 'I need to go now anyway. Have you got your mobile with you? I can let you know if I find anything out?' She raised those eyes, so like her brothers, to Becky and Becky softened.

'All right,' she said with a sigh. 'Let me know as soon as you find anything, okay?'

'Okay. Even if we find an E.C. Dunbar, we need to get the marriage details from the parish register to prove it further. If it's local, I can do that tomorrow.'

Her old friend looked so upset that Becky couldn't resist giving her a quick hug. 'It's fine. You've done so much for us today, it's wonderful. I'm very grateful to you. I'm sorry Ella felt she had to let herself impress upon you like that. It must have been scary.'

'It wasn't the most pleasant of experiences,' said Lissy guardedly.

'No, I know it wasn't,' said Becky. 'See, to her that was normal. She's trying to talk through us, trying to let us know something about her life. We know a bit more than we did, though.'

'And Adam as well. Fancy that, we've actually *seen* them today as well!' Lissy brightened up. Becky knew she wouldn't have stayed down for long. 'Jon, you'll get that photo sorted for us, won't you?' Lissy asked.

'I will,' Jon said. 'It's a priority. Well, hiding in my darkroom is a priority in view of recent events, so I think I'll go and make a start now.' He looked at Becky and attempted a smile. She gave in and half-smiled back. *Damn the man for being so attractive! What had happened to the annoying older brother thing?* Yet she went ahead and added *a little thoughtless* to her mental Jon-list. Still, if that was as bad as he got …

She tried to shake the thought away and helped Lissy pack up her belongings, eventually walking her to the door amid promises of immediate action on her behalf if at all possible. When she returned, Lissy-less, to the writing slope desk, Becky idly looked at her mobile, which was lying just on the top of her handbag. She noticed the message icon flashing and realised she had a text message. And a missed call. She'd had it on silent all morning, not particularly expecting anyone to call her at all. She cursed under her breath and picked it up. She pressed a few buttons and her heart sank. Seb. What the hell did Seb want with her? She'd made the situation perfectly clear to him; their expectations of the relationship didn't match at all. The final straw had come in the shape of a small, curvaceous blonde called Abigail. It was when Becky accidentally bumped into them in a wine bar one night that she realised what was going on.

The sweet nothings Seb was clearly whispering to Abigail riled Becky, and she had stormed up to them, told them exactly what she thought of them and left. She assumed Seb had come to her flat afterwards, as the bag she had left in the foyer containing his possessions had vanished by the time she came home from work the next day. He could have banged and hammered on the door all night, and she still wouldn't have opened it to him. And she'd switched her phone off that night as well, just to make doubly sure he couldn't contact her.

'Damn him, damn him, damn him,' she complained, staring at the message. She was aware that Jon had cautiously approached her from the side and turned to glare at him. He stood there, still in an attitude of apology, clutching a piece of shiny paper between his fingers. There was an odd smell that she recognised as some sort of chemical from the darkroom and she wrinkled her nose.

'Damn me?' he asked.

'No, not this time,' she said with a sigh. 'Damn my ex. He's trying to contact me. Well, I won't answer the phone to him and I won't reply to the text. So there.' She threw the phone down into her bag in disgust and turned to face Jon. 'What have you got for me?'

'I have Ella and Adam,' he replied. 'Not quite in glorious Technicolor, but clear enough to see them better. And I also have the photographer.'

Becky noticed that Jon was actually holding two pieces of shiny paper, one on top of the other.

'The photographer?' She opened her eyes wide. 'May I?' She tentatively held out her hand.

'If you say you'll forgive me,' said Jon.

Becky rolled her eyes. 'For goodness sake. You're forgiven, okay? I'm probably the one who should apologise. Thinking about it logically, I know what you meant. It's

72

easier for us to communicate than it is for us to talk through Ella and Adam.'

'It must have been painstaking, him trying to spell everything out,' said Jon, frowning. 'Really difficult.'

'You'll probably find they used proper sign language,' said Becky. 'Waiting while people spelled stuff out would have driven her mad. And like we said before, she could probably lip-read as well. It would have been natural for her to do that, but we'll never know for sure. Although, looking at this made me think she was talking, remember?'

'I remember. Can you see the photographer's face?' asked Jon. He leaned closer to Becky, pointing to the figure in the decanter. 'She looks a bit shocked.'

Becky felt disturbed, but in a nice way, that he was so close to her. She felt herself flush and stared at the picture, very much aware of his scent. The developing chemicals and his aftershave had, it must be said, combined to make a very attractive mixture. There was a faint smell of mint on his breath as he spoke and she found herself unable to concentrate much on the picture before her. She was aware that his mouth was moving, but she couldn't take in the words. Instead, she transferred her gaze from the photograph to the side of his face and just watched him for a few seconds until he realised he had lost her. He turned to face her and those eyes connected with hers. She thought he said her name, and then all was lost as she closed her eyes and felt his lips on hers and his arms around her. The photographs were forgotten and Becky didn't surface for quite some time.

Becky opened her eyes and the world came rushing back. Nothing had changed; they were still in the studio, still holding one another, still next to the desk with the writing slope on it. The photographs were still on the table and Jon still smelled utterly divine.

'Well, now,' Becky said. It sounded trite and pathetic, and she knew it. 'I wasn't expecting that to happen.'

'I'm glad it did.' Jon smiled. 'My only issue is, was it us or them? Are you going to pull away from me now and slap me?'

Becky shook her head. 'No,' she said. 'Not right now, anyway.'

Jon reached out and carefully tucked a strand of hair behind her left ear. He smiled into her eyes. 'You have no idea how much I've wanted to do that all day,' he said.

Becky reached up and covered his hand with hers. 'Well, you've done it now,' she said quietly. She was surprised at how shaky her voice sounded. 'I think I need some air.'

'Coffee break?' asked Jon. There was a cheeky twinkle in his eye and Becky couldn't help but laugh.

'I think so,' she said. 'Can we take them with us, do you think?' She nodded at the photographs. 'I really want to see them all properly. Now things are clearer.'

'I think they'd enjoy a trip out into Whitby,' said Jon. 'Let me just get a folder.' He tucked the pictures into a display folder and put them inside one of his bags from the studio. 'There now; if anyone sees us, it's a bit of free advertising.'

Becky picked up her bag and followed him out of the studio. 'You're so lucky to have somewhere like this in the middle of such a busy town,' she said, watching him lock up. 'You've always got a bolt-hole.'

'There's a little flat above it as well,' he said. 'I sometimes stay the night if I'm working late or the weather is too bad to travel. It's not much more than a bedsit, really, but it's mine.'

'Even better,' said Becky. 'I'm jealous.'

'Hey, if you ever want to use it the offer is there,' said Jon. Becky cast a sidelong glance at him and he laughed. 'Not like that,' he said. 'Although I wouldn't complain. I meant if you wanted a little holiday or even just some office space for your Goth write-ups.' He shrugged his shoulders. 'My landlady is very accommodating. I pay her a few quid a month and she's happy so long as she can pop in and see me occasionally.'

'*Very* jealous,' said Becky. 'Your landlady's Lissy, right?' She dug her hands inside her pockets. The wind was biting and squalling through the streets. 'We might have to sit inside the coffee shop,' she said. 'The weather's changed a bit from this morning.'

As they walked her eyes were roving around the streets, looking for the girl she had spotted yesterday. There were plenty of people about, obviously, but the fair-haired girl was nowhere to be seen. 'Oh, that's where I intended to go!' she suddenly remembered. 'St Mary's churchyard.'

'We can take a walk up there later if you want,' said Jon. 'I don't mind.'

'You've got a business to run!' said Becky. A gust of wind flipped her hair over her face and she shook it away. She stopped and turned to Jon. 'I can't let you take any more time out of the studio. Goodness knows how much trade you've lost this morning. It's probably one of your busiest days.'

There was the briefest hesitation before Jon spoke. 'I don't mind,' he said.

Becky shook her head. 'No. Let's grab that coffee and then you should go back and earn some money. There's nothing else we can do until we hear from Lissy.'

'You'll not hear the phone ring in this wind!' exclaimed Jon. 'Not up there in the churchyard. At least if I come, she'll ring me if she can't get through to you.'

'You'll not hear it for the wind either,' said Becky. 'A poor excuse. No. I insist I go by myself. I can take some more pictures, interview some more people ... do my job. Then you can do yours.' She squinted as some raindrops started falling and blew into her face. 'Come on, let's hurry before it gets any worse.'

They were lucky; a table had just been vacated in the corner of the coffee shop. Becky squashed into the space and Jon bought the drinks. He brought them over with two ham and cheese paninis and two bowls of steaming hot apple crumble and custard.

Becky sniffed appreciatively. 'Mmm, perfect,' she said. 'This is the second lunch you've bought me. Let me give you some money.' She was still embarrassed about the free dinner at the hotel.

Jon waved her protests away. 'My treat,' he said.

'Then at least give me the receipt. I can claim it on expenses,' said Becky. 'I'll say I met a local photographer in a coffee shop and bought him lunch in exchange for a story about the Goth Weekend clients or something. They're not to know you were a friend already.'

Jon laughed and passed it across to her. 'Good luck,' he said. 'Then when you get the cash ...'

'... I can buy you a coffee,' finished Becky. She picked up the panini and attacked it hungrily. 'I hadn't realised how famished I was. Poor Lissy, she's missing out.'

'She'll be fine,' said Jon. 'She never eats lunch anyway.' He placed the bag on the table between them. 'I don't want to get the photographs greasy. We'll finish eating then look at them.'

Becky nodded assent, her mouth full.

It didn't take them long to demolish lunch. The crumble was gorgeous; just the right amount of mixed spice in it and swimming in custard. She scraped the last spoonful out of the bowl and sat back.

She smiled at Jon and picked up a napkin. 'Time to see the photos,' she said. She carefully wiped her fingers and pulled the pictures out of the bag.

The first one she saw was the close-up of Adam and Ella. She stared at it for a while, trying to get inside Ella's head, wondering what she was trying to tell her; but obtusely, Ella was absent. Becky looked at Jon, wondering whether he was sensing Adam around him. Jon, however, seemed more concerned about sourcing out a coffee refill between customers, than communicating with a man who had lived one hundred and fifty years ago. Wherever Adam and Ella were, it was apparent they weren't in the coffee shop.

In the absence of Adam and Ella, Becky studied the photograph of the decanter. She saw the figure of a young woman, her hand raised as she leaned to the side of a box-like thing, which Becky assumed was the camera. From the little she could make out, Becky found the girl's expression highly amusing; she appeared to be half-shocked and half-laughing.

'Brilliant work,' Becky said to Jon, as he came back to the table with another coffee. 'I wonder who that was?'

'It wasn't cheap to get a camera like that,' said Jon. He had obviously been more interested in the way the camera was portrayed than the girl who sat beside it. 'So it had to be someone wealthy.'

'We know it was Carrick Park just by looking at that coat of arms.' said Becky. 'Maybe tonight we need to scope out the fireplaces in the hotel and try to find a match and go from there.'

'So you're inviting me back to the hotel again, are you?' asked Jon. 'Well, it's a good job I left my overnight things in my room.'

'The very same overnight things you must keep in your bedsit?' said Becky. 'You just happened to grab them after you framed that photograph last night; very convenient.'

'Very observant,' said Jon. 'It may indeed have been like that. And I didn't have far to travel back if it didn't work out.'

'Lucky for you they had a room,' replied Becky. 'And it's my job to be observant. Well, I must say I'm looking forward to tonight, then. Maybe I was a detective in a previous life.'

'Maybe you were Ella in a previous life,' said Jon.

Becky shuddered. 'I hope not,' she said.

'It's like that old poem,' said Jon. 'The one by Dante Gabriel Rossetti. Something about soulmates, and about being here before.'

'Oh, yes, I know the one you mean. "*I have been here before, but when or how I cannot tell*",' said Becky. 'And then it's something about knowing the grass beyond the door, I think.' Her voice tailed off as she realised just how powerful the words were. It was all a bit too much like the experience she had had at the hotel; seeing it as it had been and recognising it of old.

'The bit I liked best, however,' said Jon softly, reaching out for Becky's hand, 'was when he said, "*You have been mine before*".'

His words did something to Becky's insides and she felt the electricity zing up through her fingertips as he touched her. She shook her head, unable to speak, but he must have read something of it in her eyes, because he quirked that funny little smile again and let her hand go. He unfolded something from his pocket and looked at it, then put it back. He carefully spelled out the word *later* and winked.

'Jon!' Becky's voice must have been louder than she thought as several people on the neighbouring tables turned to stare. She felt herself flush scarlet. 'At least you're getting better at it,' she managed more quietly.

'Did you understand it?' he asked.

'I most certainly did,' she said. 'Look, I'm going to the churchyard now before the weather gets any worse.' She stood up and slung her bag over her shoulder.

'I'll head back to the studio,' replied Jon. He stood as well and they skirted around the other customers, Jon clutching his coffee cup as if his life depended on it. 'What will you do later? Do you want a lift back to Carrick Park with me? I assume so, as your car is still parked up there.'

'I'll come back to the studio,' said Becky. 'I doubt I'll be very long. I just want to get a feel for the place, see if I can find any interesting people wandering around the graveyard.'

'There will be plenty of interesting people wandering around the graveyard,' said Jon. 'They flock there.'

'Jon, can I ask you something?' Becky said, eyeing the coffee.

'Anything you like,' he replied.

'Didn't you used to be a smoker?'

'*What?*' The question had clearly taken him by surprise. 'I can't believe you can remember that. I was very discreet. Why do you ask?'

'You're pretty much addicted to caffeine now,' she said. 'And you weren't discreet about smoking at all. We used to watch you in the garden when you lit up, we could see the tip of the cigarette glowing and we used to laugh at you. I was just wondering if this coffee addiction is a nicotine replacement thing.'

'Maybe you're right,' said Jon. It was his turn to flush with embarrassment. 'I gave up a couple of years ago. I seem to have drunk a lot more coffee since then. I'm surprised I'm not constantly wired.'

'Observant, see?' said Becky. She tapped the side of her nose and winked. 'I'll meet you later, okay?'

'Okay,' he said. He brushed her lips with his. 'Take care and don't talk to any strangers.'

'Again, that's my job,' she said, turning away from him as she pushed her hands into her pockets again.

It was a very grey afternoon. Deep down, she hoped that she would see the blonde girl up at the church. She was one stranger she was determined to talk to, and she wasn't going to let a bit of rain and wind stop her.

St Mary's churchyard was even greyer than the town. At least in the town there were cafés and shops and museums to dart into. Becky thought longingly of Jon's cosy studio as she trudged through the churned up mud of the churchyard. St Mary's itself gleamed seal-like behind her, under its grim sheen of rain.

Becky read a few of the gravestones and took several photographs of visitors; surly youths and giggling girls who were scattered among the tombs, the place an eerie amalgam of vampires and Victorians. Yet the one person she was anxious to see wasn't there. She knew deep down that it was maybe wishful thinking, but she couldn't keep from checking all the faces of the tourists, trying to spot the girl from the funeral procession.

After an hour or so, and several interviews later, Becky decided it was time to give up. Her hair was uncomfortably flattened to her head, separating into rats tails somewhere around her shoulders. She walked over to the low wall and looked down onto the harbour, where a small boat with ragged bunting tied to the mast was cutting through the choppy water. One last picture, she thought, and she would head back. She would ask Jon if she could use the room above the studio to get some work sorted out while she waited for him. If he didn't have a computer up there, she could always write in her ever-present notebook. She smiled to herself, as she focused the camera out to sea, thinking how thankful he'd be if she turned up with a couple of coffees and …

'Becky?' She felt a hand on her arm and jumped.

She whipped around, the moment out at sea lost. '*Seb?* What on earth …?'

'I knew I'd find you.' He smiled at her, hideously over-confident as always. His carefully styled floppy hair was still about twenty years out of date. He had always seemed to base himself on a younger Hugh Grant; it was only after they had split up that Becky had realised he wasn't as bumbling and sweet as his Hollywood counterpart had always been in those films. Seb was, to be honest, rather unfeeling and self-centred. It was the way he rolled, he had told her once. Draw them in, make them tell him their stories, then sell it. He worked on a celebrity magazine, famous for its star gossip. Seb was the best interviewer they had and always managed to interview the starlets. Abigail had been a starlet. Well, she had been a reality show contestant on some nonentity channel that had about fifteen viewers, but the principle was the same. Whichever way you looked at it, Seb had been unfaithful: end of.

'How's Abigail?' Becky almost choked on the name. She itched to curl her hand up into a fist and punch him right on his perfect jaw.

'I have no idea,' said Seb easily. He shrugged his shoulders. 'She used me to meet a few people in the industry. I think she was doing some work in PR last I heard. Or shagging a footballer. I can't say for sure.'

Becky made a noise of disapproval and turned back to the North Sea. 'My heart bleeds,' she said. 'And I don't want to speak to you. Go away.'

Seb somehow moved in between Becky and the wall. *Slithered in like a bloody snake*, thought Becky. *Damn him, damn him, damn him.* He had obviously decided that she had to listen to him now, at least. She clamped her lips together, determined not to engage in conversation and determinedly looked out over his shoulder, trying to make the point that she was ignoring him. She held the camera up and fired off a few shots, knowing all the time he was there, just waiting for her to make eye contact.

'You didn't answer my texts. Or my calls. Or the doorbell,' he said, seemingly oblivious to her distaste. A gust of wind roared in off the sea and whipped his words away.

Becky still refused to look at him and continued taking random pictures. She half-wondered how many pictures of damp seagulls and scruffy dogs on the beach she could actually use.

Then Seb laughed. 'So it's like that. I see,' he said.

'Yes it *is* like that,' snapped Becky, finally moving her camera down and facing him. 'What on earth do you expect me to do?'

'Forgive me?' he said, with a young Hugh Grant smile. Becky said something particularly Anglo-Saxon, which just made him throw back his head and laugh. 'Ah, come on, Bex,' he said, using the one version of her name she hated. 'Is it going to be like this forever with us?'

'Yes, actually, I think it is,' she said. 'Now, if you'll excuse me, I have to get back into the town. I've got work to do.'

'Yes, you're covering Goth Weekend aren't you?' he said. 'I've been in touch with Chrissie.'

Chrissie was PA to the editor of the *People's History*. Becky didn't want to know *how* exactly Seb had been 'in touch' with her, but turned away, furious, intending to stomp away from him back through the gravestones.

'Chrissie had no right to tell you where I was,' she threw back over her shoulder.

Seb took hold of her elbow and spun her round to face him none too gently. He grabbed the tops of her arms and pulled her towards him. 'Bex, we were a team. We were unstoppable. Will this not change your mind?' he said. He planted his lips firmly on hers and tried to kiss her.

Becky struggled against him, but he held her tight. She

managed to launch a kick at his shin, which at least made him stumble.

'Ouch!' he said. He looked surprised, which was comical in a way. But he bloody deserved it.

'Keep away from me,' she stated. *Oh God, she could feel Ella descending out of nowhere ... not here, not in front of him ...* But he must have seen something change in her eyes; he put one hand on either side of her face and stared at her. He moved his hands to her shoulders and shook her, repeating her name.

The storm was coming in from the sea. The church in the distance was no longer welcoming; the candle in the window had guttered and the pathway was in darkness. No light spilled out into the churchyard, save the feeble glow of the winter sun as it dropped behind the church and into the hillside. She wished now that she hadn't decided to start for home without him. He'd said he wouldn't be long, but she hadn't bothered waiting. The truth was, she didn't want to be out any later than she had to be. She was so stupid. Why? Why on God's earth had she even contemplated going on ahead?

'Adam!' She called for him, but whether he answered or not, she didn't know. Her eyes searched the twilight, until she saw the dark shape of a horse riding along the cliff path. There was a man on it. He raised his hand to her and waved. Thank God, he'd finished and he'd come for her. She turned, picking her skirts up and ran up the pathway to where she had tied her horse. She fumbled with the bridle, her hands cold and shaking. She dipped her head and blew on her fingers to warm them before picking up the riding crop and mounting the animal. 'Come on,' she urged it. Her heart was hammering in her chest. She hated riding, she hated the dark – how had she thought she could possibly cope with riding in the dark?

Ella faded and Becky saw the world through her own eyes again.

'Seb, just go away,' she managed. This time, she extricated herself from his grasp and hurried away from him. He made no attempt to follow her, but she didn't stop hurrying until she had reached the town and scurried up the side street to Jon's studio.

Jon was working when Becky burst through the door. A girl who appeared to be in her early twenties was sitting at the same antique desk Becky had used when she'd had her photograph taken. The girl was swathed in a black taffeta creation and had a studded choker around her neck and a lily-white face. Becky noticed that the writing slope, though, was no longer on display among the props.

The customer looked up, startled by the clanging bell as the door opened and Jon briefly popped his head from under the cloth of the camera. He waved at Becky across the room and disappeared again.

Becky smiled apologetically at the girl and snuck around the back of the till again, shedding her coat as she went. She realised, too late, that she hadn't brought the surprise coffees.

She watched Jon at work and gradually stopped worrying that Seb was going to walk in after her. Jon had an aura of calm about him, and after the experience on the cliff top by the church, she was grateful.

The customer stood up and, casting a sidelong look at Becky, leaned close to Jon and whispered something a little more than flirtatious about getting a cup of coffee.

Becky dipped her head, smiling. So, he had an admirer, did he? The girl sashayed across to the desk and rummaged around in a purse for a credit card. She was still wearing the black taffeta. It was hers, then, and not one of Jon's multi-size outfits. She kept looking at Jon as he hovered around the door to the darkroom and she kept flicking smug little glances at Becky. *As if I don't know what's going on,* thought Becky.

She found an elastic band on the counter and busied herself with tying her wet hair into a ponytail. *Honestly,* she thought, *some people were so transparent*. She'd worked in retail briefly and so luckily knew a thing or two about credit card machines.

'Here you go,' said Becky. She pressed a few buttons and gave the girl a receipt. Her name was Mina, Becky noticed. A deed poll change if ever there was one or her parents had been fans. Good old Bram Stoker.

'Thank you,' replied Mina, and tucked it in her purse. She stared again into the darkroom.

'Oh, and by the way,' said Becky, lowering her voice and leaning closer to the girl. 'He hates coffee. It brings him out in a terrible rash – all over. It gives him migraines as well.' She tapped her temple to prove her point. 'I wouldn't.' She shook her head and frowned in a concerned fashion. 'I've known him a long time, since we were kids in fact. And I've seen what it can do to him.'

She watched the girl go even paler under her white make-up, then flush so her face became a rosy pink. She stuttered something unintelligible and took herself off to the corner of the studio, where she huddled on a chair until Jon brought her photograph through. Mina grabbed it from him and fled from the studio, slamming the door behind her.

'Bye bye Mina,' said Becky, waving solemnly as the bell clanged almost off its hinges.

'Mina?' asked Jon. 'Unusual name. Nice girl, though. She said if I ever fancied a coffee, she would ...' He looked at Becky and realisation dawned. 'Oh. Right. Ha!' He shook his head and sat down on his usual perch at the edge of the table. 'Thanks, Becky.'

'No worries,' she replied. 'Jon, my ex is in Whitby. I've just seen him at the church.'

'Who? This Seb character?' asked Jon. His face fell. 'Oh. Right. So I could have gone out with Mina tonight then?'

'No, you couldn't have done,' replied Becky without missing a beat. 'She hates coffee, it would never work out. Anyway—'

'But you *know* that she said—' began Jon.

Becky held her hand up to stop him. 'It doesn't matter. I'm just saying it wouldn't work. As for my ex, I'm more interested in avoiding him than actually meeting up with him. He found out from the editor's PA that I was here. I don't know what he hopes to achieve by finding me.'

'Does he want you back?' asked Jon.

'I don't know. He probably just doesn't like the fact that I dumped him. I guess if we got back together it wouldn't last that long because he would dump me, just so he could say he was the dump*er* rather than the dump*ee*.'

'Makes sense, I think,' said Jon. 'Did he follow you down here?' He looked at the door, as if it would somehow open up and let Seb in.

'I don't think so. I don't know if I'm honest though. If he was *really* sneaky, he would have quietly followed me and he'll be hanging around. Then he'll pop up when I leave here later. Ugh.' She shuddered. 'But that's not all, Jon. When I was up there at the church, Ella came back. It was like I was living her life for a few moments again. It was getting close to night-time, because she was frightened of being in the dark alone. I was up on the cliffs and I was waiting for someone, and I saw him coming. So I – well, Ella – got onto my horse ... and that's where it stopped. It wasn't a good feeling though.'

'And it just stopped? Just like that?' asked Jon.

'Yes. I was scared. Really scared. I wasn't scared *of* Ella. I was scared because I *was* Ella. It's difficult to explain.' She reached up to push her hair behind her ears, and realised it was already tied back. She tugged on the ponytail instead and brought it around to hang over her shoulder. 'Whatever was happening to her or was *going* to happen up there wasn't pleasant.'

'And you say she was waiting for someone?'

'It seemed like that, yes. I saw him coming up to me.' Becky closed her eyes and saw the scene again. 'He was on a horse and he was riding up the cliff path. But I don't know if he ever got to me.' She opened her eyes again. 'Oh, no! What if something happened to him there? What if, I don't know, the horse threw him or slipped, and he hurt himself? She wouldn't have heard his cries for help. If it was dark she wouldn't see him very clearly and might be blaming herself for whatever it was; blaming herself because she couldn't help him. Jon, we need to go up there and see if you can feel anything.'

'Don't be ridiculous!' cried Jon. 'It's getting way too dark out there now – just look at it!' He nodded towards the door. 'There's a definite storm brewing.'

'So it's even *more* important to go up there!' said Becky. 'All that rubbish about energy that people go on about; the stuff that makes spirits communicate more easily – what could be more energetic than a storm?'

Becky suddenly remembered the roll of thunder she had apparently heard the first day in Jon's studio, when she had been trying the dress on. 'Yes!' she exclaimed. 'That storm I heard. That was it. It was important to Ella.' Had that really only been yesterday? It seemed impossible. She jumped off the seat behind the counter and stood in front of Jon. 'Please?' she wheedled. She took his hands. 'If you won't come with me, Adam might.'

'Do we really have to go tonight?' he asked. 'Like, right now? What if Seb is still hanging around?'

Becky let go of Jon's hands. 'I'd forgotten about him,' she said bitterly. She went back to where she had dumped her coat and found her bag underneath it. She pulled her phone out and looked at the screen; one new missed call from Seb and two texts from him. 'Another bloody stalker,' she muttered. 'Yay, you *and* him, I'm so lucky.'

There was also a third text from a number she was inordinately pleased to recognise. 'Lissy sent us a message!' She looked up at Jon, smiling. 'I bet she's found something.' She pressed some buttons and read the message. It was very simple. Eleanor Catherine Dunbar!!!!!! Gonna chk St M church 2morrow 4 records. Lissy xxx

Becky held the phone out to Jon. 'She's good,' she said as he read the message.

'Told you so,' said Jon. '"St M church"? St Mary's, maybe? This Eleanor Dunbar must be local, then. Sounds good.'

'I suppose she'll look at the records from the marriage date and try to fit it all together,' said Becky. 'It might prove it was them and we will then have Ella's details. Wow. I feel excited, but a bit scared as well; especially with going up there earlier and seeing what I saw.'

'I know you want to go there,' said Jon, 'but why don't we just go back to the hotel? We can relax, you can work on whatever you need to do and then we can have dinner. It's still a form of research. We want to see the mantelpiece after all, don't we? They might have some history of the hotel somewhere. And it's warm.'

Becky gazed at him, considering the options. 'Okay, then,' she agreed reluctantly. 'It was the idea of warmth that swung it.' There was a damp feeling to her shoulder where her ponytail had been lying and she really did want to pull back a little. Ella was getting stronger, and she didn't know if she was ready for anything else before a decent meal.

'Great. Give me another hour or so, just to catch the last few people of the day and I'll be ready to take you back. Do you want to pop up into the flat for a bit of peace and quiet? You can assimilate all the information.'

'Assimilate?' Becky laughed. 'And peace and quiet? I can

sit in a corner here, out of everyone's way, and have that; but yes. I think I would quite like to see the flat. You can tell a lot about a person from their home. Remember what I do for a profession?'

Jon nodded. 'Yes. I remember. Okay, just through here.'

'Narnia again,' said Becky, picking up her bag. 'You're taking me through the back of the wardrobe, aren't you?'

'Not quite,' said Jon. 'We're going around the side of it.' He squeezed past a pile of old furniture, clearly part of Lissy's contribution, and pulled open a wooden door. It led to a crooked little staircase that looked unbelievably steep and Becky had to put both hands out and connect with the wall to steady herself while she climbed it.

She turned to Jon as she reached the top, her face feeling pink and her eyes wide. 'That throws me so much off balance!' she said.

'It's a funny one,' replied Jon. He was right behind her, the staircase no problem for him. 'You get used to it. It's all uneven and plays havoc with the average person's equilibrium.' He managed to reach around her to unlock another little door and threw it open. 'Welcome,' he said, 'to my humble abode. Oh – that's the bell ringing from the shop. I'll leave you to it.' He bounded back downstairs and left Becky staring around her in delight.

The flat was small, but certainly not a bedsit. Becky was in a little hallway, and to her right was a door which led into the lounge area. It had a sofa and a comfy armchair, and a coffee table in the middle of them. The seating area looked out over the old town and Becky knew the sea was just beyond the rooftops. From the lounge was a door, which stood open and revealed a tiny kitchen.

Back in the hallway, to her left was another partially open door, which was apparently the bathroom, as she could see the corner of a shower unit through it; which left the door straight ahead of her as the bedroom. She toyed with the idea of opening the door and peeking in, and looked over her shoulder for any sign of Jon returning. She waited for a moment until she thought she was safe and hurried the few steps along the hallway to the door. She took hold of the handle and pushed it open, her eyes expertly scanning the room. Yes, it was a bedroom, and it seemed to contain a double bed. A window to the left of the room overlooked the back street where Jon had parked the car this morning. She quickly shut the door and hurried back into the lounge.

The place was remarkably neat and tidy. It was fairly obvious that it was merely a bolt-hole and not Jon's proper accommodation as there were very few personal possessions lying around. A handful of books sat on a bookshelf in the lounge, mainly about photography, local history and antiques, and a walnut desk was pushed into the corner. There was a closed laptop on the desk and next to it was the writing slope.

Becky stared at the laptop and shook her head. Typical Jon – why on earth hadn't he sent Lissy up here when the battery died on her machine? Men! Was *exasperating* on her Jon List? Well. It was now. *Still*, part of her thought, *it means we get a little more time together to work it all out.* She supposed that *almost* made up for it; so she sent a silent thank you to Jon anyway, and went over to the desk.

There was a note beside the laptop. *Becky,* she read, *just in case you pop up here at some point, please feel free to use the facilities. Coffee, tea and snacks are in the kitchen (only long-life milk though) and the password for the laptop and WiFi are both Dracula. Yes, unoriginal, but at least I can remember them.* Jon had signed it with a flourish at the bottom.

Becky put her bag down by the side of the walnut desk and opened the lid of the laptop. She switched it on and waited for it to boot up. She might as well get some more pieces written while she had the chance.

She was very aware of the writing slope lying next to her and couldn't help but rummage through it again. She opened the section she had discovered and pulled everything out of it. Jon had put the photograph in there as well, she realised. She took it all to the coffee table and spread the documents out again. Finger spelling sheet: check. She understood that one. Music score: check. Ella loved her piano; she had practically made Becky play the damn thing. The impressions had been so strong that Becky could only assume Ella was a musician. She metaphorically raised her hat to her, impressed by the girl's talents.

She was almost sure a small breath of wind lifted a wisp of hair that had escaped from her ponytail and a feeling of quiet warmth spread across her. Yes. Ella liked her piano. Next to the music was the invitation; that was still a mystery but it had grounded them at Carrick Park perhaps. Something must have happened that evening that warranted Lydia to keep it with her special mementoes. Becky remembered the cold, dark evening she had experienced through Ella's eyes at the church earlier. It didn't, she thought, have anything to do with that night. The invitation was for the summer, anyway, and not the winter. Then there was the lavender. *No idea*, thought Becky. She didn't dare pick that up or handle it too much, but she got absolutely no sense of ownership from Ella. And finally, there was the photograph; Becky's favourite item. She picked it up, along with the two enlargements that Jon had thoughtfully put with the original.

'Ella Dunbar,' she said out loud, 'is this you then?' She thought, for just a brief moment, that she heard the word *yes* in her mind.

It must have been almost forty-five minutes later that Jon came back upstairs to the flat. Becky looked up, startled, as he drifted past her into the kitchen. It was a room she hadn't investigated properly and she saw him head to the kettle and fill it up from the tap at the sink.

He turned and raised a jar of instant coffee up. 'One for the road?' he asked.

Becky nodded and clicked to save her work onto a USB stick. 'Oh, I think so,' she said. She watched Jon putting the coffee into the mugs and noticed that he looked a little pale and unsettled for some reason. 'Are you okay?' she asked. 'I know that instant coffee may not be your favourite, but if it's all you've got ...'

'Ha! No, that's fine. I've got a percolator in here, but it's too much hassle for a quick one,' Jon said. He brought two mismatched mugs out and headed to the sitting area.

It was really dark outside now, and the town was shiny with the earlier rainfall. The lights glimmered off the rooftops and he sat down, gesturing to Becky to join him. She did so gladly and took a mug from him.

'I had a visitor downstairs,' Jon said, 'when I left you here before.'

'I know,' said Becky. 'I heard the bell ring and you left me to work up here!' She smiled at him, not quite understanding why he seemed so uneasy.

'Hmmm. It was Seb,' replied Jon, looking straight at her. 'Said something about Chrissie telling him you'd met a photographer? Seb said that he was a journalist as well, and that it wasn't hard to trace a photographer in Whitby. He'd tried a couple of others, but thought I was the most likely candidate.'

'God! What did you tell him?' asked Becky, her heart somersaulting.

'I said I'd never heard of you,' replied Jon. 'I tried to put him off the scent but I don't think he was fooled. He went away eventually. I just thought I'd better tell you.'

'Thanks,' said Becky. 'I know he can't harm me, he's just annoying, but honestly! Ugh.' She shuddered. 'The top and bottom of it is that he doesn't think I'm capable of doing my job on my own. We used to work together until I went freelance. He's annoyed at what I've achieved because he always thought he was better than me. And he's not!' She shook her head and stared into her coffee mug. There were a few blobs of milk floating on the top, she realised, but so what. She looked up again at Jon. 'I'm just as good as he is,' she said quietly, 'despite what he thinks.'

'I know,' said Jon. He reached out and squeezed her hand, looking directly into her eyes; she could tell he was sincere. 'I know.'

'Well,' said Becky, 'let's hope that he goes and torments some other poor photographer. I honestly don't even know now what I saw in him originally.' She drained her coffee, suddenly wanting to be away from the little flat. It felt tainted, somehow, that stormy evening. Seb had a lot to answer for. 'Thanks for the loan of the laptop. I got a few bits done, and I'm so pleased you put the writing slope up here as well. Have you finished for the day?' She looked at her watch and realised with a start that it was almost six o'clock.

'Yes, that's me done. Chased the last few people out and told someone to come back tomorrow.' Jon smiled. 'I had someone ask if they could wear your dress; "the one that girl's wearing in that photo." I said forget it, the dress belongs to the girl in the picture and she won't be lending it to anyone.'

'Ha ha! Thanks,' said Becky.

'I mean it!' said Jon. 'It's yours now. Do you think I could ever let anyone else wear it after everything that's happened this weekend?'

'Ah, that's so sweet of you!' said Becky, delighted. 'I'd love to know more about the dress. I'm wondering why it was so special and why they had her painted in it.'

'Maybe it was a wedding dress?' suggested Jon. 'I suppose when we get the dates from Lissy, if it matches up, then we might know.'

'That makes sense,' said Becky. 'So – if it was a wedding portrait, would they do one of her husband? Wouldn't it be on the opposite wall?'

'Not necessarily,' said Jon. 'A lot of the wedding portraits I've come across have just depicted the bride. The pairs of paintings you see tend to be for couples who are a little more established. Well, Lissy said so. She might be lying, she might just be more interested in the brides' clothes rather than the grooms', so she may be deliberately trying to throw me off track.'

'So it's not really worth looking for a wedding portrait of Adam then?' Becky felt deflated. 'I guess, logically speaking, if it was in the possession of Carrick Park, it would be on the wall. So unless it's in a portrait gallery or a private collection, we will never know. Damn.' She frowned. 'But there's no harm in checking around the hotel is there? There might not be a wedding portrait but there might be something.' She looked up, a question in her eyes. 'I'm game if you are.'

'I'm definitely game,' said Jon. He stood up, collecting the coffee mugs. 'Time to take you back to the hotel then, I suppose.'

'I suppose,' said Becky. 'I do love this little place though. Despite Seb hanging around earlier.'

'Well, you know the offer is there for you to use it any time,' said Jon. 'I'll give the place a good airing, though, to get rid of his residue. That's what they do, isn't it?'

'Maybe scatter some garlic cloves around as well?' said

Becky. 'He just sucks the life out of everything for his own gain. He's worse than a proper vampire.'

'The only problem with the garlic,' said Jon, 'is that it would stop most of my customers coming in.'

'Good point,' said Becky. She gathered the papers together from the writing slope and slid them back into the compartment. 'If it's all right with you, I'm going to take this back to the hotel.'

'Fine by me,' said Jon. 'I'll just rinse these out and be back in a second.'

'No problem,' said Becky. She tidied up her workspace and closed the laptop down, then slung everything into her bag. 'Ready when you are.' She couldn't help but check her phone again. She relaxed; no calls and no texts. She hoped that meant Seb had given up.

They drove most of the way back to Carrick Park in silence. Becky stared out at the dark moors, imagining herself in Ella's position. A girl who hated riding and relied on lip-reading would have been terrified to be out on a night like this. As Becky considered it, the sky lit up with a flash of lightning and rain began to pelt down on the car. She watched it run down the windows in silvery rivulets and thanked her lucky stars that she lived in the twenty-first century and had transport. At least they were sheltered from the weather, unpleasant as it was outside.

'It's not the most pleasant of drives when it's like this, is it?' asked Jon, looking sidelong at her.

'What? Oh, yes. I was just thinking that. You must have been reading my mind,' Becky replied. She saw the glint of his teeth as he smiled.

'Yes, you're doing that frowning thing again,' he said. 'Not far now, anyway.' He indicated and the car pulled off onto the little road that led to the hotel.

Eventually they drove through the gates and saw the hotel lit up in front of them.

'A welcoming sight,' said Becky. 'I'd like to see it properly in the daylight, mind. That's two dark nights we've had here and an early morning that was still a bit grim.'

'It probably hasn't changed much from when they were here; well, the exterior, at least.'

'I wonder what the invitation was for,' mused Becky. 'A summer evening and a dinner party; it said it was a celebration, didn't it? It doesn't really matter. It's the people I'm interested in. I imagine the weather was a lot nicer than it is now, though.' She felt a shiver like a wave of laughter flutter across her body and an image of a sky appear that was as stormy as the current evening; only she was shown a deep, velvety indigo sky and the shapes of the trees she saw shadowed against it indicated they were in full bloom.

'Or maybe not,' she said quietly. Overlaying the images was again a deep sense of happiness and joy. Whatever the evening had meant, it had been important to Ella. Becky didn't want to probe too much. If she was meant to find out, she would.

Jon parked the car and they got out, hurrying into the hotel, ducking unsuccessfully to avoid the heavy rain. They ran in through the main doors laughing at the state of each other and headed straight up the stairs. Ella's portrait seemed strangely like an old friend now, and Becky silently greeted her as they passed on their way to their rooms.

Becky was clutching the writing slope and as she shouldered her way into her room, she felt a deep sense of satisfaction that it was, at least for now, back where it belonged. She placed it carefully down on the dressing table and stepped back to admire it. Well, it might not have been in the bedroom originally, but it was part of the house. As an afterthought, Becky pulled the photographs out and placed Jon's enlargement of the couple on the mantelpiece.

'You're back as well, Ella,' she said to the picture. 'We need to find out where this photograph was taken. Leave it with us, we'll have a look around. We're going to look for Adam's picture as well, so don't worry about that.'

Becky had arranged to meet Jon at seven-thirty and go back down to the dining room with him. She checked her watch; she had a good hour. Plenty of time to have a hot bath and relax.

As she lay in the warmth of the water, feeling the gritty texture of the bath salts on her skin, she was aware that in the very next room, perhaps only separated by a wall, Jon might be doing the same thing. All right, it wasn't particularly likely that he would be using rose bath salts, but he might be submerged in water just as she was. It gave Becky a pleasant feeling to imagine this and without thinking she placed her fingertips on the tiled wall, almost feeling the thrumming of the water running through the pipes and filling Jon's bath. She removed her fingers and lay back, closing her eyes against the steam. She tipped her head back, soaking her hair and washing the storm-damp of Whitby out of it.

She remained in the bath for longer than she probably should have done, and it was with great reluctance that she crawled out of her steamy cocoon and, wrapped in another huge, white, fluffy towel, wandered into the bedroom again. Once more, she dressed; a little less formally today in beige chinos and a soft, white, cashmere sweater, and pulled her hair back into a loose bun. She made sure she had the original photograph in her handbag and checked her phone once more, just to make sure Seb wasn't hounding her. She exhaled with relief when she saw that there was only another message from Lissy, saying she would meet them the next day. Mite be some good stuff she had added at the end. Translating it quickly, Becky assumed she would be running on Lissy time and they shouldn't expect to pin her down to a particular hour. *Good stuff*, Lissy had said; Becky hoped so.

Seven-thirty saw her leaving the room, and also saw Jon leaving his room. She felt her face split into a stupid grin when she saw him, and was pleased to see that expression reflected back.

'Good evening,' said Jon.

'Good evening,' said Becky.

'Ready?'

'I am.'

'Good. Let's go.'

They walked along the corridor towards the staircase and Becky drew the photograph out of her bag.

'I've got the picture,' she told Jon.

'I can see that,' he replied. They were passing Ella again and Becky stopped, remembering that she wanted to study the date on the picture. She read the gold title; the black, cursive script small and difficult to see. *Lady Eleanor Carrick, November 1865*. Becky's lips quirked into a smile. If it was her wedding portrait and she was indeed the E.C. Dunbar who had married A.J. Carrick in the third quarter of 1865, it all fitted together rather nicely.

'Oh!' she said, suddenly remembering. 'Lissy texted. She's coming tomorrow, definitely. But she didn't mention a time.' She relayed the gist of the message to Jon who rolled his gaze heavenwards and nodded.

'That's typical Lissy,' he said. He paused in front of the portrait and tilted his head slightly.

'What do you see?' asked Becky, hardly daring to ask.

'Her hair; it's practically in the same style as the photograph. It's nice.'

'Is that all?' Becky made an exasperated sound. 'I thought it was something exciting. It was probably a fashionable style in 1865. "The styles tended to reflect their dresses", remember? You told me that yourself. See, she has it pulled back behind her ears, and there's a little twist around at the back.' She didn't wait for his reply. Instead, she turned away and headed down the stairs. 'Come on, let's try and locate this mantelpiece before dinner.'

Once downstairs, Becky stood in the hallway and concentrated on the layout of the house. 'I didn't notice a mantelpiece like that in the dining room,' she said thoughtfully, 'but that's not to say it wasn't there originally.'

'Well, you thought that room is where the piano was, didn't you say?' replied Jon.

'That's the impression I got,' replied Becky. 'What if the dining room and the bar were once one big room; it *felt* a lot bigger than it *looked* last night to me. And as we say, there was no mantelpiece in the dining room area. If the place was to be refurbished as a hotel, surely the sensible thing would be to ... aaaah! That's it. After I saw the piano last night, didn't we sit down by a fireplace in the bar?'

Jon frowned, trying to remember. 'Yes, I think we *were* by a fireplace. I brought the drinks over – and I saw it from the bar when I turned around. Good call. Why didn't we notice the coat of arms on it last night?'

'I suppose I had other things on my mind,' said Becky. 'Right, let's head that way now and see if we can settle it.'

Becky gestured for Jon to lead the way and she followed him, clutching the photograph. Her heart was beating fast, which was, she knew, ridiculous. It was, it seemed, a foregone conclusion that the coat of arms would be the same one; but for her to feel that she was standing in the same place as Ella had been that day ... she fully expected Ella to rush at her like a whirlwind and was trying to prepare herself for it.

They walked into the bar area and Jon wandered over to buy drinks, somehow knowing that Becky needed to be alone for this. Becky herself headed straight across to the fireplace. The room was fairly empty. It was a Sunday night after all, and Becky assumed that most people had gone home, ready for work on Monday.

Ella pressed in on her as she approached the fireplace, but surprisingly, it didn't bother her as much as she had feared. Instead, Becky stood in front of the mantelpiece and ran her fingers lightly over the coat of arms in the centre, tracing out the C in the middle. This was it, she was positive. Satisfied, she watched for Jon coming over with the drinks and smiled at him in greeting.

'I think we have the mantelpiece,' she said. 'Look.' She

beckoned to him and showed him the coat of arms. He leaned over and studied it. Then he stood up and took something from the mantelpiece itself.

'Certainly looks like it,' he said, holding up a photograph and matching it to the plasterwork.

'What's that?' asked Becky, pointing at the photograph. 'Where did you get it from?'

'This? It's the enlargement I did,' said Jon. 'You brought it down, didn't you? I got it from the mantelpiece.' He nodded to it. 'You must have put it there when you looked at the coat of arms.'

'No,' said Becky shaking her head slowly. 'It's not. I left that in my room. I just have the original picture with me.' She lifted it up and showed it to him. 'What's going on?'

It was a strange echo of the past; they stood in almost the exact same positions as Ella and Adam had done in the original picture and Becky knew she had just asked the same question that Ella had asked Adam at the moment the photograph had been taken. *What's happening?*

One of the logs popped and flashed as a flame burst through it, splitting the wood as if emulating the light of that distant flashbulb. Jon jumped and swore but Becky just stared at him. 'It's on my mantelpiece in my room,' she repeated. 'The photograph was there.' She looked at the mantelpiece beside her, confused and lost somewhere between her world and Ella's. She raised her eyes and stared into the mirror above the fireplace, feeling for a bizarre moment there would somehow be four of them reflected in it; but it was worse than that. There was someone staring back at her from the other side of the room, but it was not Ella. It was not even Adam or an ethereal image that might have been Lydia: it was Seb.

'What the *hell* is he doing here?' Becky said. Her face had suddenly gone all white and pinched, and seemed to reflect a queer combination of fear and anger.

She was looking across the room and, for a moment, Jon thought she had seen one of the ghosts of the people they had encountered; in the flesh, as it were. He followed her gaze and saw a young man, as solid as they were and recognised him as the person who had come into the studio asking about Becky earlier.

Becky turned back to Jon and flashed such a look of hatred at him he was shocked.

'Did you tell him anything?' she asked. 'Did you say anything at all about me?'

Jon shook his head. 'No, nothing. I wouldn't have done that.'

She shook her head as if she disbelieved him and looked away, staring back at Seb.

Jon felt about the size of the cashew nut that he spotted under the table. He took hold of her arm and shook it, trying to get her attention. 'I didn't, I promise,' he said uselessly. Becky pulled away without acknowledging him and folded her arms.

Jon watched Seb saunter over to them; a little, sneering smile on his film star perfect face.

'Bex,' he said, completely ignoring Jon. 'I knew I'd find you soon enough.'

Becky told him categorically where he could go and Seb laughed at her.

'It wasn't hard. I saw your coat in his studio.' He nodded his head towards Jon. 'I just had to wait outside and follow you. God, it was cold in that alleyway.' He spoke slowly and, Jon noticed with a rising annoyance, he had stepped right inside Becky's personal space.

'There's a name for people like you,' said Jon in a low

voice. He saw by the twitch of Seb's eyebrow that he had heard him. 'I can probably call the police right now and have you arrested.'

'Seb, I told you to leave me alone!' said Becky rather too loudly. 'Can't you take a hint?'

'Is this your new boyfriend, Becky?' continued Seb, still at the same low, measured pace. 'I know you were probably on the rebound when you picked him up, but honestly, someone like him who's got a poky little studio and relies on mad, vain tourists? It's not sustainable. Come on. I'll take you back home and we can start again. You know we worked well together.'

'No, we did not,' said Becky. This time her voice was staccato, pressing her point home. 'Go away and stop bothering me.'

'You heard her,' said Jon. Even to his own ears it sounded rather pathetic.

The corner of Seb's mouth curled up into a smile, but he never took his eyes off Becky. Instead, he held his hand out, apparently expecting her to take it and walk meekly out of the hotel.

Becky shook her head again. 'No. I said *no*, Seb.'

'Come on, mate. Enough's enough,' said Jon. He could feel that odd sensation creeping into his fingers again. It was Adam. Whatever Seb was doing to Becky, Adam didn't like at all. Jon felt his hand ball into a fist and had an image of himself punching Seb in the middle of the bar. As a rule, he was not a violent man and would more often than not try to joke his way out of a situation. He tried to calm the feelings that were rising up from the floor and engulfing him; he felt powerless against a massive rage and an unreasonable hatred of Seb.

A few people were filtering into the bar area now and Jon was aware of a group of pensioners as they tottered in and sat nearby. The old dears were oblivious to the tension and more intent on chattering about how snug the fire was. There was no way Jon was going to pursue this scene with Seb in polite company. He fought back Adam's desire to punch the man and with a great effort turned away from him.

'Seb, if you want to continue this conversation, I suggest we go outside,' said Becky.

'Your call,' said Seb, shrugging his shoulders. 'If you think I can talk to you better in private.'

Jon saw Becky narrow her eyes, and then she nodded curtly. 'I don't want to talk to you in here,' she said. 'Outside is better for me.'

Jon sensed the atmosphere thickening around them; he understood that there were too many echoes of the past and the likes of Adam and Ella weren't going to give up any more easily than Seb was – especially not on their territory.

Becky gestured for Seb to leave the room in front of her. As the man turned and started to leave, she flicked a look up at Jon. For the first time, he saw a glimmer of uncertainty in her eyes. He managed to fumble out the letters O K to her. He frowned, trying to make her see it as a question and was rewarded with half a smile and a nod of her head. He nodded back, and watched her follow Seb out of the room.

Jon waited a few moments; then he couldn't help himself – he followed them out.

'Bex, where the hell are you taking me?' asked Seb. She was weaving through the dark pathways and he could barely see where they were going. She ignored him and continued down through some trees as he stumbled after her. 'Bex!' he shouted, feeling the old anger bubble up inside of him. 'I don't know what you think you're playing at—'

'This is the summer house,' she said, turning around. 'We're going to stop right here, Seb.' She moved to face him and leaned against the door frame of the pretty, restored Victorian building. She folded her arms and her eyes drilled into him. 'Now are you going to tell me what you're doing here? I thought I'd been very clear when we spoke earlier.'

There were some glass storm lanterns inside the summer house and they threw her face into shadow. His face, he realised, was illuminated by the lights and he blinked at the brightness. He felt like he was under some sort of inquisition and made to move further towards the shadows.

Becky, however, remained firmly in the door frame – short of physically pushing her out of the way, he couldn't actually get into the summer house and, despite everything, he wasn't going to lay his hands on her. So he tried another tactic, he went for her emotionally, rather than physically.

'Becky, are you doing all this for the correct reasons?' he asked.

'Doing what?' Her voice was sharp and Seb felt a frisson of annoyance.

He tried to keep his voice calm. 'Being like this? Being in Whitby, by yourself? What are you trying to prove?'

'I've got nothing to prove,' replied Becky. She shifted position, crossing her arms the other way and following that by crossing her legs. Ah – she was being defensive then. Seb hadn't worked in this industry for so long without understanding basic body language. Yet she stared at him and met his eyes steadily. 'What makes you think I have?'

'Because you're bloody-minded and want to get back at me?'

'Maybe.'

'Look, Abbie was—'

'It wasn't all Abbie,' retorted Becky. 'That was just what made me decide.'

'Abbie was because you were freezing me out, working through your "issues".' He made quotation marks in the air with his fingers to emphasise his point.

Becky rolled her eyes. 'Load. Of. Rubbish,' she said. 'Abbie was because you couldn't keep it in your pants.'

Seb chose to ignore that comment. Abbie had been a very attractive young lady, but that was beside the point. No – best to deflect this by turning it back on his ex-girlfriend, who stood there defying him like he didn't know what.

'Becky. What are you going to do in five years' time? Ten years' time? Fifteen?'

'Same as I'm doing now, unless I get a better deal,' she said. 'Nothing's going to change.'

He laughed and shook his head. 'I don't know if you're an idiot or just stubborn.'

'Okay, that's *really* going to win me back,' said Becky. 'This conversation is over. I'm not listening to you any more.' She pushed herself away from the door frame and turned to head back to the gardens.

'Not listening?' said Seb loudly and sharply. 'Well now, there's a surprise.'

Becky swung around and glared at him. 'Words fail me. You arrogant, talentless, useless piece of—'

'Talentless?' Seb almost shouted. 'You're calling me talentless? Look here, Becky Jones, I'm the one that got us all those *Gossip World* assignments. You can't claim any rights to those.'

'I can't,' said Becky, her eyes like fire as she closed the gap between them, 'but I'm the one who wrote the damn articles because you were too busy shagging the interviewees. Or their management. Or their bloody dog-walkers.'

'That was a one-off!' yelled Seb.

'One-off be damned!' Becky yelled back at him. Their faces were inches apart and for one moment Seb remembered that spark they had once shared. And the sex. The lots and lots of sex.

He couldn't help it; he reached out and pulled her face towards him. God, she was still gorgeous, despite everything.

'What the—?' Becky clamped her hands over his and pulled them away from her face, almost flinging them back at him. 'Do *not* touch me. You *never* touch me again, are we clear on that? You don't want the whole package, so you can just get out of my life.'

Seb swore and turned away, punching the door frame so the whole thing shook. 'Bex. Listen,' he said, turning back and planting himself right in front of her. 'I've tried to be reasonable. I've offered to take you back. I am the best you can hope for now, especially if you want to stay in this business. You don't need a fruit-loop like that photographer because what can he ever do for you? I can make things work for you. I can get us assignments and pull strings and we can do it all over again. We were a good team. And if you refuse that offer, well.' He spread out his hands, palms up and looked her directly in the eyes. 'I can make things really difficult for you. I know a lot of people.'

Becky glared at him. 'Yes. And so do I. And I know the ones who will accept the fact I'm a professional, freelance journalist, and you are a useless, talentless idiot who doesn't even know how to handle your own life, never mind anyone else's. You think if you ring up and report things about me, it'll make them want to work with you?' She tapped the side of her head. 'Think about it. Who'll come out of it the best? And who's got the work on her hard drive, emailed to herself, for every damn article we ever did together that went out under our joint names? Oh. That would be me. Because you were too busy playing shag-buddies with the dog-walker to do any bloody work. And Jon isn't a fruit-loop or whatever you called him. He's a friend, and he's more of a friend than you ever were. And the fact is, I can't afford to waste any more of my life with someone like you, Seb. It's over. Accept it. Move on.'

Seb stared at her. This wasn't exactly the way he'd imagined this panning out, if he was honest. In his mind, she had accepted his terms and crumpled into a sobbing heap, declaring her life was worth nothing if he wasn't in it.

Of course he knew that those articles were all her work – he'd had very little input, if you didn't count the input he'd had in the starlets themselves. And that was something he was conscious of. If Becky wasn't working with him, he'd have to do it all himself and he knew he wasn't the best at it. That was how it had worked between them so well and for so long. He had once appreciated the fact that she was feisty and bloody-minded. Now, he wasn't so sure.

Becky looked at him one last time and shook her head. All the fight seemed to have gone out of her.

'You are unbelievable,' she said quietly. 'Please. Just get out of my life. Things are hard enough right now without you around.'

'One last thing,' he said, holding his forefinger up. He dropped his voice to match hers. 'I managed to book a room at the hotel. I will be here for a few more days. You think about what I've said to you and about everything – and I mean *everything* – that's already happened. Then you can tell me whether you think it'll work out for you in this industry or not.'

'Goodbye, Seb,' replied Becky. 'Thanks for your concern, but I don't need you. At all. I never did.'

She turned away and headed off into the darkness before he could reply. She disappeared behind some shrubs, and was swallowed up in the night.

Now he was alone, Seb shivered and looked around. He didn't actually like it in that summer house, he suddenly decided. One of the lanterns creaked as it swung in a breeze that he couldn't feel and it sounded horribly like a man, shifting his weight from one foot to the other on loose floorboards as he squared himself up for a fight.

Seb didn't hang about. He hurried away, back to the hotel using the quickest, most well-lit route he could find.

Becky would come round to his way of thinking.

Otherwise, what hope did they both have?

It was dark outside and the wind hadn't abated, but at least the rain had stopped. Jon walked around the perimeter of the hotel. He could make out the skeletal shapes of trees, the branches waving madly in the wind. He saw the two of them sitting on a seat in the courtyard at the back of the hotel. A pool of light fell onto them from a lamp – the sort of lamp they had lining the driveway to the hotel. Becky's words about Narnia came back to him from earlier and he again felt the anger rise as he realised that, for all his diversionary techniques, the mere fact that Becky had left her wet coat lying behind the counter had caused all this. Neither one of them had thought that Seb would have had the gall to search for her as he had done. The man clearly couldn't accept rejection.

Jon kept close to the edge of the building, watching the couple in the lamplight, wondering what Seb was saying to her. They were, as far as he could tell, turned towards each other, a stiff sort of formality between them. Becky sat very straight, her hands folded on her knee while Seb was the more animated of the two. Jon felt unaccountably angry at his performance. And if Becky decided to believe him and give him another chance; well, he didn't want to think about that scenario. He crept closer to them, feeling more of a stalker than Seb had been.

Jon was disturbed by a rustling in the undergrowth to his left. There was a high hedge there with a small gate he could just make out in the shadows. An entrance to the gardens, he assumed, a piece of the old Carrick Park left behind to enable guests to take a little wander in the gardens after dinner. It was probably lovely on a warm summer evening, strolling around the lawns with a glass of wine in your hand. It didn't seem as appealing in November, somehow.

He peered through the darkness and heard footsteps hurrying towards him from the gardens. There was a little, wheezing breath coming with them, as if someone had been running or walking too quickly in the bitter temperatures. He pressed himself against the wall, hoping that whoever it was didn't see him and take him as a prowler, simultaneously wishing that they would hurry up and get past him, so he could creep ever closer to Becky and Seb. Well, okay; so he was a *bit* of a prowler, he conceded, but only for that moment in time. To his horror, a security light flashed on as the person broke the beam, which must have been linked to the area next to the gate. Instinctively he closed his eyes at the bright light, appalled at the fact that he had been caught out looking exceedingly guilty. Too late, he tried to throw himself to the right, around the corner, away from the glare.

'Jon?' Becky's voice. And she sounded, yes, out of breath, but also rather shocked to see him there – as she would be, really, he conceded again.

Jon opened his eyes painfully, the light seeming to sear into his retinas, so used had he become to the soft darkness of the grounds and the small pool of light in the courtyard. 'Everything okay?' he asked weakly.

'Fine, thanks,' said Becky. 'What are you doing?'

'I was coming to save you from Seb,' said Jon, even more weakly.

'*Save* me?' repeated Becky. She opened her eyes wide. The light, he realised with a pinch of annoyance, wasn't bothering *her*, was it?

Jon shrugged. He didn't really have an answer for her. He spread his hands out in front of him helplessly.

Becky's eyes flicked down to them and back up to his face. 'Please don't do that,' she said. 'Seb just did that and it did not endear him to me. But do you know what? I did wonder if you were going to punch him earlier, because that might have been quite interesting. I feel like punching him myself now. Anyway, I think he's finally got the message, so there's really no need to rescue me.'

'Where is he?'

'I haven't a clue. I left him at the summer house. It's all floodlit and it's really pretty. If you're with the right person, that is. I told him how I felt; I told him he was out of order.' She smiled derisively. 'And then I just wanted some space, so I came back the long way.'

'How did you know there was a long way and a short way?' asked Jon. 'And considering the long way doesn't appear to have any floodlighting.'

Becky dropped her eyes. 'I just did,' she said. 'And I have excellent night vision.'

They had gone back to the house through the rain-drenched gardens, and Ella had run up the staircase. He had followed her up to the first landing and reached out to stop her before she took the flight towards the left wing.

'When we are married, I shall have your portrait hung right there.' He pointed to a space on the landing wall …

Jon made a little involuntary noise and started. Becky must have caught the movement and she looked up at him quickly.

'Never mind,' said Jon. His voice was tight. 'You don't have to tell me the details.' Then his voice hardened. It was as if he wasn't the one formulating the words, but he was the one speaking them. *'But if he comes near you again, I shall not be responsible for my actions.'*

It was at that point, Jon remembered the couple in the courtyard. He spun around to face the area. He shouldn't really have been surprised to see that the courtyard was empty and that there wasn't even a seat in it; but he was.

The rest of the evening was spoiled, of course, the spectre of Seb hanging over them as they had dinner. Becky lost count of the times that Jon opened his mouth and tried to apologise. She did a fine job of ignoring him after the first dozen or so attempts and she knew that he knew it. She felt rather flat and all the delight of discovering the fireplace had evaporated; even the puzzle of the photograph on the mantelpiece was forgotten. Becky truly didn't know what Seb had done after she had left him at the summer house. If he had tried to follow her, he would have been unsuccessful – Ella had guided her beautifully, she realised. She had woven in and out of trees and hedges, following tiny, overgrown pathways that had been neglected for years. Once, she had stopped by a tree and stood, looking around her, for a clue as to where she must go next. She had touched her fingertips to the tree, looking up at the storm-grey clouds sailing across the velvet sky and wondered if she could get a better sense of Ella out here – out in familiar grounds. Even if the pathways were dark, it was not the darkness of St Mary's, that darkness which had scared her that afternoon. This was a familiar darkness and as such, she felt safe.

Remembering the church perked Becky up briefly. 'I wonder if Lissy will tell us anything we haven't already worked out?' she said.

'It'll be good to have clarification, regardless,' said Jon. He helped himself to more coffee from the pot the waitress had kindly left on their table. By a mutual, silent agreement, alcohol was not going to enter the equation with dinner. Becky sighed and rested her chin on her hands.

She watched Jon drink the coffee, saw him pull a face, and raised her eyebrows. 'What, a cup of coffee you don't like?' she asked. 'How strange.'

'It's gone a bit cold,' replied Jon. He put the cup down and pushed it to one side. 'I'm really sorry, you know …'

'*Aaaaahhhh!*' wailed Becky. She covered her face with her hands and shook her head dramatically. 'Enough! Please. It's not your fault that Seb saw my coat and followed us here. He's ruined the night, I appreciate that. But he's gone now and that's it.' She let her hands flop onto the table and she sat back in the seat. 'I think we'll feel better after a good night's sleep, don't you? It's been stressful.' She made a dismissive gesture with her hand. 'Thanks, Seb, appreciate that.'

'Yes, it's probably a good idea to get some rest,' agreed Jon. 'We'd best head upstairs then.' He smiled at her, and despite herself her insides did a somersault. *God!* Somewhere from her subconscious floated lines from the last verse of Rossetti's poem: *And day and night yield one delight once more …*

She quashed the thought and stood up rather too quickly. Had she really been considering ... *that* with Jon? Yes, she thought. Yes, she had been. She looked at Jon and studied him as he pushed the chair back and stood up. Damn Seb! He'd spoiled everything; being with Jon like that really didn't feel appropriate any more.

Becky was sure Ella was laughing at them as they passed her portrait. She noticed that Jon hung back on the stairwell again and she turned, meaning to ask him if he felt the same as she did about the girl in the picture. She got no further than formulating the question in her mind. There was a strange expression on his face and the Jon she had grown to know seemed to have slipped behind a mask. It was his eyes, she realised with a start. For a brief moment, well, they just weren't *Jon's*. She touched his arm and willed him to look at her. After a moment he did.

'What is it?' she asked.

'She was always meant to be in that spot in the stairwell, you know,' he replied. 'Adam told her the night he asked her to marry him. They were in the gardens, there was some sort of party going on – when they came back, he told her he would have her portrait painted and he would hang it there.'

Jon looked at Becky and took her hand. He still seemed as if he wasn't entirely himself. 'And he promised her all of that, when she was standing there; right where you are. And he was here, where I am. And we were at the fireplace in the same positions as they were earlier. And that had good memories for them as well.'

I have been here before, But when or how I cannot tell. Rossetti's words hung in the air between them. *When* and *how* were the words that Becky wanted to clarify; yet she could find no words with which to answer Jon.

Jon intended to leave Becky at the door to her room. It really wasn't how he had hoped or indeed planned for the evening to end, but after Seb turned up – it just didn't seem right. What if she thought he was trying to take advantage of her?

One thing was certain though: he definitely knew that whatever sort of annoying childhood friend she'd been, she wasn't that any more. He half-wished Lissy was there, to diffuse his feelings. But on the other hand, he was extremely grateful they were alone. Fate was an incredible thing. If he hadn't have gone for that coffee; if she hadn't caught sight of that girl and paused, just in his pathway … would they have met again and found this connection between them?

Yes.

The answer in his mind was emphatic. Of course they would have done.

Jon forced his thoughts back to the present. 'I'll be right next door if you need anything,' Jon told Becky, trying to inject a note of cheerfulness into his voice.

Becky stood, her hand hovering uncertainly above the lock as she apparently plucked up courage to open the door. Eventually, she turned huge, brown eyes up to Jon. 'Please don't let me go in there by myself,' she almost whispered.

It must have almost killed her to ask him, he reflected. She hadn't really shown any fear of the dead at all so far.

'Look, I know it's stupid, but I'm a bit scared. The photo for a start – what if someone was in my room and took it? What if they've done anything else?'

She didn't need to elaborate; they both knew who she

meant. It wasn't the dead she was concerned about, then, Jon realised. He still had an uncomfortable feeling about Seb. He didn't seem to be the sort of person who would just let things go. Even now, he might be in the gardens, just waiting for a chance to come back into the hotel; possibly book a room in order to sit and stare at them over breakfast. Jon's imagination began to take flight. He opened his mouth to suggest something, then closed it again.

Instead, he nodded at Becky. 'Okay. I'll come in with you, if it would make you feel better.'

'Thanks,' she replied. She took a deep breath and Jon found himself doing the same. Becky turned the key and pushed the door open. 'I just hope they left the writing slope alone,' she said.

She walked into the room and stood in the centre of it, looking around. It was a little untidy, but no more than was to be expected of a hotel room. Some clothes were folded on top of the chair, a book was lying on the bedside table next to half a glass of water. Becky's hairbrush and make-up were on the dresser, but nothing looked as if it had been deliberately messed up.

'Does everything look all right?' asked Jon, coming to stand beside her.

'I think so,' she replied slowly, unfastening her hair from the topknot she'd tied it up in. Jon saw her cast a glance over the room and then she pointed to the writing slope, which was sitting on the dressing table. 'I left it right there, so it hasn't moved.'

She hurried over to it, her hair falling now in a dark curtain which obscured her face as she bent over the slope. Jon saw the little kink in her hair where the elastic band or whatever it was had held it in place and longed to smooth it out with a touch of his fingers.

Becky straightened up and turned to him, smiling. 'The

papers are all there, apart from that enlargement. I have no idea how that got down to the fireplace.' Again, that little quirk where she pushed her hair behind her ear. 'I think we're fine.'

'So, you're quite happy for me to go to my room, then?' asked Jon. He didn't expect her to challenge that statement, but when she paused for a split second, he felt his heart beat just a little faster. Then just as quickly, his hopes were dashed.

'Yes, you go back. I know where you are if I want you,' she said.

'Well, then. Just make sure you knock on the door really hard,' he said, 'if you want me, that is.'

'I will,' she replied.

Jon nodded and backed away towards the door. 'You sure?' he tried.

'I'm sure,' she said.

'Goodnight then.'

''Night.'

Before he realised it, Jon was outside in the hallway staring at a closed door. He waited a moment or two, then opened the door of his own room.

It must have been about quarter past one, when he heard the knocking. He woke with a start and for a moment couldn't place the noise. He realised that whoever was knocking was not about to give up any time soon.

'Becky!' he almost shouted her name. He threw back the covers and ran to the door. He pulled it open and she stood there like a wraith; her face was as white as the robe she had flung over her shoulders, her eyes darker even than her hair. Now that she had a response, she pushed her hands into the pockets of her robe.

'Jon,' she said. 'Let me in. I'm staying in here tonight.'

Jon took her wrist and pulled her firmly into the room. He led her over to the bed and sat her down on it. He was conscious that her gaze never left him as he moved to the wall and flicked on the bedroom light. She squinted a little as the light flooded the room.

'I had the worst dream ...' Her hands were still in her pockets. 'It's definitely something to do with the coast, Jon. I had this horrible dream. It started when I was reading. I picked up a book and I was looking at it, and I read some of that poem we were talking about. "*The sweet keen smell, the sighing sound, the lights around the shore.*" I thought that I must have remembered the lines. And then, in my dream, I could smell lavender – really, really strong lavender. And I could smell the sea and the fresh air. Then I started to feel all this weird stuff happening. It was dark and stormy and I was scared, and then I had the feeling I was falling and I couldn't breathe. I woke myself up at that point. And this was on my pillow.' She raised her right fist and dropped a sprig of lavender on Jon's knee. 'And this was on the floor.' She raised her other fist and opened it. Her fingers spread like a starfish and a stream of golden sand slid out of her hands and piled up on the floor by her feet.

'What do you think?' she asked eventually.

They both stared at the sand and Jon poked it with his toe.

'It was by the chimney,' continued Becky. 'I mean, it's possible that the storm blew it up from Whitby and dumped it down the chimney ...'

'Practical Becky. Well, it's possible, I suppose. It certainly looks like sand,' he said.

'I have no idea where it came from. It was just there when I woke up,' replied Becky. 'It was weird when I was dreaming of the seaside though. So, I don't want to go back in there; at least not until daylight.' She pulled the robe around her shoulders. 'So can I share the room? You can have the bed, if you want,' she added.

'Don't be stupid. You can have the bed. I'll manage,' replied Jon.

The undercurrents were ridiculous. He knew what they were both trying to say – and indeed trying to avoid saying. The words *elephant in the room* sprang to mind. But it wasn't right; deep down, he knew that. God, things must have been easier in the Victorian days. There was no question of it outside of a respectable marriage was there? Somewhere from the left of him came a deep, unamused chuckle. *Very wrong, my friend.* Jon's stomach clenched and he quickly looked at Becky to see if she had heard it too. Of course she hadn't, and anyway, her attention was still on the sand.

After a moment, Becky looked up at him. Jon tried to keep his face expressionless.

'Okay. I'll have the bed, then,' she said. It was so unexpected that Jon just nodded his head. *There's still one of them about!* he wanted to shout, *and he thinks I'm his friend!*

'Great,' said Becky. ''Night, then.' She swung around and somehow managed to ease herself under the covers, still wearing the robe. She wriggled a bit, then brought the key to her room out from the depths of one of the pockets. She placed the key carefully on the bedside table and pointed at it. 'My key,' she told him. 'I'm not taking any chances.'

Jon nodded and shuffled over to the edge of the bed, knocking the lavender onto the floor where it landed among the sand. He leaned down and picked up the flower head, turning it in his fingers the way Becky had done with the dusty specimen from the writing slope. It was different to the normal lavender that grew in gardens and the borders in places like Carrick Park. It wasn't even proper lavender – a mistake many tourists made. Jon hadn't lived by the coast all these years not to recognise it.

'Sea lavender,' he said. He looked down at Becky, expecting a response of some sort. She was turned away from him, the sheet pulled up to her chin. He sighed. He would have to tell her in the morning. No, sod it; he would tell her now. He prodded her sharply between her shoulder blades.

'Ouch!' she said. She sat up and glared at him.

'It's sea lavender,' he said. 'Just so you know.'

She stared at him for a few seconds. 'Okay. It's sea lavender. Thanks.' She shook her head and lay back down, turning over onto her side again, as if to say *and what do you expect me to do about it tonight? Nothing. That's what I'm going to do about it tonight.*

Jon sat for a moment, looking at her, then he sighed again and pulled some clothes on. She had taken all the bedcovers, of course. There was nothing to cover himself with. If he didn't want to freeze, he had two options. One was to go and plead with the night-time receptionist for some extra blankets, or another was to simply raid Becky's room and strip her bed. But after what she had told him about the room, he didn't really want to enter it unless it was absolutely necessary. The receptionist it was then.

He grabbed both keys, just in case, and crept out of the room with one last look at Becky. He decided that she probably wouldn't even know he'd gone. He walked down the corridors, a strange echoing emptiness about them that came with creeping about a mansion house at night when all the residents were in bed. In the olden days, of course, people would be stirring in a few hours; maids making fires and boiling water in the kitchens for instance.

He rounded the corner to the staircase, thinking about how harsh life was for these people and stopped suddenly. Not all the residents were in bed. He saw a figure on the staircase staring at the portrait of Lady Eleanor. Jon would have to walk past that figure to get to the receptionist. It was something he did not particularly want to do. The lights of the hotel had been dimmed and the figure's features weren't particularly clear, but Jon had a pretty good idea. He quietly turned around and padded back through the corridors.

Jon came to Becky's room and wrestled with the key. He managed to get inside and stood, his heart banging in his chest and his back to the door. He dashed across the room and grabbed the covers from the bed as quickly as possible, bunching them up in front of him. The covers smelled of the hotel's fabric conditioner and Becky's perfume, which was preferable to the strange lavender scent which still lingered in the room. It was with a sense of thankfulness that he managed to escape and make it back into his own room, switching the light off and preparing to curl up for the night on the sofa.

It might have been about half an hour later when he was eventually dozing off that he thought he heard the doorknob rattling.

When Becky woke up, it was still quite dark and she was conscious of the fact that the room seemed wrong, somehow. Feeling unsettled, she sat up and looked around. She saw a shadowy figure huddled on the sofa and her stomach flipped, until she realised it was Jon. She had no idea what time it was, but the moon was still up – a few rays were slanting through the partially drawn curtains – not enough to see clearly, but enough to tell her it was before dawn. She pushed the covers back and swung her legs out of the bed. There was a gritty sensation between her toes and she pulled a face remembering the sand from last night and the reason she was in this room.

She saw the moonlight shimmering in the mirror above the dressing table and glinting off a silver hairbrush on the unit. She didn't give any thought to how unusual it was for a man to have such an item in his room; she assumed, instead, it had been provided by the hotel. She padded over to the dressing table and stood before it. She looked at the strange, pale reflection in the glass and shivered. The way the moonlight highlighted her hair made it look as fair as Ella's. Still staring at the reflection, Becky's fingers groped for the hairbrush and she picked it up. She looked down at it wondering for a moment what she was doing. Then she remembered a flash of the dream; the shattering of the mirror and the starburst of cracks appearing in the glass. She jumped as she felt hands grasping her shoulders and gasped, dropping the hairbrush. She looked in the mirror and saw Jon behind her. He looked pretty ghostly himself, the way the shafts of moonlight washed over his face and bleached all the colour out of it.

'For God's sake!' she yelped. 'Don't sneak up on me – please!' She swung round, glaring at him, then stomped away towards the door and the light switch. She snapped it on and faced him. 'You gave me the shock of my life,' she said.

'I doubt that,' said Jon. He still looked pale, but this time it was more to do with the fact he clearly hadn't slept that well on the sofa, if the dark circles around his eyes were anything to go by. 'But may I please suggest something?'

'What's that?' asked Becky. She yawned and squeezed her eyes shut, rubbing the sleep out of them.

Jon waited until he had her attention before continuing. 'I think it's a good idea to slip away from the hotel before breakfast,' he said. 'No – I'm being serious, Becky. After you fell asleep last night, and I was on that sofa, I'm pretty sure I heard the doorknob rattling.'

'My guess is that it was the wind?' she said. 'Like the wind that deposited the sand down the chimney?' She tilted her head to one side, hoping that he would agree with her.

Instead he remained silent and simply shook his head. 'I don't think that was the wind with the doorknob,' he said. 'Seb's still here.'

Becky felt as if the floor was slipping from beneath her feet; she sat hurriedly on the bed. 'What? No. He said he was going to get a room so he could keep an eye on me and talk to me when I was feeling more "reasonable" and more "open to his suggestions". I thought he was just bluffing.'

'Well, I wish you'd told me that last night!' said Jon angrily. 'I would have damn well gone down to the summer house and made *sure* he couldn't stay. I would have put him in A & E first.' His pleasant, easy-going face hardened and Becky could tell he was imagining what he was going to do to Seb if he caught him again.

'Jon.' Becky reached up and touched his arm, forcing him to focus on her. 'That wouldn't have solved anything. If I can't stand up to him myself, what does that make me? Then he's won. He's battered my confidence, that's true, after he got me following him around on ridiculous celebrity assignments, sitting in the background watching him flirt with anything in a skirt, then getting me to write the pieces up. But I know now that I can do this myself. I've made the break. I'm doing things I enjoy and coming to places I love. I'm with the people I want to be with. I'm learning to be *me* all over again.'

'He shouldn't have put you in that position!' said Jon. 'And if I'd known all that, I wouldn't have let him stay upright in front of that bloody picture. God!' He raked his hand through his hair and moved away, prowling a full circuit of the bedroom, before coming back to stand in front of her.

Becky stared up at him, feeling for a moment that she was ten years old and she and Lissy were in trouble again. But she wasn't ten years old, was she? She was twenty-seven and just trying to regain control of her destiny after everything that had happened. No. Seb wasn't going to win this one. Jon had no cause for concern. She opened her mouth to tell him, but he spoke again.

'You know, I was going to ask the receptionist for some extra blankets last night. I was halfway there and I saw someone on the landing. I thought it was one of *our* people, but then I realised it wasn't. He was looking at the portrait, looking as if he was waiting for something.'

'Ella would have told him *nothing*,' Becky answered vehemently. 'Are you absolutely sure it was him?'

'A young Hugh Grant with an attitude?' replied Jon. He laughed bitterly. 'There can't be that many of them about. And if I'm let loose on him, there'll be one less in Yorkshire, I can guarantee that.'

Becky sighed. He wasn't about to let it drop, so she tried to change the subject. 'Where are we going to go at this time in the morning?' she asked. She fought the urge to tuck her hair behind her ears and pressed her fists into the bed. 'It's not even six o'clock. There's nowhere open.'

Jon blinked and looked down at her, as if he was suddenly drawn back to the present. 'Where can we go?' he repeated. 'Well, there's the studio,' he suggested. 'It's not the

126

most exciting of places, but it's better than here.' His face clouded again.

'That's fine,' said Becky hurriedly. 'We'll go there. To be honest, I'd rather sit in the car than ever face Seb over my toast again.' She shuddered. 'Right. Let me go to my room and get ready. Then I'll give you a knock.'

She stood up and again felt the sand beneath her toes. She kicked it away, thinking that she would, in truth, be glad to get some fresh air anyway.

It didn't take her long. She grabbed the essentials, and got dressed. She felt much more human and ready to face the world afterwards. As an afterthought, she picked up the writing slope and took that as well.

Jon looked at her curiously when she turned up at the door with her arms full of walnut.

She tilted her head to one side and gave him what she hoped was a winning smile. 'I was wondering if this could live in the flat? I know it belongs here, really, but once we both go home, well ...' She shrugged her shoulders awkwardly, as she clutched the slope to her chest. 'It just seems right. I don't want to leave it at the hotel anyway. It might get lost or damaged. They won't care about it as much as we do.' She lowered her eyes, then raised them and fixed them on Jon. 'Jon, I don't even know where you live properly. I don't know anything about you, apart from the fact you work in Whitby. Lissy was never the best with family news. Unless it concerned her, of course.'

Jon smiled at her, closing the door of his room quietly behind him. He had the car keys dangling off his fingertips, but still managed to take the slope from her.

'What do you want to know?' he asked her.

'I don't know,' she said. She raised a hand and flipped her hair back, then shook her head. Again, she made a little dismissive gesture. 'I really don't know. There's a lot we don't actually *know* about each other,' she said.

'I know,' said Jon.

'That doesn't help!' said Becky. 'We never actually had more than a fleeting conversation with each other did we? I can't quite believe we're managing it now.'

'No. I know,' he repeated. Frustrated, Becky pushed him gently. He winked at her and nodded along the corridor. 'Do you want to go that way? I'm just wondering if you want to take the chance of meeting him.'

'The servants' staircase?' Becky said suddenly. She pointed in the opposite direction. 'This way.'

'I have to trust you, I suppose,' replied Jon. 'You know this place better than I do.'

'Ella knows it. Adam should know it too,' said Becky.

Jon muttered something derisory as Becky headed off down the corridor towards the servants' staircase. She wound her way through the hotel, knowing exactly where she needed to be. Sure enough, there was a door fitted into the wall and Becky turned to Jon, smiling.

'You wouldn't know, unless you had cause to,' she said. She ran her fingers carefully down the side of the panel, feeling for a latch or a handle. Finding one, she pushed it and the door creaked open.

She looked at Jon, her fingers still holding onto the door. 'Do you think anyone heard that?' she asked.

'I hope not,' said Jon. 'It was pretty loud though.'

'That's what I thought,' Becky said with a frown. 'Come on, we'd best hurry in case we've set any alarms off.' She pushed the door fully open and, unaccountably, started to giggle. 'I feel like we're in some sort of crime thriller,' she said. 'You know, like you see on television.'

'Do you like those shows then?' asked Jon, squeezing past her and waiting at the top of the staircase.

'Yes, I love how they manage to solve an entire case within an hour,' she said. 'Oh, my, it's really dark in here, isn't it? They mustn't use it much. Just as well they've got those funny little lights. We'd probably have an accident, otherwise.'

One or two sickly white circular lights glowed pathetically in the stairwells and an illuminated sign suggested the staircase was merely a fire exit now. Becky closed the door behind them. She tried to make it as quiet as she could, but it was an old door and quite heavy.

She cringed as the door scraped along the floor again and pulled a face. 'That so wasn't quiet,' she muttered. 'Okay, down here, Jon, It's quite easy. There should be a door at the bottom leading out to the courtyard – what?' Through the semi-darkness, she saw that Jon's whole body seemed to go rigid.

He shook his head and gestured for her to lead the way. 'Keep going,' he said. 'I want to get out of here.' His voice seemed oddly tight.

'Follow me, then.' she said.

She hurried down the stairs and found the door that she knew was there. She touched the frame, a little thrill going through her. Ella must have done exactly the same. As if in confirmation, Ella's world began to creep up on Becky again. A little jolt of panic seized her momentarily, but she managed to ignore Ella and concentrate on the task at hand instead.

She leaned over and checked the door. 'I can unbolt it, but we would need the key to get out. Not to worry.' She stood up and looked along the stone passageway. Turning back to Jon, she pointed along towards the end of it. 'We can probably get out that way.'

As she began walking along the corridor, a dull glint in the darkness caught her eyes. She saw, just ahead of her, a rack of old bells on the wall. Unable to stop herself, she reached out and touched them gently. 'Imagine the stories these could tell,' she whispered. She ran her fingertips around the edge of one and stood back. 'Which one was connected to Ella's room, I wonder?' She didn't have long to ponder it. Some light was filtering through a door frame, and it seemed like a good idea to hurry towards it.

This time, she was in luck. The door opened smoothly and she stepped out into the foyer, right behind Reception.

'Good Lord,' she muttered. 'I could not have planned that any better.' The receptionist was not at her desk. It was shift change or coffee break, Becky neither knew nor cared. 'Run!' she said to Jon. 'Outside! Now!'

The pair of them ran through the hallway and jostled each other out of the way at the big main door, trying not to laugh.

'We are utter criminals now,' said Becky, once they had burst outside. 'Wow, it's cold!' The blast of wintry air caught her unawares and she shivered.

'To the car!' said Jon, rather over-dramatically, Becky thought.

'I've done all the hard work getting us out here,' she whined as they dashed towards the car park.

'I've carried your writing slope,' said Jon, fumbling for his keys. He pressed a button and unlocked the doors, putting the slope in the back footwell.

Becky hurried over to the passenger side and clambered in. She waited for Jon, twiddling with her hair thoughtfully. Loath as she was to be chased away from Carrick Park, the idea of driving in the peaceful early morning towards the coast was in a strange way quite exciting.

'Is there a way to Whitby over the moors?' she asked,

when Jon was settled next to her. He put the car in reverse and eased out of the space. Becky saw the glimmer of frost on her little car and felt slightly guilty that she hadn't moved it for a couple of days now. Still, Jon wasn't complaining – at least not out loud – so it was ridiculous to feel guilty.

'Yes. It's a detour but we can go that way if you like. I suppose people used to ride horses along the coastal pathways years ago. The more direct route.'

'I wouldn't fancy riding a horse,' said Becky, frowning at the thought.

'Cars are better,' agreed Jon.

'It's so nice to have a personal chauffeur with his own parking space in town,' she said, smiling at Jon.

'It's certainly useful,' he replied.

She could see the shadows on his face move and flicker as they drove down the floodlit driveway, highlighting his mouth and cheekbones as he smiled back. It was nice to watch him, she realised. Then her smile suddenly turned into a yawn. 'Oh, excuse me,' she said. 'That was a weird night. I think I'm going to suffer all day.'

'What were you going to do with that hairbrush?' Jon asked curiously. 'You looked as if you were ready to throw it at something.'

'Hmmm?' she replied. 'Yes. Maybe I was. It's probably good that we are leaving, actually. I think it's getting a bit intense. Don't you feel it? The more we're there, the more we sense what they felt?'

'I guess it's time for me to confess to something that happened to me, then,' said Jon. 'In the courtyard, last night. When I was waiting for you—'

'When you were stalking me,' interrupted Becky.

Jon turned to her for a moment, his eyes wide and innocent. He shook his head. 'No, not stalking, looking out for you!'

'Eyes on the road!' said Becky. 'You were, you were stalking me.'

'Well, whatever,' he replied. 'I saw a couple in the courtyard and I thought it was you and Seb. And it turned out that it obviously *wasn't* you and him because you came from a different direction when they were still there.'

Becky shrugged. 'So? That's nothing bad. It just means you were stalking the wrong person.' She yawned again. 'I am *so* sorry,' she said.

'I wasn't stalking anyone!' said Jon. 'Regardless, it wasn't you, okay? Except, when I looked back into the courtyard after you'd appeared ...'

'... they had disappeared,' finished Becky. 'Yes?'

'Yes,' he said.

'Ella knew that back door. That's all I can say. It may be just a coincidence,' she said. She looked down at her hands. 'I feel like I'm getting all mixed up with her life and her issues. I don't know when it's going to end.' She looked across at Jon, hoping for an answer.

'When we get to the bottom of it? When we find out why all this is happening?' he suggested.

'Maybe. I just hope ... I just hope she doesn't hang around all the time. I can deal with her to a certain extent, but she's getting stronger. I sometimes feel I'm more *her* than *me*. And it scares me a bit.'

And what scared Becky even more, but she wasn't about to admit it to Jon, was that she wondered what would happen to *them* when this all ended?

WHITBY

Whitby was strange in the early morning. There was none of the hustle and bustle Becky had experienced over the last few days. She got out of the car and stared around the almost deserted streets. 'When it's like this you almost think that it's waiting for something,' she said.

'I think the most important thing at the minute is getting into the flat,' replied Jon. 'Getting in, getting the kettle going. God, I've done all this without the aid of caffeine.'

He did look tired, Becky had to admit. Surprising both of them, she suddenly turned to him and wrapped her arms around him. For someone who had had so little time to get ready this morning, he smelled particularly nice.

'I don't know if I've thanked you properly at all, over the last few days,' she said. He was warm and his face was scratchy; he clearly hadn't had time to shave before their adventure. 'Thank you.' She could feel his breath on her hair and his arms tightened around her. She felt a soft pressure on her scalp as he kissed her. She drew her head back, and looked up into his face. She just knew he was going to say something; something she had been thinking herself only a few seconds before.

'Let's get inside the studio,' he said. His voice was different; sort of husky. She nodded slowly. There was no need for words.

The room was dim. She watched him light the lamp as she stood in the doorway. Her heart was beating fast. He turned to her, and offered her his hand. She took it in hers and pressed it to her chest, her eyes never leaving his face.

'Do you feel it?' she asked him.

'Do you?' he asked. He gently pulled her hand to his own chest. Understanding, she laid her fingertips against the material of his shirt and felt the rhythmic thrum of his heart, matching her own.

It was as powerful as the thunder in the trees, as great as the music she coaxed from her piano. He let loose her hand and took hold of her chin. He tilted her face up to his, drawing her body closer with his other arm.

'I will never leave you,' he promised her. The shadows flickered on the walls and cast his expression into darkness. She turned him gently so the light fell on his lips and his eyes and she reached up, touching his hair.

'I believe you,' she said, 'but tell me again so I am sure.'

'I love you,' he said.

And there were no more words and there was no more time and they moved to the bed and so it was.

Afterwards, Jon was astonished that they had actually made it up the stairs and into the bedroom. Once they had both apparently decided that this was the way forward, it was a battle to swiftly disable the alarm and unlock the staircase door before sense and reason returned. And now they lay there, locked in an embrace as the sky lightened over the town and it still seemed like a wonderful, marvellous dream. Jon fully expected to wake up in the hotel and find he was still sleeping on the sofa.

Eventually, Becky pushed herself up onto one elbow and looked down at him, a funny little smile playing around her lips. The frown, momentarily at least, was gone. 'Well. That was unexpected,' she said. Her hair was hanging down like a curtain and Jon reached up. He pushed it behind her ear for her and she laughed, cupping her hand around his and holding it there for a moment. 'Thanks, I think,' she said.

'You're welcome,' he replied. 'And good morning. Again.'

'Good morning. Was it inevitable, do you think? Or just weird because you're Lissy's brother?'

'Not weird,' said Jon with a laugh. 'But maybe inevitable. I did some research before you interrupted my sleep last night. Did you know that Rossetti poem had a different ending originally? In 1870, it went something like this:

"Then, now,—perchance again! …
O round mine eyes your tresses shake!
Shall we not lie as we have lain
Thus for Love's sake,
And sleep, and wake, yet never break the chain?"'

'No!' said Becky. The frown came back as she processed the information. At length, she shook her head. 'I had no idea. Amazing. I don't know that version. It's lovely, isn't it?'

'It's the "tresses" bit that gets me,' said Jon. 'It's just *you*.'

Becky laughed. She lay down on her back, staring at the ceiling. '"*Shall we not lie as we have lain thus for love's sake, and sleep and wake and never break the chain.*" It makes more sense if you run it all together like a sentence.'

'It's as if it's telling us that this cycle or whatever it is will just continue. I don't know if I believe in reincarnation or not,' said Jon, 'but it's telling us that we should be together properly, I guess.'

'Telling *us*?' Becky laughed. 'Maybe. Or maybe it's just Ella and Adam reliving it through us.'

'Which one would you prefer?' teased Jon. It was his turn to lean up on one elbow and look down at her. He smoothed her hair off her face and back over the pillow.

'I'd rather be Becky, I think,' she said. 'At least I'm not dead.'

135

'And thank goodness for that,' replied Jon.

Becky pulled a face. 'I should be going home in a day or so. There's a lot we need to talk about before that.'

'Let's not talk,' said Jon. 'Let's just enjoy today. We'll see what Lissy has to say when we see her. I'm sure we can work something out for, well, for later.'

'York isn't too far away,' said Becky, 'if you wanted to stay in touch; but I'm maybe not as straightforward as you think. A lot has happened in the last few years. I wouldn't want you to feel obliged, just because of Lissy, you know.'

Jon could sense her shutting down, drawing away from him almost. He took her face in his hands and shook his head. 'No, Becky. I said no talking. I don't just want to stay "in touch" either. I want to make it work – make *this*, this weird thing we have going on together work. I can't just let you disappear after we've found a connection like this. We've lost too many years as it is.'

Becky was silent. Her eyes scanned his face, seeming to search for some hidden meaning. She let out a tiny sigh. 'Some of it is Seb,' she said finally. 'Some of it is his fault. He's rude, he's ignorant and he dented my confidence. It's hard to think that you won't do the same.'

Jon shook his head. 'I'm not Seb,' he said. He touched her lips with his. And there were no more words.

By mid-morning Jon was in the studio and Becky had requisitioned the laptop in the flat and was working steadily through her list of projects. Her fingers flew over the keyboard as the words flowed and she selected photographs to accompany her articles. She had already submitted a feature to *Yorkshire Now* magazine and was ready for a break when she realised with a shock that it was almost lunchtime. Jon hadn't been up hounding her for coffee for at least two hours.

She leaned back and stretched, looking around the little room. She felt content here; she hadn't, in a long time, been able to write so efficiently and so easily. Seb again. She swore under her breath, trying to blot out the bad memories. With Jon it was so ... so *easy*, she admitted to herself with some surprise. She even dared imagine a future where, as a freelancer, she came here every day to work. Jon would be downstairs, they would meet at breaks and at lunch, but still have their own space ... yet there was so much to talk about, so much to discuss. Ella crept in, wrapping herself around Becky. *He loves you very much*.

I would like to think he might eventually, Becky confessed. She stood up and walked over to the window. She looked down on the winding cobbled street and saw streams of people wandering through the town, jostling each other. It was very different to how it had been early this morning, she thought. She searched the crowds half-heartedly for the blonde Goth girl, but she feared she had lost her chance with that one now.

She sighed and stepped away from the window. She headed towards the kitchen and clicked the kettle on. A swift forage through the cupboards produced some instant coffee and she made up two steaming mugs. Lissy would be contacting them soon, she guessed. They had time for a coffee first. And besides, she reluctantly admitted to herself, she actually *missed* him. And the last thing she wanted to do was ever feel that about a person; she never wanted to feel she was losing her independence. A brief scuffle with her conscience told her she was being rather ridiculous. As Jon had told her, he was no Seb.

Becky headed down the narrow staircase into the studio. Jon was taking payment from a group of giggling girls and seemed to be enjoying the banter as much as they were. He looked up as the internal door swung open and smiled at her. Somehow, he managed to speed up the transaction and usher the girls out of the studio. They blew kisses and waved over their shoulders at him, the bell above the door clanging as they left. Jon quickly put the 'closed' sign up and locked the door behind them.

'You shouldn't do that, someone might want to come in!' said Becky. 'I can't be responsible for you losing income just because I'm bringing you coffee.'

'It's having *you* in the studio that's distracting, not the coffee,' replied Jon.

'Well, there goes my idea of working here,' said Becky. 'I was just getting comfortable up there. Shall I leave?'

'No,' said Jon, taking the mug from her. 'I like the idea of you being up there. We've each got working space, but we're not too far away from each other.'

Becky ducked her head and smiled. 'I was thinking the same thing earlier,' she said. 'Sort of, anyway.'

'There you are, then. No reason to disappear.' He indicated for her to take the seat behind the till. 'I have no idea where my sister is, what time did she say?'

'I don't believe she did – at least not on her text,' said Becky. 'I'll go up and check in a minute. We could walk up to St Mary's to see if she's there. Or at least I can if you need to work.'

'I think it's important enough for us to go there together, don't you?'

'I'd like you to be there,' said Becky. 'But I understand if—'

Jon raised his hand to silence her. 'I'm coming with you. I don't need you to "understand" anything.'

Becky bit her lip. She didn't know when it would be a good time for him to 'understand' all about how she was now, years after he had known her before. And she didn't really want to go into it at this point in time, not when they were so close to finding something out about Ella and Adam. She studied him as he drank his coffee and, between mouthfuls, told her all about the last group of girls. She nodded at, she hoped, appropriate moments. But she wasn't listening to him, not really.

'I was right, she hasn't given me a time,' said Becky.

She had gone back upstairs to wash the mugs. Jon had followed her up a short while later, and now she was busy switching off the laptop and shuffling her work into a neat pile.

'She'll be up there at the church now, I guarantee it,' Jon said. 'It'll be "oh, I told you I'd be here, you knew where you would find me". Give her a call.'

'I'll text her,' replied Becky. She pressed a few keys and then sent it. *How are you doing? Want us there yet?* She smiled at Jon. 'Let's see if she answers.'

Almost immediately the phone vibrated. *Been here aaaaggggggeeeeesss. Come on!* Becky read it and laughed. 'She's been there ages, apparently. We have to go.'

'Told you so,' said Jon. 'Well, it's lunchtime. I'm entitled to a break. And I fancy a walk. So I will come with you.'

'Excellent,' said Becky. 'I'm very pleased.' She was pleased, she realised. She smiled shyly at Jon and suddenly he leaned forward. He took her chin in his hand and tilted her face towards him. He kissed her and it was really rather enjoyable, she realised.

'Well, I'm very pleased you're here,' he said. 'I'm hoping that you will stay forever. I've never felt like this before.'

'See,' said Becky, 'this is when I realise that I know hardly anything about you. At least you know about Seb.'

'There's not much to tell about me,' said Jon. 'A few serious girlfriends, some not so serious girlfriends, and an ex-fiancée.'

Becky made a little explosive noise. 'An ex-fiancée?' she said. 'Is she likely to stalk you the same way as that idiot's been stalking me?' She felt unaccountably annoyed.

'I hardly think so,' said Jon. 'We were about seven at the time. She was nice though. She was called Pippa … ouch!'

'Pippa! For goodness sake.' Becky made as if to slap him again and he ducked out of the way laughing.

'No, you'll be pleased to know there aren't any psycho stalkers in my cupboard,' he said. 'It's a bit unfortunate, I feel cheated somehow.'

'Do you want one of my stalkers?' asked Becky. 'I have two you know.'

'No, thanks. You should probably know that I did used to live with a girl though. She was called Fran. It lasted a few months and then she moved away. She got a job somewhere down south. I didn't want to leave Whitby and she didn't want to stay. We kept in touch and I tried to change her mind, but it all fizzled out. She was nice.' There was a faraway look in his eyes and Becky couldn't help it; she did the defensive thing.

She pushed her hair behind her ear, folded her arms tight and felt that annoying furrow deepen in her brow. 'Hmm,' she said.

Jon's attention returned to Becky and he took her hand, pulling it away from the tight little knot she had created with her arms. 'Don't worry. I'm well over her. Hopefully my next girl will like Whitby as much as I do and she'll stay here with me quite happily.'

He was smiling as he said it; smiling and looking right

into her eyes, right into her soul. Something inside her twisted. There was an appealing little glimpse there of what might be, all things being equal. But she couldn't allow herself to get her hopes up. She felt Ella bristling, fizzing almost with anger. *Answer him! Tell him!*

Instead, Becky dropped her gaze and pulled her hand away. She busied herself straightening her pile of paperwork and finally looked back at him. 'Ready?' she asked. 'For the church?' She pasted a smile on her face, trying hard to look neutral, as if she hadn't quite understood him.

For a second, Jon looked a little confused. Then he obviously decided to let the subject drop and smiled back at her.

'I guess so,' he said. 'Are you?'

'I am.'

'Then let's go.'

They headed up to St Mary's together, weaving through the crowds. Jon had taken hold of Becky's hand a few steps along the street and she hadn't pulled away, which was good, he thought. It was still cold but at least the sun was out today. It would be lovely up on the cliffs, even with the winds blowing. Becky was quiet though; too quiet. He squeezed her hand and she looked up at him.

'Are you all right?' he asked. 'Nervous?'

'A little,' she said. 'I think it's because I've built it all up so much and this is where it kind of comes together.' She frowned and waved vaguely in the direction of her ears. 'Ella,' she said. 'Can't get rid of her.'

Jon nodded and drew her closer to him. She was tense; he could feel it in the way she held herself. He wasn't really surprised. He didn't have Ella to contend with, but he could sense Adam prowling about near him. It was as if the man was following them, two steps behind. Cautiously, he glanced down at his hands. He really didn't want Adam taking him over here and now completely. Although, he thought ironically, if he did, it would mean that he and Becky could chat quite easily on the trek up to the church.

It made a difference knowing what Adam actually looked like. And dammit, that was another thing. Hadn't bloody Seb chased them out of Carrick Park before they could search for Adam's portrait? Exasperated, Jon's mind drifted back to the photograph; seeing Ella and Adam as they were caught unawares, was astonishing. Jon dealt in a visual medium and images meant more to him than words. Words were clearly Becky's department. It was frustrating. They obviously fit so well together that he couldn't understand her withdrawal in the flat, especially after they had eased into a relationship so readily. He cast a sidelong glance at Becky; she was silently watching everything that was going on around her. He knew why, and he had to admit if Ella was impressing upon her to that extent, Becky wasn't fazed by it. It was probably best not to try and converse though, at least not until they had reached the church.

They wound up the cliff path, moving into single file to squeeze past everyone. There was a small figure sitting on one of the table-like tombs clutching a pile of papers. The figure waved wildly as it saw the couple coming up the hill.

Becky raised her hand and waved back. 'She looks like she's been busy,' she said. She still felt edgy for some reason. Whatever had happened to Ella, had happened near here, she was fairly certain.

Lissy jumped up from the tomb and ran towards them.

'I've found out loads!' she said. She waved a bundle of papers under their noses. 'They *were* married. I found them in the records. Adam John Edward Carrick – and Miss Eleanor Catherine Dunbar. They were married in September 1865. Right here! Right here at this church. Becky, are you all right?' She looked at Becky with some concern. 'Last time you looked like that, you'd overdosed on vodka.'

'I'm fine,' Becky said. She smiled wryly. 'Just talk a little slower, will you?'

'Oh dear!' said Lissy. She reached out and touched Becky's arm. 'I remember what it was like when she got me.'

'It's not so bad,' murmured Becky. 'I'm getting used to it. I just hope she goes away properly soon. Anyway; you were saying?'

'They got married here.' She stood right in front of Becky and pointed earnestly at the church. '*Here.*'

Becky tried not to laugh; poor Lissy. It wasn't natural for her to be slow about anything, especially not speaking. The words just seemed to tumble out of her mouth and somehow string themselves together to make sentences. Well, if she missed anything, Jon would have to fill her in later. She concentrated on Lissy, watching as she continued her excited babblings.

'They just disappear from the records after that though. No family, no children I can find. No death records. I'm wondering if they moved away. I would need to dig a lot deeper if they went abroad. I could look up the old newspapers of the time to see if they appeared in the social columns or anything, but obviously I can't do that right away. I've done as much as I can so far.'

Lissy looked at the clumps of paper. She leafed through them and pulled another one out. She studied it for a second and nodded. 'This one is interesting.' She passed it across to Becky so she could read it.

Becky was aware that Jon had moved closer and she turned, a little startled to see how close he had actually come. She could feel his warm breath on her neck and, despite the situation and the completely inappropriate setting it did funny things to her insides. She passed the paper to him, hoping that by doing something more practical it would negate the funny feelings; it didn't.

'The Lydia we found, she is Adam's sister,' continued Lissy, talking more to Jon than to Becky.

Lissy obviously thought the paper was enough for her to be going on with. That amused Becky to some degree as well.

'Lydia married someone called Jacob. Now, from what I can gather, he was some sort of cousin. You look a few years down the line and Lydia is marked as the owner of Carrick Park, although she didn't actually live there a lot of the time. I haven't worked out what happened to Jacob yet. I need more time for that. Anyway, Lydia and Jacob had a daughter who was born in 1866. They married on New Year's Day 1866. So it must have been a very quick conception.' She winked broadly. 'Or maybe it was a very quick marriage. The baby was christened here in September 1866, though, so it makes you wonder. You'll remember my epic GCSE fail in maths, Becky,' said Lissy, turning to her and grinning, 'but I can add nine or ten months onto a marriage date.'

'What did they call the girl?' asked Becky.

'This is where it is lovely,' replied Lissy. 'They called her Elizabeth Catherine.' She smiled broadly and pointed to herself. '*Elizabeth*. Isn't that marvellous? Only she has the "z" and I have a sort of foreign version.'

'And I bet they called her Ella for short,' said Becky. 'Ugh. It's not helping me a great deal.'

'It's all written down,' said Lissy, pointing wildly at the paperwork again.

Becky raised her hand and closed her eyes. 'I know. Thanks.' She tried to comprehend all the information. Eventually, she opened her eyes again and turned to Jon. 'Where the hell did Ella and Adam go?' she asked him. 'Where did we *go*?'

She felt a tug on her sleeve. Lissy was looking at her eagerly 'Oh! I forgot to say, there were no more children for Lydia and Jacob, if that helps. So Carrick Park was never inherited by any of their descendants. Baby Elizabeth got another property, though, and Carrick Park was sold.'

'That's why it's a hotel now then,' said Becky. 'Perhaps there were too many bad memories there, so they got rid of it.' She sat down on the tomb that Lissy had recently vacated, facing Jon and his sister. She pushed her hands into her pockets and let her gaze drift across to the sea. She could almost swear the seagulls were the same ones that were there the other day. 'I think I'd like to take a little walk,' she said.

Jon came closer to her and laid his hand on her shoulder. She took hold of it and squeezed it, answering the unasked question. 'I'll be fine,' she said. 'I just need to be on my own for a bit.'

'And would you like a coffee?' asked Jon.

She stared at him. The man was obsessed by bloody coffee! Yet he obviously thought he was being solicitous.

Becky burst out laughing. She didn't care if it sounded really loud and really incongruous in the churchyard. 'Jon, *you* want a coffee, don't you?'

'I'd rather have a cigarette at this moment in time,' admitted Jon, 'but I'm being good. It just all feels a bit strange, you know?'

'They are real now, aren't they?' she replied. 'And we know what they looked like and we know about his sister, and we have her writing slope for whatever reason. Someone must have been clearing out someone's possessions for it to end up in an antiques shop. That's sadder than anything.'

'I'll get us that coffee,' he said. He looked longingly at the hill down towards the town. 'Then I'll come back up, okay?'

'No problem. Jon, do me a favour and take Lissy with you?' asked Becky. 'I don't think I can cope with any more facts at the minute. She's done brilliantly, though, hasn't she?'

'That's my little sister for you,' he replied. As if he had conjured her up by mentioning her, Lissy came hurrying up to him. She had been rummaging through the papers again and had obviously found what she wanted.

'Can I just show you this before you go?' she asked. 'I knew I had something else. It's good to have friends in high places, you know, in galleries and the like, yet my brother criticises my unusual methods. But, thank God as well for email.' She thrust something else into Becky's hand. Becky didn't bother listening to the explanation. She just read the document.

The paper was a printout showing a scanned copy of a commission. Adam had commissioned the wedding portrait of Ella as he had promised and this was clearly the invoice. But what made Becky's heart flip, was that it was signed by Lydia and not Adam.

Part Two

ELLA
1865

Ella, having pleaded a headache, watched from the bedroom window as the riding party made its way out of the grounds. She wasn't sure where they had decided to go in the end, although chances were that they had fixed on Whitby as arranged. Her attention had wandered and she was relieved that this afternoon, at least, she didn't have to try to be sociable.

She picked up the invitation again; a celebratory dinner party, no less. She loved Lydia deeply but she did not always love her demands.

Ella had known Lydia for many years, since their days as schoolgirls, in fact, and as such had been a frequent visitor to Lydia's home at Carrick Park. Lydia's older brother, Adam, owned the family estate now, and at the age of twenty-one, Lydia was anything but anxious to take an active part in running the place. No, she left that to Adam and preferred to host parties and balls and generally enjoy herself with the frivolous lack of care that seemed indigenous to her nature. Six years separated Adam and Lydia, and Lydia had always been babied and indulged by everybody in the Park.

Lydia's current house party was made up of her unfathomable cousin Jacob, whom Ella had known for years and reserved judgement upon, and a childhood friend of the family's called Helena – who, if she was honest, Ella had barely any time for. Ella was sorry that Adam wasn't here – she had always gotten on well with him and they shared a deep despair of Lydia at times. Also, Adam was not that fond of Helena, and Ella knew that if Adam had indeed been here, they would have been able to bear her slightly better together.

Ella walked over to the wardrobe and pulled it open, fingering the delicate fabrics of the gowns that shimmered out at her. It was impossible trying to decide what to wear to these social occasions that her dearest friend was so attracted too. Ella didn't particularly enjoy them; dinner parties especially. Once the wine began to flow, people began to slur and repeat themselves. It was hard work keeping up with them. She moved back over to the window, ensuring the riders had disappeared from sight.

When she was quite sure she was alone in the house, she pushed the door open and made her way downstairs to the drawing room. She knew the piano would be there waiting for her and Lydia had, after all, given her free rein, as she did every time she came to the Park.

'Darling,' Lydia would say, 'you are practically my sister. You practically live here with us during the holidays, so you can do whatever you please.'

Ella sat down and ran her fingers gently over the piano keys. She pressed an ivory and smiled as the note thrummed through her fingertips. She shuffled some scores around, chose a piece, then placed both hands on the keyboard and started to play: Mozart, her favourite. She understood the tone of the music by the vibrations, and the classical feel of Mozart suited her far more than the angry notes of Beethoven, which she often thought was ironic.

The music came to an end, and as she sensed the last few notes dying, she became aware of a shadow falling across the piano. Her stomach knotted and she turned slowly, dreading who she might see there. A man was standing, smiling at her. He was dressed as if he had just returned from a journey and was clapping. Her eyes flicked towards his gloved hands and back to his face. He had always borne a striking resemblance to Lydia, and that was still the case.

Like Lydia, the man was tall and had fair hair that turned blond in the sunlight. His eyes were a darker shade of brown than Lydia's and they crinkled up at the edges when he laughed – which was frequently. His skin was lightly tanned at the minute, thanks to the fact he had been abroad for quite some time and his travelling clothes, although dusty, were smart and well-cut. His velvet-collared overcoat hung off his broad shoulders, and Ella noticed the ends of his large necktie had become untucked from his waistcoat; and she had a ridiculous urge to straighten him up a little.

Instead, she smiled at him.

'Bravo,' he said. 'You still play very well. *Là ci darem la mano*. Mozart. I would recognise that anywhere.' He pulled his gloves off and threw them onto the table. He walked over to her and held out his hands.

'Thank you,' she replied. Then she broke into a wider smile. 'Adam – how wonderful to see you. I didn't expect you but I cannot say it is a disappointment that you are here.'

'And it is anything but a disappointment to see you,' he replied. 'I've missed your last few visits – it is a shame that I have to travel such a lot. It's been, I would say, too long since we were all together.'

Ella stood up and held her hand out. 'I have heard you are doing well. Lydia constantly sings your praises.'

Adam took her hand and bowed over it. Ella curtseyed and Adam raised his eyes to hers. There was a smile in them.

'I suspect the others have gone riding? And that you have managed to escape it yet again? Your piano playing still defies belief, by the way,' he said.

Ella didn't take offence. For one thing, she was grateful that he appeared to be speaking in measured tones. There was nothing worse than people trying to exaggerate the words. It made it too difficult to have a conversation; she had never had that issue with Adam.

'Lydia said she had invited a special guest to stay with us when I wrote last week. I had no idea it was you,' he continued.

Ella smiled back. 'Lydia is a wonderful person. I can only assume that your return is the reason for our dinner party tonight. She did not tell me you were coming, so therefore I shall have to be cross with her when I see her.'

'She has arranged a dinner party? Oh, no. Lydia is not so wonderful then.'

Ella frowned. 'I hope it will just be us. As you probably know, she has rounded up your cousin Jacob and Helena Warner. They are all staying here, but they are, as you correctly assumed, out riding at present. I am not sure when they will return. And my instinct is that Lydia is plotting something, anyway.'

She looked around, trying to locate a bell-pull. 'I feel I should try to get you something to eat or drink,' she said, 'unless anyone welcomed you when you came in?'

'I just let myself in,' he said. 'They haven't realised I am home yet.'

He indicated for her to sit down and she lowered herself onto the edge of the sofa. He turned and went to the corner of the room where he pulled a rope and then headed back towards her. She watched him come closer and silently prayed he would have sense enough to sit with the light on his face. He had the choice of two chairs and, to her relief, he chose the one facing the window. She should have known. Even as a boy, Adam had often been more considerate than his sometimes wilful younger sister.

Adam sat back and crossed his legs, steepling his fingers. 'So Jacob and Helena are here?' he said. 'How fortuitous for them. Helena has been in love with Jacob for at least a century.'

Ella laughed. 'Perhaps Lydia thought it was time to act,' she said.

'Something like that,' replied Adam, his eyes crinkling at the corners as he smiled. 'But it is you I am particularly interested in.'

Ella dropped her gaze. 'Oh, I am just the same,' she said. 'As you see, I still enjoy my piano playing.'

He leaned forward and took her hands in his. She looked up at him. 'And these?' Adam said, squeezing her hands. 'Do they still speak like they used to? I could never keep up with you.'

'Not so much,' admitted Ella. 'I try to manage in other ways now.'

'I am getting the sense that they need to flutter, Miss Dunbar. Don't let anyone stop you.'

Ella opened her mouth to protest, then thought better of it. He was right. It was more natural to her to use her hands to emphasise her points; but it was usually best just to pretend, as she always did. Lydia had tried to learn finger spelling a while ago but had lost patience with looking at a sheet of paper. Ella had given her some practical lessons and they could now, eventually, have some sort of conversation with each other. Ella smiled inwardly at the thought.

'I always meant to learn properly,' mused Adam. 'I wanted to be able to do all that with you. Oh – that must be our maid. Please, excuse me one moment. Watch her; she won't make any show of not having known I was back.' He released her hands and turned to the door.

Ella looked up, seeing a young girl come in and curtsey. The girl, Elizabeth, was a sweet little thing. She would often smile shyly at Ella when she passed her in the corridors, breaking, Ella guessed, all the household rules.

Adam spoke to Elizabeth and she nodded, scurrying off down the corridor, no doubt to gather together a tea tray.

Adam turned back to Ella. 'Do you see? Not a flicker from her. Anyway, tea will not be long. And I still cannot believe how well you play the piano. Where did you learn? I don't think you ever told me.'

'I don't know. Truthfully, I just watched people. I read scores. I followed the notes and taught myself. I understood what the scores meant and learned to place my fingers on the keys the way others did. The vibrations seemed the same. So I assumed I had done it right. Please. I don't want to talk about it any more, though. It embarrasses me.'

The honest answer was, though, that she had refused to accept she shouldn't do the same as any other young girl in her position. She painted, she read, she rode – albeit grudgingly – she sewed and she played music. The only thing she didn't do was sing. Apart from that, and despite the fact that her hearing had gradually deteriorated, to the point where she was now completely and utterly deaf, she hoped that there was nothing to recommend her as different in any way.

'Would you be interested in a little exercise after our tea?' asked Adam.

'Not if it involves horses,' replied Ella.

Adam laughed. 'So indignant!' he said. 'You have always been the same. What is it about them you dislike so much?'

Ella shuddered. 'I don't dislike horses, I just dislike riding them,' she said. 'I understand it is a necessary evil, however.'

'Well, would you prefer a more sedate walk with me around the gardens?' he asked.

'That seems much more preferable,' replied Ella. 'Oh – here is your tea coming.'

They waited until the tray had been placed on a small

table beside them, and Adam thanked the maid. Ella fussed over the tea cups and Adam waited until they each had a cup in their hands.

'So have the others been gone long?' he asked. 'Should we expect them back too soon?'

'I wouldn't have thought so,' replied Ella. 'Miss Warner suggested a long ride towards the coast. I believe she mentioned the Abbey ruins.' She coloured slightly. 'Well, I understand that to have been the plan anyway. I could not swear for definite.'

'And when did they discuss the destination?' asked Adam.

Ella dropped her head in embarrassment. 'You are teasing me,' she said, but there was a smile in her voice. She raised her eyes and tilted her head to the side, bracing herself for his next comment.

'Aha! You see – that familiar look of guilt. I know you better than you think,' said Adam. 'When was it? Did they tell you outright? Knowing those characters, it won't have been decided beforehand unless Lydia decreed it.'

'They may have been on the driveway,' said Ella slowly. 'I may have caught them discussing it before they departed ...' She left the words hanging.

'You spied on them from the window,' said Adam. 'Good girl. Well, we have plenty of time then. Come now, drink up. I want to enjoy some time with my sister's irritating little friend before they all return and spoil my fun. We could never get anything past you, could we?'

'Oh, you could sometimes,' said Ella, 'if you were devious enough to turn away from me.' She spoke without malice. Adam had always been easy to get on with. 'But as you say, Lydia and I could plan things right in front of you, and you would have no idea.'

'That damned finger spelling,' said Adam. 'Wait here.'

He stood up and walked over to a desk. On it was a walnut box – a writing slope, with Lydia's initials and the house crest embossed on the lid. He stood with his back to Ella and she watched him fiddle with the box, then turn back to face her. He held a sheet of paper aloft and smiled triumphantly. 'I knew where it was. Lydia always kept it in there. She was terrified she would lose it and it would fall into my hands and spoil her fun. Strangely enough, I managed to find the secret drawer one day when she was out. It was in there. My sister is so transparent at times.' Adam sat down and studied the paper. 'I need to revisit this, I think,' he said.

Ella quickly fluttered her fingers at him. *You will never manage* she spelled. She smiled at him as he stared at her blankly. 'Good luck,' she told him.

After the tea, Ella found a light cloak in her wardrobe and, fastening it as she left her room, met Adam at the bottom of the grand staircase. His face lit up as she came down the stairs and he held his arm out for her.

'No horses. Let us walk,' he said and guided her out of the house.

Carrick Park was an oddly built house, part Georgian, part medieval and situated on the moors north of Whitby. It was a good hour's ride across the moors into the town from the Park and Ella judged that Lydia's riding expedition might still have a while before they returned. Selfishly, she realised, she hoped that it would indeed be some time before they appeared; it gave her more time to spend with easy-going Adam and less living on her nerves in the shadow of Miss Helena Warner. There was just something about the girl she disliked.

Ella was a good judge of character; her first impressions were seldom wrong and she had wondered in the past whether this was a type of compensation for her lack of hearing.

Much as she disliked Helena, she wasn't overly fond of Jacob either; sometimes she found him looking at her strangely, fixing his grey eyes on her as if he was calculating something in his head and it made her feel quite uncomfortable. It was always a disappointment when she arrived at Carrick Park and he was there; especially, she thought with a blush, when she wanted more of Adam's attention.

Jacob was, she thought, a deeper, more brooding character altogether than Adam. His dark hair was always immaculately brushed and parted at the side, whereas Adam's fair hair was rather tousled and untidy looking. Adam spent, she knew, much of his thinking time raking his fingers through it and that was part of his charm.

Ella understood there had been some issues with wills and properties in the past and Lydia had confided in her once that she thought the house should really belong to Jacob under the normal scheme of things, but Lydia was a wonderful foil to the mild annoyance that was Helena and Jacob; and now, joyfully, Adam was here as well. Perhaps the dinner party tonight might not be as untenable as she first thought.

Involuntarily, Ella smiled as her heart lifted with the warm, summer air outside. She looked up at Adam who was apparently studying the topiary. She took in the gentle laugh lines around his eyes and the mouth that was always ready with a subtle quirk of the lips that could express so much and she felt, for once, genuinely contented. A small sigh escaped her own lips and Adam turned towards her, catching her looking at him. She blushed and looked away, feeling him shake with suppressed laughter. He squeezed her arm and reluctantly, she looked at him.

'Are you happy here?' he asked. The question took her by surprise.

'Why yes, I am,' she replied. 'Why do you ask?'

'Because Lydia's wild ideas are not to everyone's taste. She has clearly gone into town for some reason, and I do wonder what her expectations are for this evening.'

'A celebratory meal with friends and family to welcome you home?' Ella tried. 'Surely that is all?'

Adam pulled a face. 'I think there is more. I think she hopes that she can make a match between our cousin and our friend. The more I think about it, the more I sense it. Lydia is, as I say, transparent.' He felt around in his waistcoat pocket and brought out the finger spelling sheet. 'I'm keeping this for a while,' he said. 'It might come in useful for tonight. Imagine, we can sit beside each other and converse without involving them.'

'Please put it away,' said Ella, laughing. 'You cannot learn it in an afternoon.'

'I can learn what I want to this afternoon. Have no fear,' replied Adam with a smile. Suddenly, he looked up and the smile left his face. 'Dammit, they're back,' he said.

'I beg your pardon? Did you say they were back?' asked Ella. She turned to follow his gaze, her heart sinking. *Dammit* indeed. She saw the three horses cresting the drive from the moors towards the house; one tall, confident young man and two slender young ladies were riding them. She narrowed her eyes as they came closer, trying to catch their conversation.

'Apparently your sister called a halt to the expedition – something about a blinding headache. Oh!' Ella laughed. 'Miss Warner is asking her whether *that girl's* headache was contagious. That is me, of course. That was my excuse.

Now, your cousin looks to be angry about something ...'
Ella shook her head. 'He has turned away. I don't know.
Oh no, quick!' she pulled Adam into a gap in the topiary. 'I
think Lydia saw us. Are they coming?'

Part of her wanted to stay hidden away in the cool green
of the hedge, but the rational part wanted to know if the
riding party was heading her way. She certainly didn't
want them to pull up outside her hiding place with no
forewarning.

Adam squeezed her hand. 'Yes, I can hear the hooves
coming,' he said. 'Come on, we have been spotted all right.'

'Oh, please, just leave me in here!' moaned Ella,
reluctantly following him out of the hedge. She saw him
shake his head and she rolled her eyes.

They stood together on the path, watching the horses
ride up to them and Lydia, leading the way, raised her crop
in greeting. The other two plodded along behind her, in
no hurry, it seemed, to greet Adam. Ella saw pure venom
in Helena's demeanour and in Jacob's she saw a pettiness
directed at his male cousin. Ella promised herself to stay
away from them for the next few hours if at all possible.

'Darling, Adam!' Lydia cried. 'You are home. But please
forgive me – I must go to my room for a while to lie down
before dinner. This blasted head of mine. We had to cut our
trip short.' She pouted prettily and looked slyly at Ella.

Ella knew the look well. '*Come to my room*,' Lydia
mouthed, knowing that Helena and Jacob, sat as they were
behind her, couldn't see her. Ella nodded slightly, and Lydia
blew her a kiss.

'To the stables,' she said, and flicked her crop against the
horse's flank.

Adam murmured greetings to Helena and Jacob as they
approached, and Ella peeled away from the little group,
heading back towards the house. Much as she didn't want

to leave Adam, she couldn't bear being in the same vicinity as Helena for very long. In fact, even the next county would be too close for comfort, she decided.

Ella ran up the stairs to Lydia's room and knocked on the door. The door opened a crack and Lydia beckoned her in. She looked far too healthy for someone who had suffered such a migraine, and Ella told her so.

'You don't fool me,' Ella said, taking Lydia's hands. 'Be truthful, now. What happened?'

Lydia, laughing, nodded to the chairs in the bay window and they sat down.

'You are right, of course,' she said, with that mischievous twinkle in her eyes. 'I was hoping they would stay behind and let me return home. I knew Adam was coming and I was anxious to see him. I also wanted those two to spend some time together. It didn't quite work out how I had planned it.'

'Adam was right,' said Ella. 'You are plotting, are you not?'

Lydia opened her eyes wide, looking at Ella innocently. *Yes* she signed, exaggerating the gesture. Then she shook her head and spoke. 'Of course I'm not!' she said, crossing her hands on her lap primly. 'What must you think of me if I was plotting?'

'One tends to find that matchmaking is only successful if the two parties at least consider each other as potential candidates,' said Ella. 'Adam says Helena may be open to the idea, but Jacob ...' She shook her head. 'I don't know. Perhaps he's never considered her in that respect.'

'Oh, he has,' said Lydia. 'Many years ago when we were children. I'm hoping to reignite the spark he seems to have lost somewhere.' She leaned across and tapped Ella on the arm. '*You* need to help.'

'Me?' exclaimed Ella. 'What do you expect *me* to do?'

'Well, I have a terrible feeling his heart is elsewhere and we need to put him back on track. We need him to understand that the only option he has is Helena.'

'But where else would his heart be?' asked Ella, leaning forward, eager for some gossip.

'Why with you, of course!' said Lydia, as if it was the most simple thing in the world.

Ella slammed back into her seat, horrified. 'Oh, no. Absolutely not,' she said, shaking her head. 'Absolutely not.'

'Exactly. And I cannot let it happen either, as I have other plans for you,' said Lydia smiling angelically.

'I cannot let it happen either!' exclaimed Ella. 'What can I do to help?'

'Why, talk to Adam at dinner tonight,' said Lydia guilelessly. 'Let those two ... converse. I shall sit you next to Helena – now don't look like that, it's perfect – and on the other side of you shall be Adam. On Helena's other side will be Jacob, then next to him, myself. You talk to Adam ...' she waved her hand around as if to display Ella turning her back on Helena, 'and that means Helena has to talk to Jacob. And I will be there to guide their conversation. It's really quite simple.'

'Lydia, I hate dinner parties. You know that. I'm not particularly fond of Helena either. How can you do this to me and still say you are my dearest friend?'

'Come now, that may be so. But you do like Adam, do you not?' said Lydia. There it was again, the mischievous twinkle. 'It's perfect.'

Ella shook her head. She raised her little finger and pointed it at Lydia. 'You are *bad*,' she said. 'I'll do it for you, and only because it is you. But you are *bad*.'

159

'Being bad can be *so* much fun,' said Lydia complacently. 'You should try it.'

'So, are we to be entertained by your cousin's little protégé tonight?' asked Helena.

Dinner had not exactly been a roaring success. Ella had missed most of the discussions between Helena, Jacob and Lydia, but she had enjoyed sitting next to Adam. From what she understood, Helena had done her best to hold Jacob's attention, but Jacob did his best to ignore her. Jacob had also spent much of dessert trying to attract and maintain Ella's attention, which she was not particularly happy about.

And now, Helena sat daintily on the chaise longue, her rose-pink skirts all fluffed up around her, her dark hair falling from a neat centre parting into a froth of ringlets, almost to her waist. She folded her hands on her lap and smiled up at Jacob. She blinked her strange eyes innocently; a queer genetic flaw had made her the bearer of one dark blue eye and one bright green eye. Helena, Lydia had said, detested it, but she seemed to play on the fact that others thought it sweet and interesting.

'Does she play anything we would recognise?' Helena continued. 'Or is it just – well – a rather amateur parlour trick?'

Ella, seated next to Lydia, stiffened. *How dare she?*

Helena deliberately looked straight at Ella and spoke very slowly. 'Do. You. Play. Well?' she asked. Ella wondered why the girl should distort her face quite so grotesquely to ask such a simple question.

'I do,' she replied.

Helena tilted her head slightly. 'What?' she asked.

'I do,' repeated Ella. 'I play well. At least I have been told that.' She flicked a glance up to Adam who smiled at her.

'She does indeed,' said Adam.

'Oh! No. I meant *what* do you *play*?' Helena ignored Adam and looked towards Jacob. 'The inflection is lost on her,' she said. 'It is quite difficult to judge it.'

'Inflection?' Adam interrupted. 'How ridiculous! The way you addressed her, Helena! *"What?"* could have meant absolutely anything and you know it. But what makes it even more astounding, is that you actually whispered that last comment! And to answer your question, whichever way you meant it, I would like to say that Ella plays Mozart particularly well.' He caught Ella's eye and she was sure he dropped one eyelid in a wink, as if to say *stupid woman*.

Ella ducked her head, frightened that she would laugh. Lydia took Ella's hand and squeezed it. Ella turned to her, still smiling.

'Would you mind?' Lydia asked, nodding at the piano. 'I told Helena how marvellous you were.'

'Well, I do mind, a little,' she responded. She flicked a glance over to Helena. She was fluttering her eyelashes at Jacob. 'Why must I prove myself to her?'

'I am so sorry, darling,' said Lydia, 'only she asked when we were riding earlier. She asked a lot of questions about you.'

Ella looked at Lydia curiously. 'Surely I am not that intriguing?'

'It is only the piano, sweetheart.' said Lydia. She patted Ella's hand, her warm, dark brown eyes smiling into Ella's bright blue ones. 'Adam would love to hear it too, I am convinced.'

'Lydia!' said Ella, cursing the treacherous blush that flooded her cheeks. 'That is not the way to convince me. And he has already heard me anyway.' She glanced across at Jacob and Helena, effectively ending the conversation.

Helena sat picking lint from her bodice, her rather thin mouth set in a petulant line. Suddenly she pulled a face and looked up at Jacob. 'I would not care,' she said, seeming to forget that anything she said that night was not exactly private, 'but she looks quite normal. It is difficult to remember that she is like *that*.'

'*Excuse* me?' asked Ella. She pushed Lydia's hand away and stood up. Ella strode towards the piano and taking hold of the open lid, slammed it down with all her might. The vibrations passed through the floor, jarring through her satin shoes and up her body as the piano made what could only have been a hideous cacophony of chords.

Helena's hands flew to her ears and Jacob rushed over to the piano, grabbing it and holding onto it, seemingly trying to stop the noise. A few sheets of music slid to the floor and Ella glared at Helena.

'No,' she said. 'I don't think I *will* play the piano tonight. Miss Warner can do it.'

She bent down and lifted a sheet of music from the pile on the floor. She studied it then walked over to Helena. 'Try this,' she said, 'and best of luck.'

She turned on her heel, oblivious to Helena's outraged shouts, ran upstairs and into her bedroom.

She stood in front of the mirror and stared at her reflection. '*She looks quite normal*,' Helena had said. Well, of course she did. She looked exactly the same as everyone else – she would never look out of place anywhere, ever. That was the problem. It wasn't obvious. It didn't have to be obvious. It was only when people like *her* pointed it out, that she could feel the shift in atmosphere among people who didn't know her and then they all looked at her differently.

Ella picked up the silver-backed hairbrush that lay on the dressing table and hurled it at the mirror, watching the cracks burst across its surface. Seven years bad luck, was it? She wasn't superstitious, so it hardly mattered. She saw the door behind her reflected in the mirror – someone had thoughtfully moved the table there shortly after she arrived, probably, she thought bitterly, so she would know if anyone was coming into the room. It worked, however, because now she saw the door open and a figure appear in the doorway. Their reflection was obscured, but she knew who it was. She swung around and faced them.

'There was no need to come,' she said. Instinctively, she raised her hands, spread her fingers and brought them towards her body at shoulder height. *Leave me alone!* She made for the door and pushed past, not waiting for an answer. Once in the corridor, she picked up her skirts and ran. She ran down the stairs and across the hall. She reached the door, not knowing or caring if they were following her or not and flung it open; then she was outside in the fresh air and nobody could stop her.

'Where did she go?' asked Jacob, tiring suddenly of pandering to Helena's bruised ego.

'I do not know and I do not care,' whined Helena. Her eyes were red and teary, although her ill-tempered sobs and raging had finally abated.

Adam had taken the sheet music and placed it back on the piano; then he had, Jacob knew, followed Ella out of the room a few minutes later. Jacob felt a new kind of anger build up in his stomach towards his cousin. Unbelievable, leaving him, Jacob, to deal with a hysterical woman. And Lydia was no help. She had disappeared as well. For God's sake, Helena was a guest at their house, so surely one of those two should be soothing her?

He looked around desperately, wondering when he could escape. It didn't cross his mind that Ella was also a guest and thus entitled to some attention from her hosts as well.

As if sensing his anxiety to leave, Helena let out yet another wail. 'She is so mean!' she said, hiccupping dramatically on her words. 'I did not do anything. I was trying to be nice to her and it is so difficult ...'

'I know,' said Jacob mechanically. 'Lydia will speak to her when she returns, I am certain.' *Lydia*, he noted. *Not Adam*. Oh, no, not Adam, because he could see where that was leading. He'd seen the way Adam had looked at the girl and really, her attention had all been on him, Jacob, before Adam's arrival.

Damn the man! On this visit, at least, with Adam away on whatever unnecessary business he had to attend to, Jacob thought he would have been able to break through Ella's reserve and God knows he had tried to at that ridiculous dinner party. At that moment in time, Jacob despised Lydia almost as much as he despised Adam. That was typical of his male cousin though – flaunting his status at the dinner table, monopolising the most attractive woman there; and he, Jacob, had to watch that man sit at the head of what *should* have been *his* table and play up to Ella Dunbar. He had tried to get her attention, but those beautiful sapphire-blue eyes had kept slipping away from him, her body clearly aching to turn back to bloody Adam. It was getting beyond a joke now. Due to that mad relative of theirs and that damned convoluted will, Adam had effectively stripped him, Jacob, of everything he should have owned – and Adam clearly wanted the one woman Jacob loved as well.

Helena pouted. 'I still don't understand why everyone thinks she is so marvellous.' She raised those hideously strange eyes to him. 'I have known you all much longer. Can you remember when we were very little children and we used to play together in the nursery? I would come over with my nursemaid and you would be here and—'

'That was a long time ago,' said Jacob, sharply. 'We have all grown up since then.'

Helena continued to stare at him and then her face hardened. ''What *is* it about her?' she asked. 'Is she prettier than me? Is that it? Is she more talented than me?' She laughed shortly. 'I sincerely doubt *that*, actually. Jacob, you know my father can settle a sizeable dowry on me. What can *she* offer you?'

Jacob shook his head. How could he tell this girl, who he had grown up with alongside an 'understanding' of sorts, that from the moment he first met Ella, all those years ago, he had been utterly entranced? The way she really seemed to take notice of him, really seemed to listen to him and concentrate on his words had fascinated him and charmed him in equal measures. She was like nobody he had ever met before. And over the years, she had started to watch him with more interest and he knew that, when he was speaking to her, he was the only one she was aware of. Lydia had told him why, of course, had said that Ella was like that around everyone – she was "terribly polite" and going "terribly deaf", apparently, but he revelled in the fact that her world consisted of him and only him when he was with her.

So Helena Warner could, quite frankly, go hang.

'Jacob?' The woman's voice startled him and he looked at her, trying to hide the disgust he felt for her. 'I repeat, what can she offer you that I cannot?' she said, her pretty, doll-like face still contorted into a venomous mask.

'Nothing, Helena,' Jacob said flatly. 'Ella Dunbar is just a house guest, like we are. She is interesting, that is all.' And that night it had been obvious that she was just as interesting to Adam.

A roll of thunder interrupted Jacob's thoughts and Helena started. 'I hate storms!' she moaned. 'This evening just gets worse and worse.'

Lydia chose that moment to come back into the room. Jacob saw her cast a glance at himself and Helena. 'So sweet together,' Lydia murmured and wandered to the window. She lifted the heavy curtains and stared out into the darkness. 'It's terrible out there,' she said. 'I hope Adam finds her all right.' She jumped as another roll of thunder tore through the house.

She dropped the curtain against the rain, which was pelting against the glass and turned to face Jacob. 'Are you enjoying your stay?' she asked. 'I mean, apart from tonight, obviously.'

'What annoys me is her attitude!' burst out Helena. 'She is so ... so ... unsettling. She watches you the whole time. Ugh.' She shuddered dramatically.

'Helena! She is deaf, she is supposed to watch us!' said Lydia, laughing. 'How else can she understand what is going on?'

'Well, I don't like her,' said Helena. 'I don't trust her in the slightest.'

'Ella is a wonderful person,' Lydia replied. 'She is my dearest friend. I hope she becomes my sister in the future.'

'Your *sister*?' Jacob said bitterly. 'What? Do you expect Adam to *marry* her?'

'It would be rather nice,' said Lydia. She moved over to the piano and picked up the discarded Mozart score and hummed the first few notes. 'She plays this perfectly,' she said. 'It is a love song. I heard Adam singing it earlier. He said he had stumbled upon her playing it. It is just so romantic.'

'That doesn't mean he wants to marry her,' said Jacob. 'He could have heard her play anything and he would still have been singing it. Good music is like that; it stays in your head.'

'Maybe. But do I detect a little jealousy, Cousin?' said Lydia, her eyes twinkling. 'Would you rather Miss Dunbar played this for you and you alone? Oh, Helena, don't look like that. You *know* I'm only being naughty.' She walked over to Helena and put her arms around her, kissing her on the forehead. 'You and Jacob are perfect for each other, we all know that.'

'Not all of us,' muttered Helena.

Jacob pretended he hadn't heard. Instead his mind was on Ella, as he imagined what it would be like to have her play a love song to you and then look at you with those sapphire eyes while she waited, all her attention on you, for you to voice your approval.

Now she had left the house, Ella slowed down and forced herself to walk along the pathway, around the familiar sweep towards the lake. She pulled a face. She didn't like Helena at all. She had put up with more than enough from her these last few days. If it wasn't a case of spoiling Lydia's plans, she would leave just as soon as she could. Oh, but who was she trying to convince? It was Adam she didn't want to leave, wasn't it?

It had always been Adam. She recalled the crushing disappointments when she came here, full of anticipation, only to discover he was away on business. He had been the one she had wept and raged at when, not much more than a child, she had discovered there was no hope that the awful, creeping silence she had lived with would ever stop until it had swallowed up everything in its path. It had been Adam, not Lydia – because dear and sweet and wonderful as Lydia was, she had handled it even worse than Ella had. Lydia's immediate thoughts had been how she would ever enjoy the coming-out parties and balls they had to look forward to. Adam's thoughts had been of a far more practical nature. Like Lydia, Ella had no parents to guide her – only an elderly aunt who didn't quite know what to do with her. So Adam was the one she turned to – and he had barely been a man himself, but she swore to this day that his wisdom was what had saved her soul.

There had always been an attraction between them – at least on her side – and it was only today she had realised that their easy friendship had the potential to develop further. She felt herself grow hot as the colour flooded her face again and was briefly thankful for the cool air against her skin.

Ella looked up, finding herself on the path that led to the summer house. The twilight was approaching and there were some clouds glowering on the horizon. The air felt heavy and she knew that a thunderstorm was likely. The air had a special smell to it, of earth and undergrowth, and Ella could feel the pressure building up around her.

As she watched the sky, a jagged fork of lightning lit up the countryside and big, fat drops of rain started to fall. Ella reached out and laid her fingertips on the trunk of a tree. She began counting in her head, and sure enough, a few seconds later, she felt the thunder roll among the clouds and tremble through the tree. She raised her face to the sky again and closed her eyes, feeling the rain wet her cheeks. She had always loved thunderstorms, even as a child and had often pressed her hands against the panes of glass in the windows and felt them rattle and shake.

Then Ella opened her eyes and snatched her hand away from the tree trunk. There never had been and never would be a roll of thunder that would break her silence. She jumped as she felt a hand on her shoulder and swung around, her heart hammering in her chest. Adam was standing facing her in the half-light, his eyes full of concern even as he smiled that easy smile of his.

'I told you to leave me alone!' shouted Ella, shaking his hand from her. She turned away but he pulled her back towards him and placed a hand on her upper arms.

'I told you before,' he said. 'I cannot use sign language. I don't understand it. Come now, you are soaked through.'

'It is getting dark,' said Ella. She deliberately turned her face away from him. 'I don't know what you're trying to say.'

Adam leaned into her line of vision. 'Don't lie to me, Ella. Don't be so dismissive. You know perfectly well what I'm saying. And you're still getting wet. Fortunately, I had the forethought to bring this.' With some sort of flourish, he produced a soft, velvet cloak. He reached around Ella and hung it on her shoulders. He pulled the hood up over her honey-coloured hair, then manoeuvred her towards the summer house, pushing her gently ahead of him. Once inside he produced two candles from his pocket and lit them with some matches he produced from his other pocket.

Ella stared at the flames, watching as Adam moved the candles onto a small table and indicated that she should sit on one of the two chairs in the pool of light, while he took the other.

'No excuses now,' he said. 'We can have quite a conversation. You first. What happened tonight?'

'Talk all you want,' said Ella. 'I don't know what you're saying.'

'Yes you do,' said Adam. 'If you couldn't see me, you wouldn't know I was talking. But you can see me, so I'll ask you again. What happened in there?'

'I hate that woman,' said Ella dismally. 'She is poisonous.'

'Helena is in love with Jacob,' said Adam. 'She's jealous.'

'But I'm nobody to be jealous of,' exclaimed Ella. 'I'm certainly not interested in Jacob romantically and I cannot bear Helena. She is welcome to him. I know Lydia wishes them to be together and I would never get in their way. And I don't really care either way!'

'Oh that *is* good to hear,' said Adam. 'Ella, I lied when I said I didn't know any sign language.' He dropped his head and stared into the flames, then raised his head. He looked directly at Ella and she felt the atmosphere shift. She clutched the edge of the seat and stared at him waiting for his next comment.

'Ella,' he said carefully. 'You remember how I found Lydia's old finger spelling sheet this afternoon? I was hoping to have a little more practice, but – well – I shall try.' He raised his hands, looking embarrassed, and smiled at Ella. The candlelight made flickering shadows all over his face, and Ella longed to follow them with her fingertips, but she dug her fingers into the seat instead.

Adam began to laboriously shape his hands and fingers and she quirked her lips into a smile as she watched the phrase take shape.

'There is a quicker way,' she said eventually. She pointed her right forefinger against her chest, crossed it with her left hand and then pointed at Adam, again with her right forefinger. *I love you.*

Adam smiled. 'Beautifully expressed,' he said, 'but it means nothing unless it is true.' He tilted his head to one side. 'Is it?' he asked. 'It was when I said it through my fingers.'

Ella shook her head and Adam's face fell.

Then, despite herself, she laughed. 'Unless you "line" me, then no, it's not true,' she said. 'You are quite right, you need more practice.'

Adam laughed and she could see the relief wash over him. 'Then I beg of you, will you teach me?' he asked. Adam leaned towards her and took her face in his hands. 'I am willing to learn. I am willing to take all the time in the world to learn it from you. Could we have that time together, at all? The rest of our lives, perhaps?'

Ella's heart skipped a beat. She hardly dared believe he meant what she understood. 'I don't know,' she said carefully. 'What are you implying?'

'I want to marry you, Ella Dunbar. I think I have loved you since the first time Lydia brought you to Carrick Park, but I hardly dared to think that we would have any sort of future together. Look at you. You are beautiful, you captivate everyone you meet. What hope do I have, as simply the brother of your old school friend?'

'Adam! I long to say yes, but it's something I've barely allowed myself to dream about. What happens in the future? What happens when you are committed to someone like me? I would be no good for you, with all your business contacts and social events. It is difficult, Adam. I don't know how I would fit into your lifestyle. I mean, you own Carrick Park! There is a certain duty attached to it. I don't know whether I could help you fulfil that. I would be a hindrance to you – how could you stand me sitting by you at all those social occasions, missing the point of every conversation and looking ignorant in front of your contacts ...'

Adam put his finger to her lips, silencing her. 'Ella, you are anything but ignorant. You are my Ella, and that is all that matters to me. You always have been. You couldn't be any more perfect for me.'

'Adam—'

'Ella. I will ask you again. Will you marry me?'

Ella looked at him. 'I think it's too dark in here after all, despite your candlelight. I can't seem to believe what I think you just said.'

'I meant it.'

'But—'

'No buts. No excuses. Just a simple yes or no.'

There was a beat. Ella looked into the flame, then looked at Adam. She slowly nodded her head. 'Yes,' she said. 'My answer is yes. But I am so very sorry.'

'What about?' asked Adam.

'I smashed the mirror in the guest bedroom,' said Ella. 'Lydia was right. It did feel rather good to be bad.'

'Incredible,' murmured Adam. 'You are incredible.' Then he leaned over and kissed her and all thoughts of the mirror fled from Ella's mind.

They had gone back to the house through the rain-drenched gardens, and Ella had run up the staircase towards her rooms, decreeing that she would not to return to the party under any circumstances. Adam had followed her up to the first landing where the stairs split into two and he reached out to stop her before she took the flight towards the left wing.

'When we are married,' he told her, 'I shall have your portrait hung right there.' He pointed to a space on the landing wall.

'No!' she said, laughing. 'Never. I would make a terrible sitter.'

'You would not,' he said, pulling her close and cupping her face in his hands. He looked down at her. 'Will we call you Lady Eleanor, I wonder?'

'I would prefer Ella,' she replied. 'I feel nothing like a lady.'

'You are everything a lady should be and more,' said Adam. He gestured up the stairs. 'Go now, I see you're anxious to escape. I think we'll save our news for tomorrow. I'll speak to my sister and tell her I found you safely and you are resting.'

'I am sorry I spoiled the evening,' said Ella. 'I am sorry that you had to come out and find me in the storm.'

'I am sorry that you had to put up with Miss Warner,' said Adam. 'I will speak to her privately.'

'Adam!'

'No,' said Adam. 'She cannot treat our family like that. Leave it to me. Goodnight, my love.' He leaned down and kissed her, her face still in his hands.

She smiled and continued up the stairs, but before she reached the top of the staircase, she turned and saw him still standing there, watching her.

He raised his hands. *I love you* he told her.

I love you too she replied, and disappeared around the corner into the corridor.

THE PHOTOGRAPH

When Ella woke up the next morning she wondered at first whether the whole episode had been a dream. She raised herself up on one elbow and looked at the dressing table mirror. It was shattered and cracked, the silver-backed hairbrush lying on the dressing table itself.

She looked at herself, her sapphire eyes and long, honey-coloured hair reflected a million times in the shards of glass. It was real. Everything was real. There was a draught of cold air on her shoulder and she saw the reflection of the bedroom door opening. She sat up in bed, wondering who could be coming to see her.

The door opened fully and the little housemaid, Elizabeth, entered, balancing a breakfast tray. She smiled widely at Ella and came over to the bed. She fumbled around, dragging a small table over to the bedside and set the tray down.

'Breakfast, miss,' she said, pointing unnecessarily at the tray. 'For you.'

Ella knew she was speaking loudly and slowly and managed to hide her amusement. This was entirely different to Helena; Elizabeth had not a venomous bone in her body.

'The master said so,' the girl finished, nodding eagerly.

'Thank you,' said Ella. The girl nodded and smiled again and left the room. Ella looked at the food piled up on the plates and wondered exactly how long it would take her to work her way through it all. Well, for this one morning, she would luxuriate in it.

It was well after ten by the time Ella had finished breakfast and dressed. Part of her was eager to go downstairs and see Adam, but another part of her was not so eager to see

Helena. With any luck, the girl would have gone riding and she would be excused her company for a little while longer.

Ella went down the staircase, seeing again the space on the landing wall where Adam had threatened to hang her portrait. Today, he had told her, was the day they would share their news with Lydia. Lydia's habit, she knew, was to sit in the drawing room until everyone was gathered around her and then she would begin to tell them what they would be doing that day. Lydia would never change. Ella smiled, remembering the dinner party invitations she had issued to them yesterday. There had only been the four of them at that point. Lydia had obviously known that Adam was coming but, Lydia being Lydia, she did like to formalise things.

Ella pushed open the door into the drawing room and saw Lydia sitting at a table, studying a big, square box with two round pieces of glass on the front. She had a book open next to her and she seemed to be looking at the book then fiddling with the object.

Lydia looked up and waved. 'Good morning, darling. Do you like my new toy?'

'What is it?' asked Ella.

'A camera,' said Lydia. 'Is it not marvellous? I ordered it from America! How splendid it is.'

Ella, curious, began to head towards the thing, until she felt an arm creep around her waist. She turned to see Adam standing beside her.

'What has she acquired now?' he asked.

'I don't know. She says it's a camera,' Ella replied. She turned to Adam. *What is she doing?* she asked. A flash of light caught her off guard and she jumped, letting out a yell of shock.

Adam laughed and pointed at Lydia.

Ella turned back to her, thoroughly confused now.

'Oh, I am terribly sorry. I think I just managed to take a photograph of you,' said Lydia, almost as surprised as Ella was. She blinked and looked down at the camera. 'I shall have to develop it now. Adam, darling, would you?'

'Certainly,' said Adam. He hurried over to the camera and they bent their heads over it, apparently trying to work out how to take the plate out and which of the various chemicals that Lydia produced from a box beside her would work on the thing.

Ella shook her head and wandered off into the corner of the room towards the piano. Let them sort it out, she thought as she sat down and began to pick out the Mozart tune from the night before. If it was indeed a picture of her, she was in no hurry to see it anyway.

Lost in her music, it seemed a while before a rather damp piece of paper was placed in front of her. On it was a slightly blurred image of Ella and Adam, caught at the precise moment Ella had been asking what Lydia had been doing.

'Oh, no!' Ella cried, grabbing it with both hands and studying it. 'This is horrible! Look at me! Oh, Lydia, no!' She looked at Lydia, torn between being horrified and desperately amused at the image. She shook the picture at her. 'How dare you!'

'It's beautiful!' Lydia laughed, hugging her. 'Look at you both. See how handsome my brother is. And you are so pretty!' She made the sign for *pretty* as if to emphasise her point. 'You can see the light shining on your beautiful hair. How clever. What were you saying to him?' She took the photograph from Ella and looked closely. 'Oh, I see. You were asking what I was doing. You terrible girl! You see, I can still understand you, even in a picture. But what a shame some of it came out so blurred. At least your faces are clear enough.'

'Well, you can destroy it or you can hide it somewhere; it will not see the light of day,' said Ella. 'It's dreadful. And stop talking so quickly! It's impossible to keep up with you.'

'It's not dreadful,' reprimanded Lydia. 'But I will keep it, if only to prevent you from destroying it yourself. Oh, Jacob! Good morning. Come and see this.' She waved the picture in the direction of the door.

Jacob walked up to the piano, nodding at the assembled company. Adam, having tidied up some of the mess Lydia had left with her chemicals, came to stand beside Ella.

'Good morning. Let me see, then,' said Jacob, holding his hand out for the photograph.

Ella wondered if she was the only one who saw an odd look flit across his face as he held the picture, then his expression settled into its usual calm composure. 'Interesting,' he said. 'From this morning, I suspect, looking at your outfits and the setting.' He handed it back to Lydia, clearly showing her that he wasn't at all interested in it. 'Where is Miss Warner, today?' he asked. 'I was looking for her earlier. I have already been around the gardens and she was not there. The stable hands have not seen her either.'

'Oh, I really cannot say!' replied Lydia. 'I just assumed that she was around.' She looked about the room vaguely, as if Helena was going to pop out of a bureau or appear from beneath the table.

'She has gone home,' said Adam shortly. 'She came to find me earlier – apparently she had news from home and she had to leave. I was going to tell you before, but then my sister managed to take a photograph and I was somewhat distracted.'

'News from home?' asked Jacob. He looked at Adam steadily. 'Convenient.'

'Do you believe so?' replied Adam, looking at his cousin just as steadily. Jacob was the first to break eye contact. 'Well, she will be missed,' Adam said. 'But we cannot dwell on it. There are still four of us here. What, my sweet Lydia, is our agenda for today?'

'I thought a trip into Whitby, because we did not make it yesterday,' she said. 'We shall take the carriage. Oh, that is so annoying about Helena leaving.' She pouted prettily.

'Oh, I do not mind riding,' said Ella quickly. She felt responsible for Helena's disappearance and as she was sure that Adam had engineered it for her, she didn't want to cause any more disruption by insisting on the carriage.

She looked at Adam, a question in her eyes. He shook his head imperceptibly at her, seemingly telling her not to worry about Helena.

'It is not for your benefit, Ella,' said Lydia. 'I just think the weather looks rather dreary and I would rather be inside the carriage should we have another storm like last night's.' She smiled to show there was no hidden meaning in her words.

'Well,' said Adam, reaching his hand out for Ella's. He pulled her gently to her feet and drew her close to him. 'The storm did us a favour last night. I found Miss Dunbar wandering by the summer house and bade her enter in order to stay dry. While we were in the summer house she did me the honour of agreeing to become my wife. I hope you will welcome her warmly into the family.'

'Ella! You have *always* been part of our family!' cried Lydia, rushing up to her and embracing her. 'Now my dearest wish has come true and you are to be my sister. And this photograph shall be your official engagement photograph!'

'I am to have a portrait painted of Ella for the landing,' said Adam. 'Or a portrait of Lady Eleanor as she will be.'

'No!' said Ella. 'Please, to see myself in that photograph is bad enough. I don't want to be subjected to seeing myself every time I ascend the staircase.'

'I shall have to ignore your objections,' said Adam. 'I shall arrange it immediately.' He lifted a lock of Ella's hair from her shoulder and let it drop again. 'I cannot wait to see what someone like Sir Edwin Landseer makes of you. If his work is good enough for the Queen, it is good enough for Lady Eleanor.'

'Stop tormenting me!' she said. 'No.'

'Jacob,' said Lydia suddenly, 'you have not wished them well yet.' She fixed her cousin with a look that Ella knew hid a glimpse of steel. Vague and delightful as Lydia was on the surface, she was not quite as naive as she appeared to be.

'Why, of course I am delighted for you both,' said Jacob. He bowed to Ella and took her hand in both of his. He kissed it and ran his thumb gently over her hand. The gesture was so pathetically tender, she was surprised for a moment. Jacob raised his face and looked into her eyes. 'It is rather a shock to me,' he said, 'and very sudden.'

'Ella has known Adam almost as long as I have,' said Lydia. 'And I think that you, my dear cousin, need to race after Helena and make us happy with some news of your own.'

'I really cannot see that happening,' said Jacob. 'Miss Warner is a wonderful girl, but it was never going to be.'

He looked at Ella and she couldn't read what was in his eyes. Pain? Regret? Anger? Whatever it was, it made her uncomfortable and instinctively she moved closer to Adam. She saw Jacob catch the movement and his mouth twisted for a moment, as if he was biting back a comment. 'My heart lies elsewhere, Lydia. Alas, I think your matchmaking in this instance has failed you. Helena has run away. She has deserted us all, and what are we to make of that?'

'Oh, she will be back,' said Lydia. 'She cannot keep away from you.' She tapped Jacob lightly on his chest with her forefinger. 'She is besotted with you, did you not know that?'

'In the light of recent events, perhaps it is best that she *has* gone home. It is a more pleasant atmosphere all round,' replied Jacob. 'So, are we to ready ourselves for our trip then?' he asked, neatly changing the subject. 'Or do we maybe have another task to perform before that? Please, do allow me to inspect that marvellous camera of yours, Lydia. I know a little about them and, strangely enough, how to make the subjects feel at ease.'

Ella watched the conversation around her; Lydia was speaking quickly, excited at the prospect of an outing and some fun with her new toy; Adam half sat on the piano, amused at his sister; and Jacob – well, Jacob. He was as unfathomable as ever. But she knew one thing for certain – she really wasn't sure that she felt she could trust him very much.

THE DRESS
August 1865

Once Lydia had an idea in her head, she was determined to see it through. She had been consumed over the last few weeks with organising Ella's wedding. Her excuse was that Ella needed assistance and she was the best placed person to do it.

'Darling, what if you go somewhere and they chatter too quickly?' was one of her favourite rationales. 'I can help.'

'I don't need your help,' said Ella every time. 'I will ask them to slow down. I always manage when you are not around.'

To which Lydia would shake her head and say, 'No, no, no. It is best that I come.'

Ella usually found herself acquiescing, just to stop Lydia from pestering her.

It was on one such day that they had taken the carriage into Whitby to choose the material for Ella's dress. Ella was looking out of the window, watching the moors roll past her and feeling the warmth of the sun through the glass. The gentle rocking motion of the carriage was almost lulling her to sleep and she laid her fingers gently on the door, sensing the clip-clopping vibrations of the horses' hooves as they travelled along the road.

Lydia startled her by laying her hand on her knee and tapping gently to get her attention. 'What colour have you in mind?' she asked, her round, dark brown eyes even wider than usual. 'Because I have seen a beautiful pale green satin and I thought that would suit you. The seamstress said she could trim it with ribbons and beads for us as well. It will be stunning.'

'Lydia, this is *my* dress!' exclaimed Ella. 'Yet you are

telling me you have already chosen it?' She frowned. 'Lydia. How could you?'

Lydia had the grace to look slightly ashamed. She dropped her head then looked up again. 'I am sorry. I thought that it would help.'

'Once again – I don't need all this "help" you keep offering me. Honestly! I am perfectly capable of deciding on a dress. And if I want a scarlet dress, I shall have a scarlet dress. Or maybe I shall choose royal-blue. Or perhaps purple. It is *my* dress after all.'

More upset than she cared to admit, Ella looked stubbornly back out of the window and refused to acknowledge any more little taps from Lydia the whole way to the town, even though they became more urgent and insistent the closer they got to Whitby.

Eventually, the carriage pulled up and stopped to let them alight.

Ella gestured to Lydia to leave first. 'Go ahead,' she said, still smarting. 'You know where the seamstress is, not me.'

'Oh, please, don't be cross with me,' said Lydia, clasping Ella's hands. 'I was trying to help. I know I'm becoming intolerable. I just want everything to be perfect for you. I always wanted you and Adam to marry and I just cannot let go of the thought that I need to keep driving the situation.'

'You also wanted Helena and Jacob to marry,' replied Ella. 'Look what happened there. Has anybody had word from Helena since that horrible night? No. Now Lydia, I love you. You are my sweet sister. But you have to let us all make our own mistakes. If I want you to make a decision, I will ask you. What have I even organised myself for this wedding? Nothing.'

She shook loose Lydia's hands. She actually hated people touching them when she was trying to drive a point home;

it was like they were cutting her tongue out. 'And now, now you want me to let go of the whole … *dress* thing as well.' She emphasised her words with a quick sweeping motion, moving her hands down from her shoulders to the ground, spreading her fingers out to show the sort of gown she desired. 'No. I appreciate everything you are doing for me, but please, let me decide this for myself.'

Lydia nodded, looking contrite. *Sorry* she signed, balling up her fist and rubbing it vaguely around her chest area.

'And so you should be. In consideration of that, I will allow you to take me to your seamstress and we can look at the fabric *together*.' She signed the word as she spoke it, so there was no mistaking it.

Lydia threw her arms around Ella, all smiles again. 'Thank you,' she said, sitting back in the seat. It was her turn to gesture to Ella. 'After you,' she said. 'I will show you where the seamstress is, but you can make all the decisions. But I must simply insist on a pale pink for my gown. You know I look terribly sickly in green. It is, actually, maybe best that we have decided against the pale green for you. I will be standing next to you all day – I want to look my best as well, you know. I cannot have a greenness reflected upon me. It would look terrible, I know it would.'

Ella smiled and blew a little kiss to her. 'I shall look forward to seeing you in your dress,' she said. 'You will be a wonderful foil to me.'

The seamstress had worked for Lydia's family for years. She had made dresses for Lydia since she was small, and had known her mother very well. Lydia looked a lot like her mother; she had the same slim figure, despite her height, and the same exuberant attitude and knew the seamstress appreciated how she had kept using her services, even after her parents had died.

Today, Lydia led the way through a narrow door in a building off a side street from the town. It was a small place, but very welcoming. The seamstress lived above the shop and used much of the space downstairs as storage for her fabrics and trimmings.

Lydia turned to encourage Ella to hurry up, and saw the girl staring around her in wonderment.

'I didn't expect it to look like this,' she said, turning to address Lydia. Ella's words, as always, were clear and precise and rang around the little workshop.

Ella smiled. 'Miss Waters, allow me to introduce my dear friend, Miss Ella Dunbar,' said Lydia, reaching for Ella's arm and drawing her closer.

The seamstress smiled and curtseyed. 'Miss Dunbar,' she said.

Ella smiled at the seamstress and held out her hand. 'I am delighted to meet you,' she said. 'I have heard so much about you.'

'And I you,' said Miss Waters. 'You are marrying Master Adam, yes?'

'That is correct,' said Ella. She turned to smile at Lydia. 'Lydia said I should come to you for my wedding gown.'

'Ah, yes,' said Miss Waters. She disappeared behind the counter. 'The pale green, was it not, Miss Lydia?'

Lydia darted over to the counter and hung over it. 'No!' she said to the seamstress, quite loudly. 'We had a discussion on the way here. Ella needs to choose her own!'

Miss Waters looked up, surprised. 'I thought you said, miss, that it was the green.'

'Let her choose her own!' said Lydia quickly.

'Is there a problem?' asked Ella coming over to them.

'Lydia?' She touched her arm, apparently confused. 'What is the matter?'

'Oh! Miss Waters is simply checking she has enough samples for you to choose from,' said Lydia. 'That is all.' She smiled disarmingly.

'I see,' said Ella, half-smiling. 'Well, I may be able to save her the bother. Miss Waters?' The seamstress popped up from behind the counter and looked at the girls. Lydia hoped that Ella wouldn't notice the ream of pale green satin in the woman's arms.

'I have just seen some satin over there. Would it be possible to look at it a little more closely?'

'Oh!' said Lydia. 'Already? Well, I am sure you can look at it.' She drew Ella from the counter, seizing her opportunity to get her friend away from the pale green material. 'Show me. Show me where it is.'

'This one,' replied Ella. She pointed up at a roll of satin. 'It is that lovely creamy-white stuff.' She turned to Lydia. 'I think maybe with some swansdown and crystal trimmings? Would you agree?'

'Ohhh. Utterly perfect, darling!' said Lydia. 'See, I knew it would be fun coming for your fabric today! Would you agree to some white tulle, perhaps? Some frills of some description?'

'That sounds delightful,' said Ella. 'See, *now* you are being useful.'

Lydia smiled and tugged her gently to the side as Miss Waters was approaching them from behind with a small stool. The seamstress set the stool down and clambered up to reach the fabric.

She pulled the ream down from the shelf, climbed back down and headed over to the counter. 'Here you are, Miss Dunbar,' she said, rolling it out. 'Feel that. It is beautiful and soft, is it not?'

Ella reached out and ran her fingers along the surface of the material.

Not for the first time, Lydia was a little jealous of how elegant her friend's hands actually were. Lydia was the unfortunate bearer of short, stubby fingers and her hands were, it had to be said, rather large considering the rest of her proportions. That was her excuse as to why she could never play the piano, anyway.

'It is, it is wonderful,' said Ella. 'If I tell you what I am considering, would you tell me if it is possible to make it?'

Ella tilted her head to the side, a habit Lydia knew her brother found most endearing. A little bubble of love and warmth burst inside her, making her so pleased that her plans had worked out so happily. Adam, she decided, owed her a great debt.

'I can make almost anything,' said Miss Waters proudly. She puffed her chest out like a little pigeon. 'You just tell me what you want.'

'That *is* good to know,' said Ella. Innocently, and without missing a beat, she looked straight at Miss Waters and smiled. 'I would also like a bridesmaid's dress for my new sister here. I think that pale green satin she had set aside would be marvellous on her. I see you have it all ready there, anyway. I think maybe she would like some beads and ribbons as trimmings?' She nodded to Miss Waters and turned away.

She smiled sweetly at Lydia as she passed her. *Sorry* she signed.

Lydia knew she didn't mean it in the slightest.

Some time later, Lydia and Ella left the seamstress, happy in the knowledge that Miss Waters was now settled with a nice commission and the promise of a neat little sum of money.

Ella linked Lydia's arm and pulled her close. 'I am *sure* you will not look that terrible in green,' she said.

Lydia pouted. 'You are wicked at times, Ella Dunbar. But I expect I deserved it.' She sighed. 'I swear I will not meddle in your affairs any more.'

'Oh, I'm just teasing you. I asked her to use the pink in the end, don't worry,' said Ella. 'I asked her to do so when you were being miserable in the corner, staring at the pink satin. You were the one who told me how nice it was to be bad, remember?'

'Ella! You don't have to practise that skill on me!' said Lydia, trying hard to look indignant. 'It was for ... other people.'

'Mmm. I suspect I could have been rather evil to Helena,' replied Ella, 'given the chance.'

'Yes. I wish she would contact us,' complained Lydia. 'I just don't know what happened.'

'I wonder if Adam said anything to her?' suggested Ella. 'Oh, well. It is done.'

'Anyway, how did you know that I was lusting after that perfectly delightful pink satin?' asked Lydia.

Ella laughed. 'I see a lot more than people think. I rely on seeing things. There is not much that escapes my notice.'

'Sometimes I envy you,' said Lydia. She stopped and turned to face Ella. 'You just astound me. You play that piano better than anyone I know. You enchanted my brother, which, believe me, many women have tried to do. And you are just incredible.' She shook her head. 'I have never told you any of this before. But I wish I was more like you.'

'No.' Ella shook her head. 'I often wish I was just like everybody else. Just ordinary. It can be difficult, especially at night.' She frowned. 'Sometimes I worry about that side of things.' She looked at Lydia. 'I am sorry. I am speaking out of turn.' She flushed and turned away, tugging Lydia along with her. 'You have no need to know any of that.' She put her head down, desperately embarrassed.

Lydia stopped, forcing Ella to stop with her. She took her face in her hands and spoke to her. The girls were the same height – Lydia's eyes were exactly on a level with Ella's. 'It will be perfect,' she said. 'This is Adam. He knows everything about you. Just trust him.'

'But we can never have a conversation at night!' said Ella desperately. 'I dread the winter and the dark evenings. How will we manage?'

'You do not always need words,' said Lydia. 'Just trust him.' She stood a little way back and smiled impertinently. 'And there is always lamplight and candles if you do need to converse.'

Ella started to laugh. 'You always make me feel better!' she said. Then, suddenly, 'Oh! I say, is that not your cousin Jacob? He is heading this way. You didn't tell me he was in the area.'

'I didn't know!' said Lydia. She swung around and they both faced the man who was heading towards them. She looked back at Ella, surprised. 'He didn't say he was here. Jacob! Darling!' She waved at the man and he raised his hand in acknowledgement. He broke into a run and came up to the girls.

'Lydia! Ella! What a coincidence. I was in the area and I thought I would come into the town. I didn't tell you officially, as I have no time to visit you. I do hope you will forgive me. My services are required elsewhere today and I must travel back mid-afternoon. Truthfully, I was frightened to tell you I was here, in case you urged me back to the Park and I was forced to decline the invitation.' He turned his full attention to Ella and his eyes met hers, with something like a challenge in them. 'Am I in trouble for not confessing my intentions?'

As Helena had so cattily mentioned, inflections were difficult for Ella at times and she frowned a little, wondering how exactly he meant those words. She realised, at least, that he was here unexpectedly and, for once, she was grateful Lydia was with her.

'Lydia is very much in charge,' said Ella. 'So I should ask her.'

'I would not normally miss such a chance to see you,' he said, still looking at Ella. 'It has been too long.'

'July, was it not?' interrupted Lydia. 'Only one month since you visited us, Jacob!' She laughed. 'Or does time fly for you?'

'Any amount of time away from the Park is too long,' he said. 'May I join you two ladies or are you on pressing business that does not require a man? I do have an hour or two to spare myself. And now we are together, we should make the most of it.'

'We have been organising Ella's wedding outfit,' said Lydia. 'So exciting!'

'I see,' said Jacob. 'Well, I do hope the seamstress does her justice.'

'She will,' said Lydia, smiling at Ella.

Ella was quite grateful for the pause in the exchange; she was getting dizzy looking from one to the other and had maybe fully understood half of the subsequent conversation. 'I myself have some other business to attend to while we are here,' said Lydia.

She turned her back on Ella and said something to Jacob. Ella saw him repeat the word *present* and she tried to suppress a smile.

Lydia turned back to Ella. 'Please, would you amuse my

cousin for a little while, Ella? I will meet you at the carriage at two o'clock. Is that reasonable? Then we shall be able to get back to the Park for tea. Jacob, will you be able to squeeze us in?'

'Unfortunately not,' said Jacob. 'As I say, I must leave later this afternoon.' He offered Ella his arm. 'But are you to come with me, Miss Dunbar, for a short while at least?'

'Apparently so,' said Ella, looking at them both, slightly confused.

'I would appreciate your company,' said Jacob. 'Shall we take a walk up the cliff path, along past St Mary's?'

'If you wish,' she said. She took his arm, not entirely comfortable with the proposition, if she was honest, and they headed off, away from the town and up to the cliff path.

JACOB

The sea was glassy and calm, reflecting the azure of the sky. One or two fishing boats were bobbing around and the gulls dipped and dived around them, hoping for some scraps.

'It is peaceful up here today,' said Jacob, leading Ella to the wall where they could look out over the coast.

'There were quite a few people in the town. It was rather crowded,' replied Ella.

'I would not have gone there today had I not needed to speak to my contacts urgently,' replied Jacob, 'but I am pleased I ventured out.' He smiled at Ella. The girl was half-turned, facing him, her hands neatly and primly crossed in front of her. 'Not only did I unexpectedly see you and my cousin, but I also get to take advantage of the view with such a delightful companion.'

'Have you heard from Miss Warner?' asked Ella.

Jacob felt a sharp stab of annoyance that Helena Warner should weave her way into his precious time with Ella. It wasn't as if he would get many more moments like this with her, not since Adam had claimed her as his own. A little like Carrick Park, really.

'No. I have heard nothing from her,' he said. 'Not even a letter. It is most strange. She was in a terrible mood that night. She must have been angrier than we imagined.'

'Angry?' repeated Ella. 'But Adam said she had news from home. I thought that was why she left?' She looked sweetly confused, a little frown deepening in her forehead. 'Oh dear, I did not mean to cause a rift between you all, but I must confess that I had my suspicions.' Ella blushed, obviously reliving the evening. She lifted her hands and crossed them the other way, pressing them back into her skirt.

'It is not our concern,' said Jacob. 'So, your wedding plans are progressing well?' he asked her, not really wanting to hear the answer, but he thought it would at least draw her into conversation with him.

He was rewarded when Ella's eyes lit up and she nodded enthusiastically, the little ornaments in her hat bobbing up and down. 'Oh, yes. Lydia has done so much for us, we are very grateful.'

An idea began to worm its way into his head and he rocked back on his heels. He simply had to take the chance with it. 'And has Adam been by your side constantly during this last month?' he asked. He could hear the slight, nervous raise in pitch in his voice as he asked such a loaded question and was pleased that Ella couldn't. For sure, that would scupper his plans all together.

The light in the girl's eyes flickered a little and her smile wavered. 'He has been busy,' she said, 'but I understand that. He has the estate to run after all.'

'If I were lucky enough to be marrying someone like you,' said Jacob, deciding to push his point home a little more, 'I would never dare let them out of my sight.'

Ella dropped her gaze. 'Oh, I am nobody special,' she said, staring at the ground by their feet, as if she were embarrassed. Then she lifted her gaze and stared resolutely out at the sea, clearly uncomfortable with the praise.

'I only ask because I realise how busy Adam is,' said Jacob, waiting until he had her attention again. 'Has he spoken to you about the Park's history?'

'No, I know very little about it,' said Ella. She appeared to relax a little, more comfortable with the subject.

'It was our great-grandfather's property,' said Jacob. 'He entailed it to his daughter, rather than any of his sons. Adam is descended from the daughter whereas I am descended from the eldest son.'

'Oh!' Ella looked surprised. 'Lydia might have mentioned something a while ago ...' She shook her head. 'No. I apologise – I speak out of turn. I doubt I heard it correctly.' She blushed again. 'But I just assumed it was the usual sort of inheritance. I suppose that must have made things difficult for the families.'

'It did,' agreed Jacob. 'Fortunately it does not affect my relationship with Lydia and Adam.' He knew he was lying through his teeth. He hated the pair of them. Then he forced a smile onto his face. 'We almost grew up together at the Park, you know.'

Ella smiled. 'You were often there when I visited, especially, I recall, when we were younger.'

'Once we boys were sent away to school, it was never practical to spend as much time there,' said Jacob. 'Lydia is four years younger than me, Adam is two years older. I was like the middle child. I always enjoyed it more when you were there.'

'It must have been wonderful to be part of such a large family,' said Ella smiling. 'My parents moved abroad when I was very small, but they thought it best to leave me in England. They did not want to confuse me with foreign languages. They died within days of each other shortly after they moved there, apparently of a fever. I cannot miss them, because I never really knew them.' She spoke without bitterness.

'Who did you remain in England with?' asked Jacob.

'A terribly old aunt, who died last year. Since then, I think I have spent more time at the Park than I have at my family home. Lydia has been a wonderful friend to me.'

'I see.' Jacob moved to face her and took her hands in his. He looked at her, marvelling, and not for the first time, at the clear sapphire-blue of her eyes. 'Ella, pray forgive me for saying this, but are you sure you are marrying Adam for the correct reasons?' He continued, speaking slowly so she fully understood him. 'You are not simply lonely? And you do know what a responsibility it is for anybody to be connected to the head of that family? They own property all over the country and the business is expanding abroad. Adam suggested he may need to spend a considerable time in Italy shortly, and then more than likely he will need to move to Paris and Switzerland. I do not mean to scare you, but he will expect you to go with him.'

'I know, and I am happy to go,' said Ella. 'I have nothing to stay in England for except Lydia, and she will most likely come as well.'

'Lydia will have to stay here, Ella,' said Jacob. 'Somebody will need to be here to look after the interests of the Park and the business at home. The agents cannot do it all. I have offered to assist, knowing this day would come, but they will not hear of it.'

'What are you trying to tell me?' asked Ella. 'You have lost me.'

She did look bewildered. It was maybe time, Jacob thought, to drive his point truly home. And if Adam got hurt in the process, he really did not care.

'You will be on your own in a foreign country with foreign staff and nobody around who will speak reasonable English,' Jacob said. 'I say this because I care about you. How will you manage? Have you really thought about it? It is natural to be concerned about your future, Ella. Sometimes, even angels fear to fly. It is often safer for them to stay on familiar territory.'

Ella flushed scarlet and stared at him. She did not answer immediately. Then eventually she said in a funny, stilted little way: 'Thank you, Jacob. You are being honest and I appreciate it. But I have no wish to discuss it further.'

Jacob nodded and let go of her hands. She shifted position and stared out to sea again. Jacob stood back and did the same. He had planted the seed, anyway. She would be far better off here, in England, with him. He knew that, but she just needed to understand that herself.

Lydia had been at the carriage waiting for them at two o'clock as specified and they said their goodbyes. Jacob held Ella's hand a little too long when he kissed it to bid her farewell, and he promised to see her again soon, which did not make her particularly overjoyed.

Lydia chattered all the way back, and Ella smiled and nodded at what she hoped were appropriate intervals, but she wasn't paying attention. Instead, she was thinking about Adam's absences and the conversation she had just had with Jacob. She guessed, correctly, that she would be expected to officially be the hostess at any events they held both at the Park, and abroad. If Lydia was there to help her, that was truly marvellous and she had never given any thought to the fact that Lydia would *not* be there. Yet if Lydia was not there, where did that leave her? She was completely unschooled in anything like that. Her foreign language skills were non-existent – she knew a little basic French which she had learned due to pure stubbornness, but that was it. The more she thought about it, the worse it became. She might be expected to entertain a room full of – God forbid – foreign Helena Warners.

'I cannot do this,' she said suddenly. The carriage was bumping over the gravel of the estate drive on its way to the house. 'I cannot marry Adam. It's just *wrong*.'

'Ella!' cried Lydia. Her face was horrified.

Ella held up her hand and closed her eyes, shaking her head. 'Please. Don't ask "why". I just cannot do it.'

The carriage pulled up and Ella flung open the door, not waiting for anyone to assist her out. She ran up the steps and burst through the main doors. Not looking in either direction, she hurried up the grand staircase and into her room.

Elizabeth, the maid, had been passing through the hallway when the door flew open and Miss Ella had run past her. She squashed herself into the wall as Miss Lydia followed her. Miss Lydia was shouting after her, which was a bit silly of her, seeing as Miss Ella wouldn't ever hear her shouting; but she did seem upset.

Elizabeth waited for a moment, then moved to the bottom of the stairs. She listened carefully and could hear the doors slamming and lots of shouting going on. It didn't sound good and she pulled a face. She hurried upstairs and went along the corridor towards Miss Ella's room and she pressed her ear against the door.

'It was a ridiculous idea!' Miss Ella was shouting. 'Cancel everything. I will leave as soon as I can. I will not waste any more of your time.'

'Don't be so *stupid!*' That was Miss Lydia, screaming at the top of her lungs. 'I cannot understand what brought this on. Ella!' A momentary pause. 'Look at me, Ella. Ella! Stop it! Just stop that immediately.'

Elizabeth tried to peer through the keyhole of the door, but all she could see was a dark blur. One of them must have been standing in front of the door.

'Ella!'

'Get off me!'

'Ella, why will you not look at me? *Ella!* Oh, I give up!'

The shadow moved and the door handle turned. Elizabeth jumped out of the way and Miss Lydia stormed out. She slammed the door behind her with all of her might and it bounced back off the hinges, swinging ever so slightly open. Elizabeth waited until the corridor was clear and then she peered through the crack. Miss Ella had the wardrobe door open and was flinging clothes onto the bed.

Elizabeth thought quickly. She would have to hope that everyone forgave her, but it was too important to let it go. She just had to wait and watch, then act as she needed to.

Ella stared at the pile of clothes on the bed, wondering how she was going to get everything back to the town house in York. The thought of the imposing, stone-built house was unappealing, stuffed full as it was of her aunt's possessions. If she could ever bear to empty it, it would be better. The only saving grace was the piano in the room at the back of the house which overlooked the garden. Other than that, it had nothing to recommend it at this present moment in time. Much as she loved York, once she had spent time with the Carricks, she always felt unsettled. There was something freeing about being so close to the sea, feeling the breeze on her face and breathing in the salty scent of the ocean.

She turned her back on the pile of clothes and headed towards the door. If she was leaving the Park, she had to visit one particular place one last time. She hoped that they would forgive her eventually – she couldn't bear the thought of never seeing them again. What else, really, was there in her life except Adam and Lydia? Fortunately, she would never have to earn a living, but the thought of spending her days rattling around her aunt's house on her own was intolerable.

Ella slipped out of the door and hurried along the corridor. Instead of turning left, however, to descend the main staircase, she headed right and made her way to the servants' staircase. When they had been younger, she and Lydia had enjoyed playing hide-and-seek. One of the favourite places to hide had been in the servants' hall. Inevitably, whichever small girl had taken refuge there would have received little treats and a considerable amount of petting from the cook. Soon, it was no longer "let us play hide-and-seek", but "let us play at being servants" and the two of them would sit there wearing ridiculous little white hats for as long as they were not missed upstairs.

It was difficult to recall now, but Ella could vaguely remember a muted buzzing around them. It must have been the sounds of conversation and pots boiling and the fire crackling and it had been comforting in a way, but gradually that had slipped away as well until all she was left with was the warmth on her skin from the fire and the delicious smells of baking instead.

Now, the adult Ella felt around the panelling in the wall and managed to prise the door open. It opened smoothly without it jarring or scraping under her fingertips, and she exhaled with some relief, hoping that nobody would have actually heard her breaking into such forbidden territory. The last thing she wanted was to find Lydia pursuing her, trying to make her change her mind again about marrying Adam. Pulling the door gently shut behind her, Ella rushed thankfully down the stairs and into the servants' corridor.

It was only a little way along until she found the doorway that led out into the courtyard. Nobody seemed to use the courtyard. In all the years she had been coming to the Park, it had been her thinking space and nobody had ever come out to bother her. It was probably something to do with it being at the back of the house and the fact that it faced north. The courtyard was also surrounded on three sides by huge walls. None of the main rooms looked onto it, but a previous resident had built a small fountain there and Ella had been disappointed to realise that the fountain was long since disused. Still, there was a bench there, and it was enough for her to simply sit on it and close her eyes. She would feel the peace around her and wish with all her heart that she belonged properly at the Park. Up until a few hours ago, that dream had been a reality.

Now, thinking about what Jacob had said to her, it seemed ridiculous even to contemplate the thought that she could marry Adam and be part of his life. She knew she had expressed those feelings in July and Adam had assured her she was being foolish. The cold, hard reality, though, was not that simple.

Not many things about her life upset her, but that did.

The bench was in the corner of the courtyard, quite close to the fountain. Ella sat down and took in the worn stone angel that reached up to the skies and she imagined the water shooting up from the angel's hands and falling down into the pool, breaking the surface into ripple after ripple. She wondered if there had been fish in the pond at one point, and who else had sat here, looking at the very same fountain over the years.

Beyond the fountain was a pathway that led straight through a gate in a wall and she knew that beyond that were the moors. She could see, in her mind's eye, the worn tracks across the grass which took the rider down to the cliff path and towards Whitby. It was a route that she had followed whenever she had been forced to ride the little black pony that was kept especially for her. The family joked that it was the fattest, least-exercised pony in the entire stables and Ella could not dispute that.

She closed her eyes and tried to let the place work its magic on her, but it wasn't happening. Adam's face kept interrupting her thoughts, and she wondered how she could possibly tell him of her decision. He had disappeared four days ago, full of remorse for leaving her again and she remembered him as he had been then.

He had taken her face in his hands and kissed her. 'I will not be long. I promise that I shall return as soon as possible. Stay out of trouble,' he had told her.

It was painfully obvious to her that her desertion would destroy him, but she had no option. What Jacob had said rang true. Without Lydia she could not hope to settle abroad and Adam would have to realise that.

Ella felt a few spots of rain against her upturned face and brushed them away angrily. The sun was still warm on her skin and she guessed that a summer shower had blown in from the coast. A few more spots hit her face and she frowned. Unless this was a real storm, she was determined to stay there. It might be the last opportunity she would ever have. She opened her eyes, hoping to judge by the clouds whether she needed to return indoors or not.

Instead of a cloud-filled sky, she saw a clear blue one. And instead of a worn old stone angel, she saw it as she had always dreamed it to be. A jet of water was shooting heavenwards, diamonds sparkling in the stream as it arched and fell down to the bowl beneath it.

'No!' she exclaimed, leaning forwards. Another jet of water shot out of the fountain; some of the stream curved away and sprinkled droplets on her, the direction not quite vertical. She stared at it, transfixed, then became aware of someone walking across the courtyard towards her: Adam.

'*My gift to you*,' he signed as he came closer, indicating the fountain. '*An angel for my angel.*'

Ella stared at him, the emotions fighting within her. Rage, anger, fear, love ... none of them had precedent, just yet. 'Adam!' It was all she could manage.

He came closer and stood in front of her. 'Do you like it?' he asked. 'I wanted it to be a surprise. Someone told me you needed to see it today.'

His eyes flicked across to the small windows in one of

the walls. Ella glanced across and saw a figure disappearing behind the glass. She caught a flash of black and white; she could tell it was a maid's dress and hat.

'Elizabeth?' she asked, still staring at the window. She looked back at Adam.

He nodded. 'The fountain still needs some work on it. As you see, the water is not quite right. Maybe there is a blockage.' He frowned at the angel, then came and sat by her. 'Do you like her?' Ella nodded, unable to answer. 'Good. It is a little early, it was to be a wedding gift, but Elizabeth suggested it to me. She thought she would be in trouble by speaking up.' He smiled. 'I wonder why she felt the need to speak today? Can you answer me? Would you prefer to move somewhere drier?'

'I like it here,' Ella said. 'I want to stay next to the angel. She is just as beautiful as I imagined she would be. Thank you.'

'Yet you are still unhappy,' he said, taking her face in his hands and looking into her eyes. His own eyes softened and he tilted his head to the side, mirroring his favourite action of hers. 'Have I done something to disappoint you?'

'No! Not at all!' she said. 'It's just that I didn't expect to see you today. I made a decision earlier and to be truthful I would rather I had *not* seen you. It would have made this moment easier.'

'What is it?' His eyes were now full of concern. 'I finished what I needed to do, and I hurried home to see you. I have travelled since daybreak without stopping.'

It was true; she could see that lovely, velvet-collared overcoat was crumpled and his necktie once more was loose and had escaped from his waistcoat.

'I know and I am very grateful. Adam, I shall always be grateful to you.' She lifted her finger and traced the laugh lines at the corner of his eyes. He looked tired and unshaven and she knew he spoke the truth. 'I shall always love you, but I am not the right person to marry you. You need someone else. Someone who can be everything you need in a wife. That is not me and I can never be that person.'

'What? Where did this come from?' asked Adam. She could tell by his face he was completely thrown by her words. All pretence of fun was gone.

She shook her head and turned away. 'You know it is the truth,' she said quietly. 'I have been thinking about it a lot. I cannot come and live abroad with you. It is ridiculous to think I would manage there. So I am leaving. As soon as I can, I will arrange to take my possessions back to York. I am letting you go, Adam. I don't want to, but I have to. It's not fair on either of us.'

'Ella! No!' he said, taking hold of her shoulders and turning her towards him. She stubbornly refused to look at him and he shook her gently until she gave in. 'What has put such doubts into your mind? Any ventures I have abroad will be dealt with in one of two ways and it is entirely your choice. We will all travel together; you, Lydia and myself, and my agents here will deal with the British interests. If we choose to stay here, I have agents in all the countries I deal with. They can work for me. I will have to make some short trips, but that is no different to our lives now.'

'But Jacob said the agents were not capable and Lydia was not to travel with us.'

'Jacob?'

'Yes. He told me he had offered you assistance but he had been refused.'

'It is *Jacob* who put these doubts in your mind?' asked Adam.

'He told me Lydia would have to stay here and I would be left on my own with the foreign staff. I rarely admit defeat, as you know, but this is beyond me.' Ella said the words she had always hated saying: 'I cannot do it.'

Adam stood up sharply. His face was furious. He looked down at her and she shrank a little under his gaze.

'You are angry with me. You have every right to be,' she said. Then she too stood up, never one to be faced down. 'I will leave as soon as possible. Goodbye, Adam. I hope you understand.'

She turned away and started towards the house, but he grabbed her arm and pulled her back towards him. 'No, Ella. You are not leaving. Damn Jacob, he is a liar. He always has been. He is bitter that I inherited the Park and he wants my life; so therefore he also wants you. That is the only reason he spoke as he did. It will *not* happen. Our plans remain. If I have to, I will sell the interests abroad to keep you here. Heaven knows I have enough income from England to rely on.'

Unexpectedly, he bent down to her and kissed her shoulder. He gradually moved up along her neckline. Now he was kissing her jawbone and she closed her eyes, a little gasp escaping from her lips.

She could feel his warm breath on her neck and, despite the situation and the unusual setting, it did strange things to her insides. She opened her eyes. The water was still streaming out from the angel, tossing prisms of colour into the air and she thought that she had never experienced such a perfect moment in her entire life. Her decision was made.

'The servants, Adam,' she said eventually, trying to draw away from him. 'They can see us ...' But if he answered, she did not hear him.

There was only one dress on the bed when Ella returned to her room; a frothy, golden coloured confection that had always been her favourite.

'Elizabeth!' she said, seeing the maid with her hand poised, apparently replacing the last of the other outfits.

The maid looked around guiltily, her face flushing a deep scarlet. 'I am sorry, miss,' she said. 'Did I do wrong? Please don't tell me you want these back out. Please don't tell me you're leaving.' The girl was speaking quickly, the words tumbling out of her mouth and Ella raised both her hands.

'Please – more slowly, Elizabeth,' she said.

'Oh, miss,' said the girl. She came and planted herself squarely in front of Ella. 'Am I in trouble? I knew the master had come home and I couldn't help but see you were upset, miss.' She bowed her head.

'Elizabeth,' Ella said gently, guessing correctly that the girl was still talking. 'Look at me, please.'

The girl lifted her head and another scarlet rush flooded her cheeks. 'I'm sorry, miss. I knew he was planning that fountain, like, and I wanted you to see it. I don't want you to go, miss.'

'It is all right, Elizabeth. I am staying,' replied Ella. It was Ella's turn to blush; she could feel the warmth spreading over her own face and she pressed her hands to her cheeks. 'I was being silly. And how could I leave after seeing the angel working? I think I owe you my thanks, to be truthful.'

'Really, miss?' asked the maid. Her eyes were wide and terrified. 'I was so worried, miss. I thought it wasn't really my place, you know.'

'You did what you thought was right,' said Ella, 'and thank you also for returning my clothes to the wardrobe.' She walked over to the dress and fingered it. 'Thank you for leaving this one out. I shall wear it for dinner tonight.' She smiled at the girl.

'Yes, miss,' said Elizabeth, curtseying. 'I'll be going now, miss. Thank you.' She backed out of the room and shut the door gently, leaving Ella alone.

Ella turned to face the dressing table and picked up the silver-backed hairbrush that lay there. She turned it over in her hands, remembering the mirror incident that she was not exactly proud of. She caught sight of herself in the replacement mirror. She still looked the same. There was nothing to recommend her as different in any way. She stood up straighter and smoothed her skirt down. Then she smiled at her reflection. She put the hairbrush down on the unit and turned away from the mirror. She was as good as anybody, if not better, and she must never forget it again.

THE WEDDING
September 1865

The wedding had been an outstanding success. Lydia told Ella that she was ready to defend it to the hilt if anyone should dare complain about even one aspect of it. She had worn her pink dress, of course, with Ella's blessing, and spent much of the day fussing over the trims and ensuring the skirt hung perfectly.

'I know, of course, though,' she told anyone who would listen, quite graciously, 'that I am simply secondary to Ella, and so I should be. Even I can see that.'

Miss Waters had surpassed herself with Ella's dress. The skirt fell in heavy panels to the ground, and froths of white lace were layered on top of the satin. It was trimmed with tulle frills and swansdown, and tiny crystals caught the light and sparkled all over the dress.

Seeing Ella wearing it had Lydia, for once, lost for words. She simply stood clapping her hands, bouncing on the balls of her feet and shaking her head.

Ella had found it all hysterical. The finishing touch was a floor length veil of the same white lace and a small posy of late roses. Ella had found a little bunch of daisies in her room beforehand, and, smiling, tucked a few flowers into the posy.

'Who are they from?' asked Lydia. 'Who would leave daisies here for you?'

'I suspect it is Elizabeth,' replied Ella. 'I saw her scurrying away along the corridor earlier.'

'She is a sweet girl,' said Lydia. 'Are you ready?'

'Almost,' said Ella. She stood in front of Lydia. 'How do I look? Tell me?'

Beautiful, signed Lydia. 'I cannot speak, you are beyond words.'

Thank you, replied Ella, laughing. 'Tell me,' she said more seriously, 'is Jacob here?'

'I don't know,' replied Lydia. 'He didn't respond to the invitation. I hope he will just turn up. Men are hopeless at responding to social invitations. If he had a wife, we would have been assured of seeing them here today.' She set her lips in an annoyed little line.

Ella dipped her head, pulling some flowers to a more pleasing shape. She knew, of course, why he hadn't responded. She had to demand that Adam actually allowed them to send an invitation – he was all for cutting his cousin off completely, and she refused to be the catalyst for that. She had longed to be part of this family and now she was, she was not about to start tearing it up.

'Perhaps he was simply concerned,' she had pleaded. 'Who is to say that I even understood him correctly?'

Adam had given in, but she knew he was hoping that Jacob wouldn't appear. Ella had told Lydia none of what had gone on. Lydia still simply thought that Ella had suffered from terrible pre-wedding jitters and had long since forgotten about it.

The ceremony itself was held at St Mary's, overlooking the sea at Whitby. Nobody gave Ella away. She walked down the aisle preceded by Lydia, her eyes on Adam as he waited at the altar for her. His expression told her all she needed to know, dispelling any remaining doubts she may have had about marrying him. She was aware that the pews were full of people, some of whom she knew and many of whom she did not. She did not care. It had pleased Lydia and all Ella wanted was Adam. She didn't care if there was a great deal of ceremony or very little, so long as the end result was the same.

The sun was shining when they walked out arm in arm, casting hues of a thousand different blues into the ocean and she felt her heart lift. This place was where she belonged.

'I will remember this moment forever,' she told Adam as he helped her into the carriage. Lydia had ensured it was decorated appropriately with mounds of pink and white flowers and matching ribbons, which would stream behind them as they travelled along the cliff path back to the Park. 'I do not believe I could have had a more perfect day at all.'

'If we had been married in rags by a travelling gypsy preacher, I could not complain,' said Adam with a tender smile.

'I was thinking much the same,' said Ella.

Adam moved her veil away from her face and kissed her. 'I could not have wished for a more beautiful bride. Every time I look at you I am astonished and humbled that you should have chosen me.'

'Shhhh,' said Ella, placing her fingertips on his lips. 'I keep telling you, I am nobody special. I am the same as everyone else. I should be honoured that you chose me. You could have had anybody.'

'But I wanted you,' he said, leaning into her. And there was no more talking for either of them for the entire journey.

Lydia took care of the socialising at the wedding breakfast, chattering to various people yet, Ella knew, staying close enough to the couple so she could step in if required. The weather was a glorious, Indian summer day and Ella had suggested they serve the champagne in the gardens. It was a joyous success and people were scattered around the lawns, laughing and talking in little groups. Ella and Adam were entertaining a rather ancient great-uncle and his companion when she saw him: Jacob had come after all.

Ella had looked up and seen a man sitting on a horse, half-hidden by the shadows against the wall, quite a way from the company. Her eyes were extremely sharp, and she could tell that Jacob was not dressed for a wedding. Instead, he looked rather unkempt. He wore no coat, waistcoat or cravat; just a loose, white shirt which was partially unbuttoned and a pair of riding breeches. His dark hair was a mess and bore no evidence of any brushes or comb and his eyes were black hollows in his unshaven face.

Ella and Jacob stared at each other for quite some time, and even at that distance, there seemed to be something in his expression that she couldn't quite place. An immediate concern for his welfare pressed into her mind and she had just decided to alert Adam when Jacob dug his heels into the horse and galloped off around the side of the house, towards the courtyard and out, she assumed, towards the cliff path.

Ella tried to turn her attention back to the great-uncle and nodded and smiled at appropriate intervals – her usual tactic when she was preoccupied and not following the conversation – until Lydia appeared next to her and raised her eyebrows. Lydia knew Ella too well, of course. There was an unspoken question in her look.

In response Ella gestured for Lydia to move to the side of the group. *Jacob may be here* she spelled out, making sure that Adam could not see what she was saying. Lydia was very good – she betrayed no emotion, she simply nodded. *But if it was him, he must not want to join us* continued Ella. *Please do not tell Adam.*

Adam will be very unhappy if he hides from us, replied Lydia. *Where is he?*

I think the courtyard, answered Ella.

Will I go?

No. I will. I may be mistaken.

Lydia nodded, and moved towards Adam and the great-uncle, smiling widely.

Ella reached for Adam's hand. He turned and smiled down at her.

'Please excuse me for a moment,' Ella said. 'I need to go into the house.'

'Hurry back,' he said, lifting her hand and kissing it. She nodded and hurried away, slipping around the side of the house, following the pathway which led into the courtyard.

It was ridiculous, perhaps, to expect Jacob to still be there when she reached the courtyard. Ella ran into the space and stared around her, trying to work out if he had indeed gone out through the gate to the cliff path. Her gaze then alighted on the angel statue. The water was shooting up perfectly now; Adam had been true to his word and restored it fully for her, but there was something amiss about it. She went over to it and looked more closely, tilting her head to the side, trying to see what looked out of place. It was only when she walked around the statue and came to the back that she saw it; the wings had been smashed off the back, and a heavy mallet lay in the water. Her heart lurched. There was no way Jacob, if indeed it had been him, could have done it in the brief time she'd taken to get to the courtyard. That meant only one thing; it had to have been done earlier in the day – probably when most of the household had been at the church in Whitby. Jacob's words came back to her. *It is natural to be concerned about your future, Ella. Sometimes, even angels fear to fly. It is often safer for them to stay on familiar territory.*

Lydia ran across to Ella when she returned to the party on

the lawn. Ella shook her head at her, hoping to indicate that she had been wrong and Jacob had not arrived after all. She didn't feel as if his presence was something she could admit to, which was silly, because if Adam ever found out who she was protecting, he would explode. Ella didn't fear for herself, it was Jacob she was concerned about. She thought that Adam would be able to make things extremely difficult for Jacob, and she did not want to be responsible for that.

'Did you discover who it was?' asked Lydia, when she had managed to get Ella on her own.

'No. But whoever it was destroyed my fountain,' Ella replied.

'Oh, Ella! Is the fountain beyond repair?' Lydia took hold of Ella's hand and squeezed it sympathetically.

'I hope not,' said Ella. 'Never mind. It is only her wings. You cannot see the damage from the seat.'

'That is not the point. I am sure Adam will be able to engage a stonemason to work on it. Are you all right?'

'I am not very happy about it, but it could have been much worse,' replied Ella.

It was very true.

ELLA
November 1865

Two months had passed since the marriage and Ella had to admit that many of her fears were unfounded. They had honeymooned in Scotland, a place Ella had never been before. Adam took great delight in showing her the sights, her absolute favourites being the raging waterfalls that tumbled over rocks and crags, splashing up into boiling pools of foam.

'Who would have thought that these places existed!' she exclaimed, hanging over a rail that ran along the edge of a rough wooden bridge and looking into the depths of one such pool.

Adam hung over the rail with her and stared down into the seething mass, then he tapped her hand. 'You will have to shout up,' he told her, pulling a face. 'I can barely hear you.'

Ella laughed. 'I can understand you perfectly,' she said.

The leaves were changing colour with the autumn approaching fast, and all around them was the scent of fresh, open air and earth. It was an unspoiled few weeks, and they returned to Carrick Park with some regrets.

'I would like to visit for longer next time,' Ella told Adam as they journeyed home. 'Perhaps next year, we could go again?'

'I think that is a superb idea,' he replied. 'Well said, Lady Eleanor.'

'Oh stop it! Stop calling me that!' complained Ella. 'You know my name is Ella. It will never be any different.'

'And I hope that you are never any different either, my love,' said Adam. He smiled down at her and took her hand. 'I have already commissioned that portrait. Mr Landseer is to start work next month.'

'Oh, no!' cried Ella. 'Can I not persuade you to change your mind?'

'Not at all,' replied Adam, 'but I shall be happy to let you try your damnedest.'

Ella coloured, knowing exactly what he meant. In the end, her doubts had been laughable. As Lydia had told her, it was Adam and he knew her well.

Ella was still protesting at the portrait commission when they reached the entrance to the Park and Adam was still teasing her, when he suddenly stopped and gently pressed his fingers against her lips.

'I must insist on a revered silence for this part of the journey,' said Adam. 'This is my favourite view of the house. And this is the first time you will have seen it like this, the first time you have returned from a long distance and know the Park is truly your home.'

'It has always seemed like my home,' said Ella. 'From the first moment I set foot in the hallway, I never wanted to leave. I hated going back to York.'

She watched out of the window of the carriage as they turned a corner and the house came into view. The sandstone glowed warmly in the low, wintry sunlight and the windows sparkled. 'I still cannot quite believe it,' she said. She pulled the window down and hung out of it, feeling the coldness rush past her face and inhaling the salty air. She closed her eyes for a brief moment and enjoyed the feeling of being part of the moors and the coast once more.

The carriage pulled up in front of the house and the front door burst open. Lydia ran down the steps towards them, a vision in a heavenly blue dress. Ella was still halfway out of the open window and began to wave madly at Lydia, laughing at the joyous expression on the girl's sweet, open face. Lydia flung her arms out wide and continued running towards them, shouting their names.

'Adam! Ella! Welcome home!' She finally drew to a halt beside the carriage and reached up, grasping Ella's hands as she approached. She looked over Ella's shoulder and frowned. 'I will not fall, Adam, so stop insisting I will,' she commented. Ella turned and saw that Adam was laughing.

'You will, mark my words,' he said.

Lydia pulled a face and turned her attention back to Ella. 'Oh, I have missed you so much, sister,' she said. She began to pull on the handle, trying to get the door opened until the coachman bowed and indicated she should move away. She stepped to one side, impatiently tapping her fingertips on the fabric of her skirt, and then surged back in towards the carriage when the door was opened. She reached up and helped Ella out, then tried to do the same for Adam, who, in his turn, waved her away.

Lydia pouted at him, then turned to Ella.

After embracing her, Lydia held Ella away at arm's length. She looked her up and down critically. 'You look just the same,' she said.

'Why would I look any different?' asked Ella.

'Because I have not seen you for so long!' moaned Lydia. 'I am so pleased you are home. We have a special guest as well. We will all be together again. Well, almost all of us.'

'Who is it, Lydia?' asked Ella, her smile faltering. *If Helena has turned up* ... she thought.

'I told you. A special guest.' Lydia smiled beatifically. 'You will see. Now come on.'

Lydia linked arms with Ella and walked with her to the house, Adam following them. It was when they stepped inside the door that Ella saw who the special guest was. Jacob was standing on the landing, his arms behind his back, waiting for them to come in. His appearance was immaculate again; that wild look had gone and he stood there, practically the image of the Master of the House.

Ella's heart lurched. She felt Lydia tug her arm and dragged her gaze away from Jacob.

'A perfect surprise guest, would you say?' said Lydia.

'A surprise, certainly,' said Ella, trying to keep her voice steady. She took a deep breath and pulled away from Lydia. 'Jacob. How lovely to see you,' she said. She held out her hand and he came down the stairs and took it. 'It was such a shame you could not make it to the wedding,' she continued. 'It would have been wonderful to see you. I can only think you were otherwise engaged during the ceremony.' She looked him directly in the eyes, daring him to disagree.

Jacob gave her a queer little look that told her he understood exactly what she was doing, and he dipped his head in a small bow. 'Thank you, Lady Eleanor,' he said. 'It is an honour to be here. I hardly dared hope I would be invited back to the Park.'

Now it was Ella's turn to dip her head. She understood *that* one perfectly. 'I do believe it was Lydia who invited you, Jacob, but we will certainly do our utmost to welcome you. Adam?' She turned and drew him forwards. 'Greet your cousin. Let us all be friends. Now, if you please, I would like to rest. It has been a long journey. I will leave you to catch up with one another.'

Adam and Jacob hardly looked thrilled to be thrown together and the two men faced each other, the air practically fizzing with animosity. Ella was awfully glad she was not going to be witness to any conversation they might have. Indeed, had they been stags, she thought, they would be locking antlers very, very soon. 'Well,' she said, quickly, eyeing up the two men, 'I shall see you all at dinner.'

You will see me sooner, Lydia told her.

What about my husband? Ella replied.

He can talk to Jacob. I have not seen you, he has.

Ella laughed, then she kissed Adam, feeling a little guilty about leaving him to the mercy of his cousin, and nodded to Jacob. 'Until dinnertime,' she said.

Sure enough, it did not take long for the door handle to turn and Lydia to slip into the bedroom. Ella had left the door unlocked, knowing that of the three people in the house who would have cause to visit her that afternoon, two she would welcome with open arms. The third person would be wise to stay away.

'Tell me all about it!' demanded Lydia, sitting down opposite Ella on the sofa in the window. 'Tell me about everything. I mean it.'

'What is there to tell?' teased Ella. 'We had a marvellous time and the country was beautiful. Rather, you need to tell me how things have been here.'

'Your news is far more interesting,' said Lydia. She rested her chin in her hands and stared at Ella. 'Far more interesting.'

Ella laughed and shook her head. 'Maybe, but that will wait. I want to know about *you*.'

'I plodded on. It was terribly boring and terribly dreary. I even went so far as to write to Helena but she did not reply. So I invited Jacob. I dislike my own company as you know. It was far too quiet about the place.'

Ella smiled. 'Well, it will not be staying like that for long. We are all home safely.'

'I know!' Lydia suddenly brightened up. She clapped her hands. 'You *are* all home. How exciting! Your letters kept me cheerful and I especially liked the last one, when you told me you were going to come home.'

'It was time to return,' replied Ella. 'Adam needs to settle a few things regarding the estate and I was missing you.'

'I am not the reason you came home and we both know it,' Lydia retorted. Her eyes sparkled with mischief. 'But I *am* glad to see you.' She stood up and stretched. 'I am leaving now. You *do* need to rest, you look terrible. Rather ill, in fact.' Lydia made a great production of signing the word to emphasise her point. 'I will see you later.' She blew a kiss and headed out of the room before Ella could retaliate.

Ella rushed to the mirror, horrified. She peered into the glass frowning. Yes, she looked tired, perhaps, but that was only to be expected. She certainly did not think she looked terrible or indeed ill. She had looked worse, and she was fairly sure, she would look worse again. She narrowed her eyes. *Thank you* she said, aiming her comment at the door reflected in the glass. She had not anticipated *that* sort of comment from Lydia. But actually, the idea of resting did not appeal in the slightest. Ella decided she would much prefer to be outside.

Ella looked out of the window and saw Lydia dragging Adam around the gardens, pointing out what he had missed during the weeks they had been away. She was telling him off for missing the flowering season of something, apparently. Adam was nodding and agreeing, but more probably for the sake of peace than anything. Ella smiled and found a warm, fitted coat in the wardrobe. She put it on and started towards the door. A movement of the handle brought her up short. She hadn't locked it after Lydia left, had she? She cursed herself and watched helplessly as the door opened.

Elizabeth, the little maid stood there with a tea tray and

a shy expression on her face. 'For you, miss,' she said. 'I'm pleased to have you back.'

Ella noticed that there was a posy of Gypsophila on the tray, neatly arranged in a small jug. 'Oh, thank you, Elizabeth,' she said. 'And thank you for the daisies. I didn't get a chance to see you properly to thank you before.'

'You are very welcome, miss,' said Elizabeth. The girl placed the tray on the small table and stood in front of Ella. Carefully, she held her hands out, palm upwards and slowly closed her fingers twice. *You're welcome.* 'I've been practising, miss,' she said, blushing. 'Just one or two things, to make it easier, like.'

Ella clapped her hands. 'You clever girl!' she said. 'Remind me to give you some lessons soon.'

'Oh, yes, miss, thank you, miss,' she said. 'That would be very kind of you. I hope the tea is all right for you. I put some of cook's ginger biscuits there too, if you want them. Thank you again, miss.' She curtseyed and backed out of the room, shutting the door carefully behind her.

Ella thought what a sweet girl Elizabeth was as she helped herself to a biscuit and some tea. It was so good to be back. Scotland had been wonderful, of course, but her heart lay here, most definitely.

The biscuits were very good and hence they did not survive long in the room. Feeling much restored, Ella started out again on her quest for fresh air. She headed out of the room and walked along towards the main staircase. She stopped suddenly, seeing a figure standing on the main landing, looking at a watercolour of Adam that Lydia had done years ago. She had thought it rather good at the time, and she had had it framed so that it could be displayed in the most prominent position in the house. Over the years, people had forgotten it was there and nobody ever took any notice of it; which made it all the more astonishing that Jacob had chosen exactly that spot to stand in. It meant that if Ella wanted to go anywhere at all, she would be forced to pass him. Then, she imagined, he would make some light conversation about it and she would be trapped with him, and then who knew what he would start a conversation about next. The thought made her feel sick and she truly did not want to be anywhere near him.

Instead, she turned and hurried back along the landing to the servants' staircase – her secret route to her own private sanctuary in the courtyard. As she had done so many times before, she prised open the door and dashed down the stairs. The door was, as always, unlocked, and she darted outside, taking deep breaths of the cold air as it flooded her warm face. She leaned back against the door for a moment, letting herself calm down, and then went over to the statue. The water was not spouting out of the top today, which, she realised, was more than likely due to the fact that they had just returned and Adam had not requested it to be set up yet. Her heart beating fast, she went around the back to check on the wings. She hoped that two months of Yorkshire weather had not damaged the statue any more and she made a mental note to ask Adam if he could arrange for it to be dealt with before the winter really set in.

As she went around the back of the angel, Ella was brought up short. After a moment, she reached forward and traced out the carvings on the now-perfect wings. Each feather was fashioned perfectly and it was almost impossible to tell that there had been any damage at all. The new set of wings had somehow been keyed into the statue and Ella's heart lifted. As she touched the wings, she sensed a strange pounding beneath her fingertips. She frowned and moved her touch quickly to the angel's hands, where she felt a strange gurgling sensation through the lead piping that came through the upturned palms.

'Goodness!' she cried. She just had time to duck out of the way and run over to the bench before the first jet of water shot out of the top of the fountain and soaked her. The throbbing had to have been the pump gearing up for action. She looked around at the deserted courtyard, trying to see who she could blame for switching it on, and saw Adam's face peering around a corner.

'You beast!' she cried, running over to him. 'I thought you were with Lydia. How *could* you? I could have been soaked!'

He laughed, gathering her up in his arms. 'You could have been,' he said, 'but you were not. Besides that, I thought you liked waterfalls?'

'I never expressed any desire to bathe in one,' she complained.

'I had it repaired – again!' he said. 'I left instructions with Lydia. She did well, did she not?'

'Very well,' Ella replied. 'Thank you.' She laughed. 'I seem to have done nothing but thank people since I returned home. People have been so kind and welcoming.'

'That is because everybody loves you,' said Adam, taking up a strand of her hair that had come loose and tucking it behind her ear. 'Returning home, however, would have been much improved without some elements.'

Ella lowered her gaze, unwilling to engage in conversation about Jacob; she knew, of course, that he was the element Adam was referring to. 'Well, now we are home,' she said, trying to change the subject, 'perhaps you should make that appointment we discussed with the solicitor.'

'Yes, you are correct, of course. I shall go tomorrow.' Adam smiled. 'Practical Ella. Yes, let us get the important things sorted out.'

'May I come with you?' she asked. 'I would like a trip into Whitby. It will be good to see the town again.'

'That would be delightful,' said Adam. 'I shall arrange the carriage.'

'Oh, no, I would like to ride,' she said. 'My horse probably needs some exercise and I have spent too long sitting in carriages these last few weeks. I feel the need for some exercise myself.'

'But—'

'Indulge me, please.'

'Very well, if you are certain.'

'I am.'

Adam nodded, his brow creased just a little. 'Then I will tell the groom to saddle him up.'

'I shall tell him myself,' said Ella, 'just in case you conveniently forget. I have neglected the poor horse and I feel horribly guilty. I need to go to the stables.' She reached up and kissed Adam. 'I shall go now, in fact, and I will see you later.' She turned and headed towards the stables, determined to make a fuss of the little black pony. She had, it must be said, missed him more than she thought possible.

Ella's pony was a ridiculously fat little thing. He always looked rather stupid, Ella thought, but he was gentle and slow and that was what she needed. As she was now living here permanently, though, she needed to be more confident on him. It was far easier to get a horse ready than hitch up a carriage if she wanted to head into town; and she had resolved to start riding again as soon as possible after returning to the Park. Therefore, she would go out tomorrow with Adam by her side and see how she felt. She knew he wouldn't rush her and that she would be safe with him.

The little black pony was apparently quite happy to see Ella. He snuffled into her hand and she laughed at the warm, ticklish sensation his breath had on her palms. She stroked him, feeling the flabby muscles under his skin and the easy rise and fall of his chest beneath her fingers. He was a lovely animal, she decided, and once again resolved to try and ride him more often.

She saw a shadow pass across the stable and assumed it was a stable hand. She turned to speak to them, to tell them that she needed her horse groomed and saddled tomorrow, and instead she realised she was face to face with Jacob.

'Ella,' he said. 'I thought I might find you here.'

'Jacob!' she said. 'Unless you were following me, I doubt that you would know where to find me. The stables are somewhere I rarely visit.' She felt uncomfortable being in such close proximity to Jacob, and moved slightly, trying to put the horse's flank between them.

'I was not following you, Ella,' said Jacob. He said something else that she didn't quite catch and she studied him for a moment. It was quite dark in the stables and she wished he would stand more out of the shadows than he was. It was difficult to read him, but she was not going to ask him to move. Instead she left the safety of the horse and walked out of the building. Jacob followed her. She wondered if he required an answer to his last comment or not.

Then he made it easy for her. 'So, am I forgiven or not?'

'Forgiven?' she almost shouted. 'For what? For destroying my possessions? Or for following me? Or for daring to come back to the Park knowing what you know about the situation? Lydia will no doubt have kept you up to date on everything in our lives, and I find it difficult to understand how you just happened to still be at the Park when we came home. If you are hoping Adam will put some extra – what do you say – codicils – into his will, then you are mistaken. Codicil is a word I am unfamiliar with but I understand what they do.'

'I know nothing about your situation,' said Jacob. 'I came because Lydia invited me, and yes, I did want to see you. I shall not pretend otherwise. She has not discussed you and Adam.'

'Knowing Lydia, I find that difficult to believe,' said Ella coldly. She was spared any further discussions with him by the appearance of Johnson, the head stable hand. She turned her back on Jacob and smiled at Johnson.

'I shall be taking Blackie out tomorrow. Please will you ensure he is ready to go at lunchtime?' she asked.

'Are you sure, ma'am?' asked Johnson.

Ella bit back a sarcastic retort. Her reputation, or something, at least, had obviously spread throughout the staff.

'Very sure,' she said.

'Very well, ma'am,' said Johnson. He bowed. 'Blackie will be ready after lunch.'

'Thank you,' she said. She turned and began to walk back to the house, but Jacob hurried after her. Then he dashed ahead and stood in front of her, blocking her way. She glared at him.

'I only wanted to ensure you were doing the right thing,' he said. 'I was trying to protect you. Adam and his life may not be the most suitable lifestyle for you.'

Ella held up her hand. 'Please, Jacob, just *stop*. I married Adam; that is my choice and if I made a mistake by doing so, I shall find out in my own time. I do not need you to tell me.' She made to walk past him and he grabbed her hand, pulling her to face him. 'Get off me!' she shouted, shaking her arm furiously.

'Not until you listen to me,' he said. 'Can we put all this

behind us? I cannot bear to be near Adam, but I am afraid I must be if I want to spend time with you and Lydia—'

'Adam has done nothing wrong. You have no reason to dislike him. The only issue I can see is that you are jealous that he inherited the Park. Adam does not know about the fountain and no, I shall not tell him. He would have no hesitation in making your life extremely difficult if he knew. I do not want to be responsible for that.'

She sighed, suddenly feeling tired. She was tired from the journey, from the situation with Jacob; she was tired from everything. 'Look, Jacob. You are a good man, I am sure. You have no official claim on Carrick Park, but you are family. When I thought I would never see the place again, I felt miserable. I would not want to put anyone else in that position. So, yes, you are forgiven. But I will never forget it. And please do not ever, *ever* put me in that situation again. I just want to move on. I have other things to think about.'

She started walking off again, pulling the coat close to her body. Jacob appeared in front of her again like a jack-in-the-box. 'What now?' she asked sharply.

'I just want to say thank you. I appreciate it,' he said. 'May I accompany you back to the house? Perhaps we can spend a little time together before dinner – the four of us. Perhaps you could play some music? I have missed that.' He held his arm out to her, hoping, apparently, that she would link it.

Ella could not be bothered to argue any more. She hesitated a moment, then accepted his arm. 'Very well. I too have missed my piano,' she said. 'I may be persuaded to play a little tonight. I shall see how I feel.'

They began to walk back towards the house. By mutual, unspoken agreement, they took the longer route that did not pass near the courtyard. Being with Jacob for a few minutes longer was a small price to pay, Ella considered, than to have him desecrate her private space again. His mere presence there would poison it at the moment.

She cast a sidelong glance at him. He seemed to be deep in thought and she was grateful that there was no conversation to be attempted. She had been truthful; she did just want to move on, but she did not want to let her barriers down too quickly. He was still rather a complex person, and she would rather tread cautiously, just for a little while longer.

The evening was not as bad as he had anticipated. Adam had made it quite clear that he was unhappy about his presence, but Jacob was well used to brazening it out. And, despite his deep-rooted hatred of Adam, he did his best to be polite and respectful to his cousin. He just had to remember that Ella was the all-powerful one in this little game. If he upset her or crossed Adam, he would be out of the Park and, as Ella had told him so bluntly, his life would be ruined.

Jacob wasn't ready to let go of the Park or of Ella yet. That business he had been attending to in Whitby the day he met Lydia and Ella? He hoped he had found a loophole in the ridiculous will that had caused this upset. He just needed an expert opinion, which he was confident would soon be forthcoming. Then it would be interesting to see which direction he chose.

After all, if the estate was entailed to the *women* of the family, Adam was there by default anyway. Thanks to that little blonde maid, he had finally gotten his hands on the will – it hadn't been easy, but once she had realised who was in charge and how he could assert that authority, it suddenly became much simpler. And then, once the loophole was prised open, he, Jacob, could have a lot of fun deciding which of the women of the household to pursue.

He looked across the drawing room at Adam, who was pulling the seat out from beneath the piano for Ella. She, in her turn, was looking at Adam, who then met her gaze and leant forward, saying something which only she was aware of. She smiled and ran her fingertips lightly along the keys of the piano, then sat down.

'They are so happy together,' Lydia said, sitting down next to him. She picked up some sort of Gothic horror novel and began reading it. 'It is so nice to all be together again. Such a shame the weather is turning quite dreary. I wonder what tomorrow will bring?'

'Where is my Mozart?' shouted Ella suddenly. She was up on her feet again, rummaging through piles of sheet music. 'I particularly wanted the Mozart.'

'Oh, poor Ella,' said Lydia, lowering the book and looking at her over the top of it. 'I know she loves it, but …'

Ella looked across at Jacob and Lydia. 'Does either of you know what happened to my music?' she asked. Her face was red and angry-looking.

Lydia lowered the book further and replied. 'Perhaps someone tidied it away by mistake? I shall speak to the servants tomorrow. Play something else, my love. Or play it from memory?'

Ella shook her head. 'No. I would rather have the music, I think. It has been a while.' She stomped around the piano and found some more pieces of music, which she proceeded to read then discard, one after the other.

Lydia shook her head and raised the book again. 'Oh, she will play something eventually, I am sure. She will not be able to sit there and ignore that instrument. I shall wait until she calms down before I ask her to try something else again.'

Jacob had half-smiled, still watching Ella look through the music. 'I am in awe of her talent,' he said, just loud enough for Lydia to hear. 'I am sure we have all missed listening to her these last few weeks.'

'I have,' said Lydia. 'I am so pleased we are all together again. I often think about Helena, you know. It is so strange. She just disappeared and you were always so close.'

'Things change,' said Jacob. He picked up a discarded book and began to flick through it. It was a history of Whitby and very boring. 'The weather forecast is not supposed to be very good tomorrow,' he said, trying to divert the subject away from Helena. 'I heard one of the servants mention that the harbour master was expecting a gale warning.'

'Oh dear, I must tell Adam. He was intending to go into the town tomorrow,' said Lydia.

'Why should that stop him?' asked Jacob, surprised. 'Surely the storm will be out at sea, it should not affect his business in the town.'

'Well, because Ella is going with him,' said Lydia, making sure her book was high enough to prevent Ella lip-reading. 'And you know what she is like. She is bloody-minded and determined to go with him and it really is not a good idea. Adam said she was arranging to take Blackie. Heaven knows that she and Blackie are not the steadiest combination at the best of times.'

'Good grief!' replied Jacob. 'But she will not be advised against it, I imagine.' He omitted to say he had found her in the stables only that afternoon.

'No. The only thing,' said Lydia, her eyes still on Ella, 'is if we can arrange a plot of some kind.'

Ella was still complaining loudly about the lack of that particular Mozart sheet music and Adam, trying not to laugh, was engaging himself in showing her different pieces to play as an alternative.

'I could go,' said Jacob, turning slightly in the seat so Ella could not see him either. 'I could follow them, and I could ensure she returns home safely if Adam is delayed and we really do get a storm. I will set off later than them, of course, so it does not look suspicious. I have business of my own to attend to anyway.' His heart began to beat just a little faster.

If Lydia agreed, then he was not the one who could be called to task should Adam and Ella discover his plans.

It was perfect. He had the opportunity to spend a whole afternoon legitimately near Ella.

There was a pause while Lydia apparently ran through the alternatives in her mind, then she smiled. 'Yes,' she said. 'I think that is an excellent idea. We must not tell them, of course. We will be in such trouble if they discover our motives.'

'Indeed,' said Jacob quietly. He watched Ella thoughtfully, seeing the graceful way she moved, the curve of her cheek, the slight tilt of her head as she listened to Adam. 'Our motives must remain secret,' he told Lydia. 'They must never know the truth.'

And so it was that Lydia waved Jacob off the next afternoon.

'Now, do take care, darling,' Lydia said, following him to the door. 'It is looking rather dark out there already.' She shivered, peeping out of the door. 'Rather you than me.'

'I am sure any storms will be confined to the sea,' said Jacob, not really sure of that fact at all. 'I will bring her back safely, do not worry.' *Her*, he had said, not *them*. He hoped that Lydia had not picked up on that. She did not seem to have done; rather, she was now huddling by the fireplace in the hallway, having given up on the outside world.

'It is bitter!' she said. 'Ella has no sense.' She shook her head then opened her mouth, as if to qualify the statement. Then she sighed and gave up. 'No sense at all. What *am* I to do with her?'

'I suspect you cannot do much with her,' said Jacob. 'Oh, well. I shall head off into the town. I know where they are going and I shall hopefully be able to reach them.'

'Just make sure they do not see you!' said Lydia, giggling. 'Otherwise we will both be in trouble.' She blew him a kiss and he left.

His horse had already been brought around for him, and he mounted it easily. He kicked it and started off across the estate. He would take the shortcut past that damned angel fountain Ella loved so much. It led straight onto the cliff path and from there it was a pleasant enough ride on a fine day. Today, it probably would not be so pleasant. He could already feel the wind gathering pace and there were some spots of rain in the air.

He skirted the courtyard and cast a derisive look at the fountain. He wished he had damaged it some more that day, but he had made his point. He had spent all the previous night in a hostelry in Whitby – God knows how he had managed to ride to the Park the next day. He just needed to be near her one last time. He had arrived, just as the wedding procession was leaving the Park. He had caught a glimpse of her in the carriage and felt his heart twist. That was it; his last chance to stop her – gone. The angel had looked just like Ella; it had the same sweet expression on its face and the same long, wavy hair. But the way he saw it, he had thought that Ella was as trapped as that statue was, tied to Adam and the estate and never free to spread her wings.

If Jacob had Ella, the Park could go hang. He would have taken her away from all that, from the pressure of business dinners and important colleagues to entertain. She would hate it. He would have walked out of all their lives and not bothered with the rest of it – as long as he had Ella. Now, it seemed, all that was left to him was to get the Park.

It never crossed Jacob's mind to think that part of the reason he was so fascinated by Ella, was her determination and, as Lydia had said, her bloody-mindedness. Just look at today. She hated riding, yet she was determined to go into Whitby just to prove a point; just to prove that she *could* and nobody was going to tell her she couldn't, until she made up her own mind about it. He kicked the horse again to speed it up and get it onto the cliff path more quickly. He looked up at the sky. It was definitely darkening. He hoped it would hold off until Ella got home safely that night. Adam should have known better than to take her into Whitby. No matter what the business was he had to deal with at the solicitors – and Jacob had a good idea what it entailed – surely it could have waited just one more day?

LYDIA
November 1865

Prowling around the drawing room, Lydia felt ridiculously nervous. She was anxiously clasping her hands together and muttering under her breath, alternately praying then demanding that everyone should return soon. It was late; far too late for them all to be out in this sort of weather. She jumped as another roll of thunder rattled the casements and the lightning lit up the room, despite the heavy drapes. It was worse, even, than the storm they had experienced in July. Dinner was always served at six. It was now seven-thirty and nobody had returned from Whitby yet.

'Hurry up!' she said to the empty room. 'Where on earth *are* you all?' She turned and began another circuit of the room. She brushed past Ella's piano and pressed a few keys far too hard out of pure frustration. She could never get a decent tune out of the thing and tonight was no different. Was it only last night that Ella had moaned about her Mozart score disappearing? Lydia had hidden behind that appalling Gothic novel, knowing full well that the sheet was concealed within her writing slope. Yes, she was a terrible tease; she knew that. But she had been bored and the evening had been dark and dinner had been disappointing and Ella knew it mostly off by heart anyway; all these excuses. She felt about an inch high, today. One learns by one's mistakes. She would never tease anyone again, ever, if only they would all come back within the next half hour.

Lydia left the piano and headed towards the door. As she approached it, she heard a commotion in the hallway. She heard Jacob's voice calling her name frantically.

'Lydia! Lydia!'

'Oh, thank God!' she said and ran the rest of the way to the door. She pushed it open, ready to greet the three soaking wet miscreants, expecting to see them all dripping soundly on the floor and looking guilty. Instead, there was only Jacob there. His face was white, his normally perfect appearance most certainly dishevelled. There was blood on his face.

'Lydia! Oh, Lydia!' he raced across to her, his arms outstretched. 'I'm so sorry. The cliff path. It has crumbled away. And then I got lost in this damned storm … I ended up thrashed by some trees …'

He embraced her and she could feel that he was shaking.

'Jacob! Darling! Well, that explains why you are so late. At least you are all here now. Where are the others? Poor Ella, she hates the dark. She tells me that she loves storms but I am positive that she must hate them when they are like this. Is she all right?' She peered around him, trying to see the door. 'Where are they? Did you get her home safely?'

'No, you misunderstand me. I am alone, Lydia. I was hoping they had arrived without me. Are they not here? Please, tell me they are here.'

'No, Jacob. They have not come back yet. Oh, no! They must be still out there somewhere.' She pulled away from him, taking hold of his hand almost subconsciously.

He squeezed it, making her look at him. 'I saw them in town. Yes, they spotted me and I was not popular, but Ella persuaded Adam that we should all meet at the church to travel home together. They never turned up. I waited there for hours, Lydia, please believe me. I do not know where they are if they have not come back.'

'Why on earth would I doubt you?' asked Lydia. 'I trust you, Jacob and I am sure Ella would have done her utmost to keep to the arrangements.'

'But if they did not come to the church as arranged, and they have not made their way home, I truly don't know where they are. Perhaps they stayed in the town? I hope they did.'

'I hope they did too.' Lydia's eyes were wide. 'If they didn't, they could be anywhere.' The moors were dark and lonely, and very unfriendly on such a night. 'Ella is not confident on a horse, poor thing. She will be even worse now. Adam will be taking it slowly, keeping her calm, no doubt,' she said unconvincingly.

Jacob was shaking his head. 'The cliff path is all but destroyed. We will have to hope they took shelter in the town. We will have to return tomorrow and try to locate them if they do not turn up tonight.'

'They will turn up. Won't they?' she asked.

Jacob shook his head. 'I hope so,' he said.

'Oh, dear Jacob, you're shivering,' said Lydia. She rubbed his shoulder ineffectually. 'Go upstairs and change into something dry. I will have someone send some hot water up for you.'

'I am going out one last time,' he replied. 'I will not go far – I just want to satisfy myself that they definitely are not out on the moors.'

'Jacob!' cried Lydia. She was torn; she wanted Jacob to stay inside, but she desperately wanted Adam and Ella to be found. She made a funny little gesture with her hands, more reminiscent of Ella than she realised. 'I do not know,' she said, echoing the sign.

'I need to go, Lydia,' said Jacob. 'Please. I will return as soon as possible.'

'Then let me send someone with you,' she said desperately. 'I cannot have you lost as well.'

'Dearest Lydia. Do not worry.' Jacob then did something entirely unexpected. He leaned down and, gently taking hold of her chin, he tilted her face towards him and kissed her. 'I will not be long, darling, I promise.' He held her startled gaze then let her go. 'Sweet Lydia.' He lowered his voice. 'I never realised how I felt about you until tonight. It was only the thought of seeing you that kept me going on that journey back.'

Lydia felt her heart twist oddly. It was the first time he had ever given such an indication to her; and she had to admit that the thought, here and now, with the storm raging outside and the relief of seeing him safely returned to the Park, was not exactly unpleasant.

She replied in a voice that was uncharacteristically shaky. 'Just bring them back safely, darling. One thing at a time.'

Jacob looked at her, his eyes dark and troubled. 'One thing at a time, my love,' he repeated. He traced the curve of her jawbone with his fingertip. There was a promise of something else in those eyes that Lydia had never seen before, in any man; apart from the look in Adam's warm, brown eyes, every time he saw Ella. Jacob nodded and turned. He strode across the hallway and threw the door open. He disappeared into the night, slamming the door shut behind him and Lydia was left alone, staring at the closed door, wondering what exactly was going on in her heart.

Another hour passed and Jacob still had not returned. The morning room looked out over the driveway and Lydia had thrown open the drapes. She sat there, staring blankly into the darkness, hugging herself and listening to the thunder. The lightning ripped the skies open, and every time the brightness slashed through them, Lydia hoped to see three figures straggling towards the house on horseback.

She didn't know how much longer she sat like that, but the memories of what happened next were burnt into her heart permanently. It all seemed to happen at once. First of all, the door flung open and Jacob appeared, striding across the room. In his hand was a riding crop covered in mud. Lydia stood up and ran across the room to him.

'I found this where the path collapsed,' he said.

Lydia stopped dead. She was not the sort of woman given to fainting, but at that moment she felt the ground shift beneath her.

Jacob's arm was around her within seconds, steadying her. 'I do not know if it is one of theirs or not,' he continued. 'It might not be.'

'They all look the same,' said Lydia. Her voice seemed to come from very far away. 'It could be anyone's ...'

'Miss Lydia, Johnson wishes to speak with you.' That was the butler coming into the room.

Lydia swung around to face him. 'Then send him in!' she cried.

The butler nodded and gestured for Johnson, the head stable hand, to move forward and enter the room.

The man was dripping wet, clutching something in his hands. He was unused to being in the house; he was far more content in the stables. His eyes were terrified and he stared at Lydia as if frightened to speak.

'Miss Lydia, one of the horses has returned,' he said. 'But there be no personage with it. Only this, caught in the bridle, like.' With a trembling hand, he held out a scrap of cloth.

At that point, it felt as if the walls closed in on Lydia. Johnson's face melted and blackened like a piece of paper burning in the grate as Lydia crumpled elegantly onto the floor into blessed unconsciousness. Johnson had shown her a torn piece of green, muddied velvet – the same green velvet that Ella's riding habit was made from.

The next few days passed in a blur for Lydia. There was a sense of hustle around the Park, people coming and going, people asking for statements and details of what had happened. And Jacob – always Jacob – dealing with the visitors and dealing with her as well.

One day, he brought her a tiny bunch of dried lavender to try and cheer her up. It was such a thoughtful, kind gesture it drove her to guilty tears, making her angry at herself for what she was putting him through. Shamefully, she hid in her room, refusing to see or speak to anyone but him. She didn't want to believe that this was happening; she wanted to wake up one morning and have Ella and Adam back. But that morning never seemed to come.

Even more shamefully, she took comfort of quite a different sort from Jacob. She had never believed herself capable of that: *ever*. She was lively, well-brought-up and sensible. So why did she give herself up to him so easily? It was a question she was to ask herself regularly over the next few months, with, it had to be said, varying degrees of self-flagellation and blame.

Then of course, they needed to arrange a wedding: a very speedy wedding. And then she couldn't think exclusively about Ella and Adam any more, she had other worries. Sometimes, as she lay next to Jacob and stared into the night she wondered how life could have changed so suddenly over the course of one day. Then the tears would slide silently down her cheeks as she blamed herself for the whole thing.

She imagined doors opening and shutting, pianos playing, Adam's laughter, floating along the corridors. Yet there was never anybody else there, and it wasn't even something she could share with Jacob, for fear that he would think her an utter, utter lunatic.

JACOB
May 1866

There was no need for them to know what had happened that night, and so long as he had breath in his body, he was never going to tell. And besides that, he had other problems to deal with. The night that he returned from the coast, the night of the storm, he had seen Lydia come out of the drawing room and look at him, full of fear. In the lamplight, her hair was almost the same honey-gold shade that Ella's was; her height, her figure, it all reminded him of Ella. It was when she made that funny little sign that he could almost swear it *was* Ella standing there.

The next few days had been the strangest he had ever encountered. He had lived in a dreamlike state, talking to people about events he wasn't supposed to have witnessed, lying about the things he did know and praying that Lydia would never find out. One of the nights, he had lost control completely. Again, it was because she looked so much like Ella that it had happened. Lydia had been more than willing; she had lost her brother and best friend all in one evening. Her parents were dead. She had nobody except Jacob to confide in or to seek comfort from.

The whole time he had imagined that this is what it would have been like with Ella. And then when cold, hard reason and daylight crept into the room, he realised it wasn't Ella. It would never be Ella. Of course, it was too late by then – but at least he could take control of the Park if he was forced to settle for Lydia. Every cloud, they said, had a silver lining.

So they had both carried the charade through to its logical and embarrassing conclusion, and now – now he was staring at a letter from Helena Warner, which had been posted from an address in Switzerland.

Jacob.

It is only right that you should know you have become a father. Yes, I do believe you are looking forward to a similar event with your wife – I can hardly bring myself to write that word – but your son and heir arrived Tuesday of last week. In case you are interested, which I doubt, he resembles you more than me, apart from the fact that he inherited my eye colour. I trust you will make suitable arrangements. You can contact me through my agents. I also pray that we never have to meet face to face ever again. I want nothing from you, apart from this child to be supported.

Sincerely
Helena Warner

Jacob crumpled up the paper and put his head in his hands. He cursed that night in July. Again, someone had been there when Ella was not. That time it was Helena. And now this; this was yet another secret he could never tell Lydia. And Adam – he had known, hadn't he? He hadn't believed her story about hearing news from home. Rather, it had been the humiliation which sent her running away that day, and Adam had guessed.

It was, perhaps, a blessing that Adam was dead. Jacob knew that Adam was dead without a doubt. And he was sure that Lydia knew without a doubt as well. And there he was; back at the beginning again – because he could never tell her how he knew that. It was enough to drive a man mad.

Jacob looked up and stared at the fireplace. After a moment, he straightened out the letter and copied the address down. Then he tore the paper into tiny pieces and scattered it into the flames.

LYDIA
July 1866

Lydia rummaged through the desk in the study. She needed an envelope desperately and Jacob was bound to have one in here. She dragged a sheaf of papers out and saw an envelope hidden among the pile. She liberated it and was trying to neaten up the remainder of the papers, when she caught sight of the corner of a cream card sticking up from the back of the drawer, just as if it had been pushed there and not quite dropped through into the next one down. She poked her fingers in and pulled it out. She read it quickly and saw it was an invitation to a dinner party. Her heart lurched as she realised which party it had been. This room had been Adam's, and now it was Jacob's. She could understand why Adam had kept the invitation, even appreciate the fact that it had slipped between the drawers and that was why Jacob had never discovered it. There was no other reason for it to be there.

From what she understood, anything to do with Ella was borderline acceptable. Anything to do with Adam was not. Therefore, something that would have united the pair of them was tantamount to sacrilege. She would never forget the day she discovered that Jacob had called in men to raze Ella's angel fountain to the ground; only on the basis, she thought, that Adam had restored it and gifted it to his bride. She felt the old anger boil up within her. Not for the first time, she wondered if she, Lydia, was simply second – or even third – best? She hadn't forgotten Helena. And this apparent obsession he had with Ella – it made her worry; it made her worry for the child. Next month, she would have a baby. It was a terrifying thought, thinking that its father might love a ghost instead – thinking that they had wed for the wrong reasons. She flushed. She couldn't say that. They had needed to marry, there was no question about it.

She took hold of the invitation and made to tear it up, the memories still painful; but as she stood by the desk, she became aware of a faint noise from the next room. Someone was in there playing the piano. She frowned. She was alone in the house, Jacob was out on estate business and they had no guests. It had to be a servant. She walked out of the study and headed towards the drawing room. Honestly, she wouldn't object if they only asked her first. They had a piano down in the servants' hall, but she would be willing to bet they would try to play a better instrument when they thought nobody was around.

Lydia threw the door open, ready to reprimand whoever was in there. To her surprise, the room was empty. And what made it even more strange was that the lid of the piano was down. She looked at the invitation in her hand and felt something like a breath of air on her neck. And then there was a brief thought; perhaps it would be foolish to destroy it after all? She shivered, and, before she could change her mind, quickly stuffed the invitation into the nearest receptacle – her old writing slope. Besides that, there was something telling her that she wasn't entirely alone in that room, either.

'Ella?' she tried. Then she felt extremely silly. Ella would never even hear her, would she? So why would she, Lydia, even expect an answer? She didn't wait to test her theory, but instead turned and hurried from the room as fast as she could. She refused to believe that the noise she heard as she slammed the door shut behind her was the lid of the piano being crashed down. It was simply an echo: it had to be.

It was a few hours later, when Lydia was lying on a day-bed trying to rest, that there was a knock on the door. She half-opened her eyes and turned her face to the door.

'Come in,' she called. It had been pointless trying to sleep anyway. She was hot, she was uncomfortable and it was broad daylight outside. She might as well see who or what the company consisted of. She welcomed anything that would keep her from thinking about that mad little scenario with the haunted piano, anyway.

One of the young maids slipped through the door and stood before Lydia, looking terrified. Lydia knew the girl had adored Ella and therefore she, in her turn, had quite a soft spot for the maid. Jacob disliked her being so fond of her, which made Lydia, perversely, treat the girl even more familiarly than she would have ordinarily done.

'Good afternoon, Elizabeth,' said Lydia, smiling at her.

'Good afternoon, miss,' said the girl, curtseying. 'Miss, I was told I could tell you this, if you don't mind me disturbing you, like. They said I could do it, means as it was such a special thing, like.'

'Of course you can disturb me,' said Lydia with a smile. 'I am not doing anything important and it is nice to see a friendly face.' She pushed herself up into a sitting position and the girl scurried forward, plumping the cushions up behind her.

'Is that better, miss?'

'Wonderful, thank you. Now what is it?'

'Miss Ella's picture has been delivered, miss!' said the girl. Her cheeks shone with pride and she stood a little straighter.

'Ella's picture? Oh, how marvellous!' Lydia clapped her hands together. 'I need to see it immediately. I shall come down.'

'Oh, miss, don't exert yourself!' said the maid. 'It ain't – I mean, it's not – going to run away. I hope your idea worked, Miss Lydia. It was ever such a good idea, wasn't it?'

'Exert myself be damned,' said Lydia. 'I am not ill. And

yes, let us hope it worked. Come on, help me up and I shall come downstairs.' She held her hand out and the girl dashed forward, holding her hand as Lydia hauled herself to her feet. The girl's hands were so rough, Lydia thought with a pang. She was such a sweetheart. She would, she determined, make a post for her to help with the baby when it arrived. In fact, Elizabeth was a rather sweet name as well, if the child was a girl – then she could be called Eliza, or Lizzy, or even Ella. She smiled to herself as Elizabeth helped her into a robe. That was another thing she would suggest to Jacob. In fact, she thought with a hint of bitterness, he would probably like the name Ella.

Lydia sat in front of the mirror and Elizabeth came up behind her with some combs. Lydia knew that her hair was a mess and her face looked red and puffy. She certainly didn't feel as if she had blossomed throughout this pregnancy. She just felt rather fat and awkward. She smiled a little, wishing Ella had been around to listen to her complaints. Yet, ironically, had Ella not disappeared, she would never have been in this situation. Perhaps she would have had to listen to Ella's list of complaints instead.

'I miss her,' said Elizabeth quietly as she fastened a comb into Lydia's hair.

'Were you reading my mind?' asked Lydia, smiling at her in the glass.

The girl shrugged her thin shoulders. 'Maybe. I can always tell when you think of her from your face, if you don't mind me saying so, miss. But I don't want to speak out of turn, like.'

Lydia sighed and shifted position slightly. She rested her hand lightly on her stomach. 'You are not speaking out of turn. You are speaking the truth.' She moved her hand and began to fiddle with the ribbons on her robe instead. She dropped her head, and stared at her hands. 'I miss her dreadfully.'

'She ain't coming back, is she miss?' asked the girl.

Lydia looked up. Elizabeth looked close to tears.

'I do not think so, darling,' she replied.

'Is she dead, miss? Her and the master?' The girl's bottom lip trembled and Lydia got the sense that it was the first time she had voiced her concerns. 'Only sometimes I imagine I see her, you know. I imagine she's in the courtyard and I see her talking to the master. Then I goes out and she's gone. And sometimes I hear the music, miss. Like the posh stuff she used to play all the time? But the room's empty, see, and she's not there.'

Lydia closed her eyes, squeezing them shut as if to block out the thoughts. 'I am the same,' she said eventually. 'I see her and I hear her everywhere. I thought I was going mad.' She laughed cynically. 'Maybe I am. Maybe we both are. Maybe one day she is going to walk back in and laugh at us and say, "that was a wonderfully spontaneous trip. Adam and I are so pleased to be home. Did you miss us?" But somehow, I doubt it. I just wish I knew what had happened to them.'

'Don't suppose we'll ever know, miss,' said Elizabeth. There was a waver in her voice and then she couldn't hold back the tears any more. 'I miss her so bad,' she sobbed, 'and when that picture is there, I know we can see her again but it'll make things worse, I just know it. She was going to teach me stuff as well, we were going to spend some time together, she said.'

'Shall I admit something to you?' said Lydia. 'The photograph we gave to the artist to use was the second one we'd taken that day. My husband took it and Ella looked so beautiful in that picture. It was perfect for the artist to copy from. The first photograph I took was a mistake and I threw it away.' She laughed humourlessly. 'Ha! I am so stupid. It was all I had of them and I threw it away. Oh, I teased Ella, I said I would keep it and I did not. And I feel guiltier about that than anything because it was so natural and you could just see that they belonged together. And now I will never see my brother again, either, and I miss *him* so much as well.' She covered her face with her hands. 'Oh dear God, I miss them *both* so much.'

She felt Elizabeth's arms come hesitantly around her and she was grateful for the comfort.

'Miss, don't be cross with me, please,' whispered Elizabeth after a moment, 'but I did a bad thing with that photograph.'

'What do you mean?' asked Lydia, turning to face the girl. 'I threw it away, what could you possibly do with it?'

'I took it out of the rubbish, miss, and I put it in a really safe place. It's under my mattress, miss, and it's yours whenever you want it. I just wanted to see them safe, miss, and it was just my way of trying to help them. I thought that was what was giving me the sights and sounds and things – because I had hidden it, like, and I shouldn't have done.' The girl's face was pale and frightened. 'I'm sorry, miss.'

'Do not be sorry!' said Lydia. She felt stupidly light-headed and relieved, then she surprised herself by laughing out loud. She hugged Elizabeth awkwardly, twisted as she was at such a peculiar angle. 'That is actually rather perfect news and the second good thing that has happened to me today. The first was hearing that the portrait had arrived. Elizabeth, I am going to tell you a secret. I want you to put the photograph in a special place for me, can you do that? I do not want my husband to know about it, so you have to be careful. He hates having anything around the house that reminds him of Adam. Thank God he's never realised I moved that terrible portrait to the west wing corridor. He seems to moderately tolerate anything to do with Ella, but anything to do with Adam – my beloved brother – he will not even entertain it.' She paused for a moment. 'I never realised he felt that way about him; all those years of bitterness. He was such a good liar. I feel ashamed to realise I never noticed. You see, that's because I'm so damn self-absorbed.' Her eyes filled with tears.

'I think, Elizabeth,' she continued carefully, wiping her tears away, 'that he blames Adam for whatever happened to them. Now, do you know where my writing slope is?'

The girl nodded, her eyes wide. 'I do, miss. It's a beauty, that is. I polish it every week,' she said proudly.

'You are very sweet. Well, I shall tell you how to get into the very most *secret* part of it. And you can put the photograph there. I trust you. And if ever you want to see it, you must come to me and ask, and I will give you permission. Do you understand?'

'I do, miss,' breathed the girl. 'Master Adam was so lovely as well, he was so kind to me.' Her eyes began to brim with tears and Lydia patted her arm.

'Good girl,' said Lydia, feeling quite emotional herself. *Damn this pregnancy!* She had never been like this before. She sat up straighter and set her shoulders determinedly. 'Now, Elizabeth, listen carefully – these are the instructions.'

Lydia saw the large canvas standing in the hallway, still wrapped in its protective coverings. Two young men were standing by it, messengers sent by Landseer himself, no doubt, to deliver it and receive payment.

'I hardly dare breathe!' Lydia exclaimed. 'Please, would you unveil it for me?'

Her heart was beating fast as one of the men started to slowly unwind the cloth. The size of it meant that Ella – or Lady Eleanor, as she would be known formally on this portrait – would be almost life-size, and, effectively, standing in front of Lydia one last time. She knew where she would mount the portrait; on the staircase as it turned to the left, exactly where Adam had requested it. Frankly, she didn't care whether Jacob approved or not. He didn't know she had continued with Adam's commission and he damn well didn't know she was planning on hanging it on the landing.

Lydia clasped her hands together to stop them shaking and watched as layer after layer of cloth fell away. She caught glimpses of Ella's creamy-white wedding dress, and even from that, she could see the skill of the artist bringing Ella to life.

Lydia turned away from the portrait, unsure for a moment if she could actually look at Ella, face to face. She stopped the men with a gesture and caught sight of Elizabeth dotting around the doorway. Lydia met the girl's eye and smiled at her.

She beckoned her over. 'Come, Elizabeth. Come and see it with me. I need you here,' she said. Her voice sounded stronger than she felt.

'But, miss …' said Elizabeth, apparently conscious of her position in the household. 'What will they all think?'

'Thinking be damned,' said Lydia. 'I am the mistress. I decide who does what. I have decided you need to come and stand by me.'

The girl sidled over and hesitantly stood by her mistress.

'After all,' Lydia said, leaning down and speaking quietly into the girl's ear, 'you were the one who wore the dress for the sketches.'

'Miss, it was an honour,' whispered Elizabeth. She blushed scarlet.

'Well, I would have done it, but circumstances conspired against me,' said Lydia. 'I fear that it would not have looked the same. Ella was always very slender. I am *not* slender at present. All they could take from me was the hair colour. And I do not think I did a particularly good job of describing her eye colour, but I did my best.'

'Yes, miss,' whispered Elizabeth.

'Now,' said Lydia, turning back to the young men. 'I am ready.'

'As you wish,' said one of the men. They flipped the covering off the portrait and Lydia caught her breath.

'My God,' she said. 'It is her. It is Ella.' She reached out her hand and touched the portrait lightly with her fingertips. She traced Ella's hair, her lips, her cheek. She smiled at her and tilted her head to one side. 'You are perfect, my darling.' She took in the dress, the soft folds of fabric, which glowed luminously against the background and finally touched the plain gold wedding band which graced Ella's finger.

Lydia dashed away a tear and stood up straighter. She turned to the messengers, confident again. 'It is excellent. Please tell Mr Landseer that I am extremely delighted by it. My brother would have been more than delighted. And now, I believe that I must pay my debts.'

'The worst part, my lady,' replied the young man. He winked at Elizabeth. 'It has to be done, though.' Elizabeth giggled and Lydia found it rather amusing.

'Elizabeth, my dear, please would you take these gentlemen downstairs for a cup of tea? I am sure cook will be able to find some cakes for them as well. I need to sign the invoice and I feel rather tired and emotional. You can understand, surely?' She smiled at the messengers. 'If you return in perhaps an hour, I may have done it?'

Elizabeth and the young man smiled at each other again. 'Certainly, miss,' replied Elizabeth. 'This way, sir.' She curtseyed rather prettily, Lydia thought, and headed towards the servants' quarters.

Lydia took another look at the portrait and turned away, heading towards the study. *Always the matchmaker*. She opened her eyes wide. It was unmistakably Ella's voice. Lydia swung around and stared at the picture. For a moment she did nothing; then she slowly lifted her hands. *Always*, she replied. *Yet you and Adam were meant to be together. And it would have happened without me, we both know that*. Then she dropped her hands. She could have felt foolish, but she didn't. She walked slowly to the study and passed the drawing room on her way. She paused by the closed door and pressed her ear against it. The sound of piano music was drifting through the door. Mozart, of course. Lydia ducked her head and half-smiled. She wouldn't go inside. Ella was welcome to play as much as she wanted to; she wasn't going to stop her.

But what she was going to do, and damn anyone who tried to stop *her*, was head off along the cliffs. She couldn't ride there, of course, which was utterly dreary, but what she could do was ask one of the stable hands in a very pretty fashion to take her up there in the little phaeton; despite the fact Jacob had banned her from travelling anywhere until the child was born. If poor little Blackie pulled the carriage, they wouldn't go very fast at all and she would be completely safe, and that way she would feel as if she had Ella with her again.

THE CLIFF PATH

It hadn't taken long to persuade the young stable hand to do as she bid, and Lydia was now safely ensconced in the carriage, rumbling slowly along the cliff path. Blackie was terribly plodding, which was part of his charm – and probably the reason that Lydia didn't notice the ruts and the holes in the road as much as she might have done. She did feel, however, rather uncomfortable, squashed into the narrow seat and once again silently blamed Jacob for her current hideous condition.

'Stop here, please!' she called as the driver rounded a corner and the vast expanse of the ocean opened out before her, sunlight twinkling off the waves and the water reflecting the deep, cornflower blue of the sky. Ella had loved it here. She had always talked about how free she felt at the coast. At that moment, trapped in her heavy, lumbering body Lydia felt inclined to agree.

The driver did as she bid and drew the carriage to a halt. He dismounted and came over to the side of the phaeton, bowing as he offered Lydia his hand so she could climb out.

'Thank you,' she said. 'Will you wait for me here, please? I will not be long.'

The driver nodded and she set off along the cliff path. Her heart was hammering in her chest, playing a terrifying rhythm, and she wondered afresh what she was doing here. She just wanted to erase those memories of the night of the storm, she decided – she wanted to see the coast in all its beauty and just be with Ella for a little while away from the confines of the Park. Carrick Park was no longer a happy place and Lydia determined once again that, as soon as she realistically could, she would get rid of the accursed house.

A warm breeze was blowing off the sea, which in itself was rather pleasant and unusual. Lydia paused, watching a sailing ship skim across the horizon. The North Sea was not the warmest of places, but the beaches here were sandy and friendly. Lydia disliked the southern beaches. They had been to Sussex on several occasions, taking the air at Hastings, and she smiled as she remembered Ella wrinkling her nose and staring out at the vast carpet of pebbles and stones that lay before them.

'To think those pebbles might stretch all the way to France,' she had said. 'One wonders if the French beaches are just the same as these ones.'

'We will go and find out one day,' Lydia had replied, tucking her arm into Ella's. 'We shall ask Adam to take us, and if he will not, we shall row across in a boat ourselves.'

Ella had smiled at her, her eyes sparkling with mischief. 'Now that will be an interesting experience,' she had said and they had both laughed at the ridiculous idea.

Lydia thought that it was such a shame the beach here hadn't been so friendly that awful night in November and she felt her heart twist at the idea. She turned away from the view, saddened again, and walked a little further along the path. She hadn't been here since it had happened.

She walked for a few minutes more, feeling about as elegant as Blackie had been when he was waddling in front of the carriage – and suddenly she was there. It looked as if a giant had taken a huge bite out of the edge of the cliff and she felt herself grow a little faint. She held onto a branch of a stubby, windswept bush and waited until the ground righted itself; then she let go and carefully lowered herself onto the grass, sitting down and never taking her eyes off the gouge in the cliff.

It was here. Here was where her brother and sister-in-law had seemingly fallen to their deaths. She was surprised the air wasn't any thicker with menace and the emotions that must surely have gone through their minds as it happened.

She didn't dare linger on the images that presented themselves to her – she didn't want to try and put the pieces together, to try and work out who had gone first. She hoped that neither of them had suffered; the thought of one of them realising the other was dead, even for a short time was unbearable. She raised a hand and wiped her eyes as the tears started to fall.

What a mess. What an absolute, utter mess. How could she have descended to this? She was married to a man who she now disliked intensely, she hated every minute of being pregnant with a child she didn't want and she had nobody else to turn to. She was twenty-two years old and she was trapped in a life she would never wish upon anyone. The spoiled darling of Carrick Park was exactly that now; just merely spoilt.

As the tormented thoughts went around and around in her head, she realised that, in her desperation, her fingers had clutched onto something next to her on the ground. She looked down, barely registering the silver foliage and the knobbly flowers at first; then she understood it was sea lavender. Lydia pulled a few of the heads off the cushion of greenery and stared at them, shredding the flowers off the stalks as her mind churned. Lavender. This was one of the gifts Jacob had given to her just after it happened. She had put the spray into her writing slope and hadn't given it much thought since. She hadn't realised the stuff grew along these cliffs and she looked up, scanning the area for any more clumps of it. There were none.

As she stared around, she saw again the chunk out of the cliff side and shuddered. Jacob must have known it happened here. That must have been where he had found the riding crop and the lavender and brought her some to—

To do what? To make her feel better? To remind her of what had happened? To remind her callously that he knew where Lydia's life had ended as well as theirs? She scolded herself for being overly dramatic, but the truth of the matter was that Jacob was as cold towards her as she was towards him. She was definitely third best. And perhaps, a little voice asked her, if she didn't look so much like Ella in the dark, would it even have gotten to this point?

'Lydia?' A female voice interrupted her thoughts and Lydia hurriedly dashed some more tears away before awkwardly twisting around to see who had spoken.

'Rose!' she said, surprised. The woman was Lady Scarsdale – one of their closest neighbours and the owner of Sea Scarr Hall, not far from Staithes. Another blade seemed to pierce her heart and twist itself a little more. They had all attended a ball at Sea Scarr, just after Adam and Ella had become engaged.

'Lydia. I'm so surprised to see you out unattended. I'd heard that you were very unwell after the birth and—'

'Excuse me?' Lydia stared at the woman. She struggled to her feet and faced her old friend and sparring partner. She did nothing to hide her condition and went so far as to pull the fabric of her gown closer to her body, revealing more than was generally acceptable for a woman of her station. 'Do I *look* like I've given birth?' she demanded. 'Ask me next month, perhaps, when the child is due.'

She had the satisfaction of seeing Rose colour a bright, splodgy red.

'Oh, dear. Oh, I *am* sorry. I must have been mistaken.'

'Mistaken?' Lydia drew herself to her full height. 'And who passed on that information to you, may I ask?'

'I am so sorry. Please, forgive me. It is my mistake. I thought he had said that was the case. I must have misheard.' Rose turned, trying to cover her embarrassment and hurry away.

Suddenly, there was a roaring in Lydia's ears and the answer came out of nowhere. She spoke loudly, but her voice seemed to be coming from very far away and sounded as if it did not belong to her. 'Did my husband tell you that?'

Rose paused in her flight. 'I may have interpreted it that way, Lydia. I cannot say for sure. He said you had childbed fever and you had not recovered that well. I truly thought it to be the reason I had not seen you for so many months.'

'You have not seen me because I have barely been out of the house,' said Lydia. 'My husband has prevented me from going anywhere too public and we do not seem to receive visitors any more.'

'Lydia! I came to the Park just after the tragedy happened. I was turned away and advised you were unwell. I waited for you to recover and contact me but you never did.' The woman's face grew concerned. 'I have clearly misunderstood the situation. It must not have been your child I saw him with. When I think of it, the little one had strangely coloured eyes and I wondered if all was well when I saw it. It seemed a large child for being delivered so early, as well – he said that was part of the reason you had suffered so badly. I am terribly sorry.'

Rose's eyes were wide. Lady Scarsdale loved gossip, and Lydia briefly wondered how many other people had heard the same story for Rose would not have hesitated to share the news. So, as far as local society was concerned, she had borne the child too early and was languishing in her confinement. Wonderful. Just wonderful. And that was even before they speculated on the date of her marriage. Well, thank God for the fact they had agreed to pretend they had married in good time for this baby. The only person who knew the truth was the vicar – the witnesses had been passing labourers who agreed to the task upon a handsome payment from Jacob. It had all seemed vaguely fun at the time and Lydia had thought how much Ella would have loved all the secrecy. But it wasn't fun any more.

'Well, I have *not* had the child,' said Lydia forcibly. 'I do not know who the child is or the identity of the mother, but as you can clearly see it was not me.'

'As I say, my dear Lydia, I am mistaken. I must go. I am so sorry. I will come and visit you soon, I promise.' Rose ducked her head and hurried away.

'No, you will not,' muttered Lydia. Then she shouted out to the retreating figure, 'And please ensure our mutual acquaintances know the truth, Rose! I would hate to be the subject of speculative gossip, as you can imagine!'

Rose practically broke into a run and Lydia watched her disappear over the path. She gave her enough time to put a reasonable distance between them and then set off back towards the phaeton, her mind whirling. She could not comprehend how her life could possibly get any worse, but she thought she was about to find out.

Lydia had left instructions that the portrait of Ella should be hung on the stairwell in her absence. And she was delighted to see that her wishes had come true.

As soon as she walked into the house and turned left up the staircase, the portrait of Ella stopped her in her tracks.

'Oh, my goodness.' Lydia reached out and touched the picture. 'How perfect.'

'Yes it is, miss.' Elizabeth crept up behind her, clutching a vase full of fresh flowers. 'I keep looking at it and seeing her there.' She laughed a little. 'I keep asking to do jobs upstairs, miss, so I get to see her. I was just taking these to your bedroom. I'm sorry I didn't use the servants' staircase, miss.' She raised the vase.

'I am so preoccupied with Ella's portrait that I had not realised,' said Lydia with a smile. 'But flowers, that is very kind of you. Did you manage to amuse yourself with the young man while I was away?'

Elizabeth blushed. 'He's very nice.'

'I am pleased about that as well.' She reached out and patted Elizabeth's shoulder. 'If you need a day off to see him, then I am sure we can arrange that.'

Elizabeth blushed again. 'Thank you, miss.'

Lydia smiled and opened her mouth to respond, when the entrance door clashed open and both women turned around.

Jacob was standing at the bottom of the grand staircase, staring up at the portrait. 'What the hell is that?' he shouted. 'What is *she* doing there?'

'Adam would have thanked me for this,' replied Lydia. 'And do not tell me you would not be happy to see Ella every day, looking at you when you walk up the stairs to your bedroom.'

Lydia was conscious of Elizabeth disappearing like a wraith into the bedroom corridor above and she really didn't blame her. She watched Jacob storm up the stairs and, when he was a few steps from the top, she turned and headed up the second flight so she was in the corridor, looking down at him.

Jacob drew to a halt in front of the picture. 'It is *not* staying there,' he said, looking up at it.

'Why not?' asked Lydia. Her voice was dangerously low and she gripped the bannister.

'Because I say so,' he said. His face was pale and his composure clearly wavering.

Lydia couldn't help it; she laughed derisively. 'You *say* so? Just as you *said* I had a child and was confined to my bed? Well, now. I disagree.'

She was gratified to see a flicker of unease pass across his face. 'Who told you that?'

'It doesn't matter. What *matters* is that you said it. Why, Jacob? I will not settle for third best and—'

'Third best?' he shouted. He climbed a few steps and stood, staring up at her.

'Third best,' she repeated. 'Ella first. And then Helena. And …' It was Lydia's turn to feel that sense of unease. 'Helena,' she repeated slowly. 'Rose said the baby looked strange. It was something about its eyes.' She stared at Jacob and in that moment she understood. 'Oh *God!* It's Helena's baby, isn't it? And what the hell were you going to do with me and *our* baby when it came?' Instinctively, she brought her arm around and laid it protectively over her stomach. 'What were you going to *do*?' Her eyes moved to the portrait and all of a sudden it started to make sense. *Third best.*

But before she could formulate any words, Jacob started up the stairs two at a time. 'I had not decided,' he yelled, 'but it is nothing I cannot do now!'

Lydia flung both her arms out in front of her, purely as a defence mechanism. Then it all seemed to happen in slow motion.

She felt Jacob's strong, hard chest connect with her open palms and someone or something gave her the strength to push against him as hard as she could.

Her screams combined with his as he missed his footing and tumbled backwards down the staircase, hitting the wall of the stairwell head first and coming to rest beneath the portrait in a twisted mess. He lay deathly still in an attitude that left Lydia in no doubt as to what had happened to him.

Then Lydia opened her mouth and screamed again. And this time she couldn't stop.

The noise brought people scurrying from every corner of the house – the first person Lydia was aware of was Elizabeth, who wrapped her arms around Lydia and gently drew her away from the top of the stairs, moving her to where she couldn't see the carnage or smell the blood that was pooling on the landing.

''Twasn't your fault, miss, 'twasn't your fault,' Elizabeth kept saying. 'Trust me, miss. I'll see you right. He slipped, miss, fair and simple, he slipped. You never touched him, miss, no not at all. I saw it all, miss, I saw it when I was coming along the corridor. 'Tis a tragedy, miss, but it wasn't your fault.'

'But you were in my bedroom,' said Lydia, on a hysterical sob. 'You couldn't see it. You couldn't see it.'

Elizabeth guided her to a chair and pushed her down into it. 'You didn't do it, miss. Trust me. I saw it all.' The girl's voice was low and controlled.

Lydia raised her eyes to the maid's and her gaze met the other girl's with an understanding that was deeper than either of them could vocalise.

'You as well?' Lydia whispered eventually.

Elizabeth blushed and dropped her gaze. 'Like I said, miss, you didn't do it. And I shall swear that until I go to my grave. We can't help the master and the mistress, but we can damn well help you.'

And as the girl's eyes met Lydia's again, she knew that was all she could hope for.

Part Three

BECKY
November

There was certainly a lot to think about. Becky was genuinely struggling with trying to fit everything together. The one thing that annoyed her the most was the fact that Ella and Adam had disappeared. It didn't take a genius to imagine that whatever it was had been pretty bad. There was definitely something Ella was trying to tell her. She was becoming more and more insistent, and Becky still hadn't managed to shake her off.

The cliff path was narrow and, where it petered out onto the real cliff edges, no more than a single track. The wind was biting, streaming right across the North Sea and battering Becky as she walked along with her head down.

The one piece of the puzzle she still didn't fully understand was the lavender. She wanted to think that it was a love token, given to Lydia Carrick by Jacob, the cousin Lissy had told her she married; but that just didn't seem right, not entirely. She paused by the railings and leant on them, staring out to the sea, hoping for some sort of divine inspiration. She felt the wind on her face and a few spots of rain or salt spray that were carried inland with it. Her hair was whipping about and she knew she must look a mess. Angrily, she pushed her hair behind her ear, but the wind loosened it, blowing it against her cheeks again. Standing there in the completely silent world that Ella had lived in felt surreal. *So this is what it would be like?* she thought. She didn't like it; and yes, it upset her. Not many things about her life truly upset her, but the thought of living permanently like Ella had to, *did* upset her.

Becky's gaze wandered onto the longer grass at the cliff top. It looked like the cliff had been the victim of some sort of erosion and she saw that a big chunk was missing a little further along. The cliff edge came up pretty close to the railings. In fact, she noticed the railings turned into a fence from that point onwards, and she walked along the path, focused on that bit. A cyclist whizzed past her and she jumped as he sped by, feeling a massive rush of air. He seemed to be ringing his bell furiously and now, not only was she upset, but she was annoyed that he had so very nearly knocked her over.

'For goodness sake!' she yelled at his retreating back. She couldn't even hear herself shout. She resolved to keep more closely to the railings. Squashing herself right in next to them, she continued walking.

Just as she approached the beginning of the fence and the semi-circle that had disappeared from the cliff side, her attention was caught by a haze of purple that was hidden within the dry, yellowy grass. She stopped and leaned over, trying to see what it was. A group of tall, knobbly flowers sprang up from a silvery green bush of foliage and Becky knew immediately what it was: it was lavender. Or more precisely, it was sea lavender.

She was no botanist, but she knew that November was really not the right time for lavender to be flowering, whether it was sea lavender or not. She guessed that it probably bloomed around about July to the end of October at the very latest. So either these had been extremely well sheltered or …

Her heart lurched. 'Was it here, Ella?' she asked. She gripped the damp wood, her knuckles showing white through her skin. Unable to help herself she leaned further across the fence to get a closer view. Her foot slipped backwards on the muddy grass and she kind of half-lurched, half-tumbled as the rotten wood gave way under her grasp and pitched her forwards, head first, towards the cliff edge.

The figure came riding up to her, stark against the night sky. Forked lightning flashed around her and yes, she was frightened. Storms had never frightened her, but this one did. She knew the cliché about the Heavens opening, and then it truly happened. There was no warning; just a sudden, terrifying blackout and then the rain lashed down out of nowhere, blurring what little distance she could see up ahead. 'Oh God!' she screamed. Close to tears, she urged the horse towards Adam, so relieved to see him there. 'I am sorry,' she called, hoping he would hear her. 'I should have waited for you. I should have come back to Whitby to find you.'

But the man was not Adam; it was Jacob. He was trying to tell her something. She tried to see him clearly, tried to read what he was saying, but it was just too dark now and the rain was blinding her.

She shook her head. 'Jacob, I am sorry, I don't know what you are saying. I must go and find Adam.' She tried to pass him, but he took hold of her arm.

She saw him shake his head. 'No.' Ella just about managed to understand.

She frowned. 'Why "no"?' She gestured towards the town with her riding crop. 'It is that way. I know where I am going, I just need to keep to the cliff path.'

'The cliff path is crumbling away, Ella,' Jacob shouted, 'and the storm is too bad. It will not be safe. The rain …'

He tried to signal what he meant, but she just shook her head again, close to tears. 'I cannot do it, Jacob; I cannot understand you. Please let me past. I need to find my husband.' She tried to make the horse skirt around him, but the gap was not very wide and the horse stumbled. Jacob grabbed the reins and pulled the animal towards him. Then he didn't know exactly what happened. One minute Ella was in the saddle, the next, apparently unseated by the horse's stumble, she was gone. The last thing he heard was a rip, a scream and a sickening series of crunches and thuds as she disappeared over the side of the cliff.

'Ella!' Jacob let go of the reins and the animal reared, pulling away, eventually finding enough solid ground to enable it to run off across the moors. Jacob leapt from his horse and ran to the edge of the cliff. He slipped and skidded, somehow managing to right himself before he too went over the edge. There was nothing but darkness beneath him. 'Oh God!' he shouted. 'Ella!' At that moment a flash of lightning lit up the scene below him; all there was to be seen were massive, jagged rocks and wild waves, crashing against the cliff side.

'Ella?' Jacob heard the voice only faintly at first. It was a man's voice, breaking through the darkness. He felt sick and his stomach lurched: Adam. He heard the horse's hooves stamping through the mud, and soon they were near him.

'She cannot hear you,' Jacob said. His voice was flat and toneless. He did not turn to greet Adam, he just continued to stare over the cliff, praying that some miracle might have happened.

'Jacob?' shouted Adam. 'What are you doing here? For God's sake, man, were you following us? Where is Ella?' He jumped off his horse and ran over to his cousin. 'Where is she?'

'I don't know,' replied Jacob. 'I saw a horse on the horizon a few moments ago but it might have been anyone's. I cannot say that I have seen her. Is she not with you?' Now he turned to Adam. He hated the man; he absolutely hated him. He had always hated him. 'She should have been with you. What was in your mind to let her travel alone on a night like this?'

'What was in yours,' Adam fired back, 'to follow us into town? We are not your concern.'

'I came to find her and bring her home, as you should have done. You should not have left her!' shouted Jacob. All the bottled up rage spilled out. 'You think you know so much about her, but you do not. Before you came back in the summer, she was mine. I could tell it was me she wanted. But all the time, throughout all of the years we grew up together, you always took what was rightfully mine.'

'We have had this discussion before!' snapped Adam. 'And that is not the issue tonight. The issue tonight is where is my wife? I did not know that she had left Whitby until a street trader told me he had seen her mount her horse and go. Dammit, if I had only forced her to come into the offices with me!' He raked his hands through his hair and looked frantically around him. 'Which way did she go?'

'She went back to the Park,' said Jacob dangerously. 'That is where she was heading.'

'I do not believe you,' shouted Adam. 'You never saw the horse heading that way did you? What have you done to her? Where is she?'

'You should not have left her!' yelled Jacob again. 'You do not deserve her!'

'Jacob! Tell me where she is! For God's sake, she could be anywhere.' Adam looked around, as if the girl would magically appear out of nowhere. 'Ella!'

Jacob laughed. 'I told you, she will not hear you.'

Adam opened his mouth to reply, just as a flash of sheet lightning lit up the coast, as clearly as daylight. He squinted at the sudden brightness and turned his head away.

And then, Jacob realised, Adam saw it. He saw Ella's riding crop lying among the clumps of flattened grass and the withered sea lavender; and, Jacob also realised, that Adam could not have failed to see where the top of the cliff had sheared away and exposed fresh mud, shining blackly under the lightning. Adam lurched forwards and grabbed the crop. He was almost upright, when Jacob launched himself at his cousin and knocked him to the ground.

The men laid into one another, fighting as if a lifetime's resentment had exploded into that one moment on the cliff top. They swore at one another, Adam accusing Jacob of all sorts of atrocities, which did not stop at Ella.

'I have my suspicions about Helena!' Adam screamed at one point. 'I can guess what you did to her that evening.'

'She is a liar, a vicious liar. I never touched her.'

'She accused you of nothing. Why would you assume that she did, if you were not guilty of something?'

Jacob punched Adam in the jaw, trying to silence the words. 'It was your fault. If you had not left her to find Ella … if you had let me find Ella … but no. No, you would never have let me do that, would you?'

'You think I would have let you near Ella? I have never trusted you, ever. And I would never trust you with my precious Ella.'

Adam had Jacob on the ground now; he was taller and stronger, the punches becoming more aggressive. Jacob, pinned down on his back, groped around the area, looking for something to defend himself with, something to get Adam off him. His fingers found a rock and closed over it; he brought the rock up, slamming it into the side of Adam's head. There was a gasp and Adam's eyes opened wide. Then he went limp and fell, tumbling away from Jacob and lying motionless in the mud. Jacob rolled away from Adam, half-crawling, half-scrambling as he tried to put some distance between them. Adam never moved. Jacob, breathing heavily stared at the man, waiting for him to move; to moan; to do anything. But Adam did not.

It was probably at that point when reason fled from Jacob's mind. First Ella; now Adam. It really only took an instant to decide. Shakily, he clambered to his feet and walked over. He took hold of Adam's arms and dragged his body to the cliff side. More land had been dislodged and the semi-circle of landslide was even bigger now. He moved, so he was well away from the erosion, Adam's body lying between him and the cliff edge. He squatted down and rolled the body towards the edge. It only took one final push, and his cousin was hurtling over the edge to join Ella.

Becky would never know how she hadn't gone tumbling over that cliff the same way that Ella and Adam had. She lay there for a while with her eyes squeezed shut, feeling the mud and the coldness soaking through her clothes. She couldn't get the pictures out of her head and she felt sick.

When the images faded a little and she finally found the courage to open her eyes, she found herself staring into a chasm, dizzied by the waves crashing on the shore below, the white tips of them creaming into the rocks and spilling back over themselves. She was clutching onto two tufts of sea lavender; as if *that* would save her – yeah, sure. Her heart pounding, she held her position carefully, trying desperately hard to *listen* to the sounds of the North Sea. Ella had gone, she couldn't sense her any more at all – but it was all terribly dull and faint around her, the crashing of the waves was no more than a whisper. She closed her eyes again and swore. Great. That was all she needed.

She carefully edged herself backwards and shuffled somehow towards the cliff path. Just as she was almost there, she felt someone grab her ankles. She yelped and twisted around, half-expecting to see Jacob standing there, ready to pick her up and toss her into the sea with the rest of them. *Dear God, save me!* But it wasn't Jacob; however, it was almost as bad.

'Seb!' she managed. 'What the *hell* are you doing here? For God's sake will you stop bloody stalking me?'

'I'm not stalking you!' said Seb. He looked genuinely concerned. He tugged half-heartedly at her ankles until she kicked him away and managed to crawl out from the wreckage of the fence.

'I can't deal with you at the minute,' she told him. 'I just can't.' She tried to stand up, but her legs felt as if they were made of jelly. She swayed, trying hard to stay upright and not actually pass out either. She dipped her head and ground her fists into her eyes. All she could see were the images that had flashed into her head. She'd never be able to prove it, though. Never. But she knew it was the truth.

She was aware of a quiet muttering sort of noise. She opened her eyes and saw Seb talking away to her. *Here we go again*, she thought angrily. She composed herself and focused on him. What on earth did he want now?

'Seb, slow it down, please,' she said unenthusiastically.

Seb stopped talking and his face darkened. 'I'm sick of repeating myself to you,' he said. 'That's the one thing that always bugs me. I came here to get you back. All I wanted was another chance. And maybe I was, well, *wrong* in some of the things I said and did. But we can all learn from our mistakes, can't we? Anyway, it's lucky for you I came up this way, isn't it? Before you bungee jumped off the cliff.'

'Enough!' snapped Becky. 'Look, Seb. I won't pretend that we didn't have some fun. We did. But you blew it. That thing with Abbie – the whole set of … *things* that led up to that. And what you just said there, about me bugging you and the things you said at the summer house. We've been through all this.' She pushed her hands into her pockets and met him directly with her gaze. 'Seb, I liked you. Yes, we did some good work together but when everything else happened I just knew it was no good. It would never work with us. At the end of the day, you just couldn't cope. And I would never, ever be able to let my guard down with you – and I can't live like that.'

Seb opened his mouth as if to defend himself, but he shut it again. Instead he shook his head and shrugged his shoulders. 'So that's it?' he asked. 'That's your choice? I liked you, Bex,' he said eventually.

He looked at her with that calculated Hugh Grant puppy dog eye thing which actually annoyed her all over again.

She shook her head. 'You're never going to like the whole of me,' said Becky. 'Let's just agree to leave it there, yes?'

Seb opened his mouth to respond, then he stopped and his attention was caught by something behind Becky. He looked startled, then confused, then all of a sudden he was on the ground; decked by a well-placed punch from Jon, who had come running up behind them.

'And stop bothering her!' yelled Jon, staring at Seb who was sitting on the ground looking, to Becky's eyes, comically shocked. Jon stood over him, breathing heavily and glaring at him.

'Jon, he's not bothering me!' said Becky. 'Honestly, it's fine. We're fine. We've had a chat.' She reached out and grabbed his arm. He was ready to land another punch, his fists were curling up. She tugged on his arm. 'Stop it. Right now,' she commanded.

Jon's eyes narrowed and he looked at Becky. 'Are you sure?' he asked. 'Really sure?'

'Really sure,' she said, looking directly into his eyes. They weren't exactly Jon's eyes for a moment. Then she blinked and the look had gone. 'Absolutely sure,' she said.

Then she couldn't help it. She swore later that it was the stress. She kind of spluttered, then she sniggered and then she started laughing; she was laughing so hard, that she had to bend double and try to catch her breath through it all.

'Oh, Jon, I'm sorry. I'm so sorry. I didn't … I didn't *hear* you sneak up …' And she was off again. She knew Jon must think her crazy, but she really didn't care. She was also aware of Seb clambering to his feet and dusting himself down, trying somehow to maintain his dignity.

Becky managed to stand upright and looked around as a hand rubbed her arm. Lissy was there, of course. She had obviously been given the coffees to hold as Jon hurtled up the cliff path to rescue Becky and was balancing the paper cups dangerously.

'I've never seen him do that before,' she said, leaning close to Becky. 'I didn't know he had it in him.'

'Me neither. But it's the best entertainment I've had all day,' murmured Becky. The girls stood together as Jon awkwardly held a hand out to Seb.

'Sorry, mate,' he said. 'Just thought, you know …'

'Yeah. No problem,' replied Seb, but he didn't take Jon's hand. 'Good luck with it all.'

'Thanks,' replied Jon.

Seb took a last look at Becky and nodded at her. 'Good luck. Whatever happens,' he said.

Becky knew those words were loaded and she felt herself

colour. 'Thanks, Seb,' she replied. 'Guess I'll see you around.'

Seb raised his hand in a goodbye and strode away along the cliff path, his shoulders set and angry-looking. The three of them watched him go.

'Well,' said Becky. 'That was exciting. Hopefully he got the message this time.' She turned to face the others. 'I think I know what happened with Ella. I'll tell you as soon as we get back to the studio.' She looked directly at Jon. 'Please? I have to get something and it's in my bag.'

'No problem,' said Jon. He looked faintly ridiculous. His dark hair was stuck up on end with the wind and he looked as shocked as Seb must have felt. 'I'm so sorry. I just don't know what happened there. He's lucky it was just the one punch – then sanity kind of took over. I could have kept going, I swear. Poor bloke.'

'I can probably help you with that one,' said Becky. She tried to tuck her hair behind her ear and gave up. She took hold of Jon's hand instead. 'He *is* lucky it stopped there. Come on. Let's go.'

'So this is where it's taken us,' said Jon, his arm wrapped protectively around Becky as the wind whipped up from the North Sea. They stood high up in St Mary's churchyard, overlooking the harbour and the pier.

'Or brought us back?' suggested Becky. 'We have to tell their story somehow. I think that's what they would have wanted, don't you? Why they looked for us? We're probably ideal candidates; words and pictures, and all that.'

They had been to the studio, and she had told Jon and Lissy what she had experienced on the cliff path. Everyone knew the story now, and both Jon and Becky, by mutual consent, felt the need to go back up on the cliffs. Lissy had graciously agreed to stay behind and man the studio. Or 'woman' it, as she told them. She was a girl of many talents.

Becky laughed nervously, now. 'I don't know. I'm more or less convinced we aren't reincarnations, but who knows? Maybe we just have to go with it. We'll soon find out if we're not meant to be together.'

'Always so glib,' said Jon, turning her around so she had no choice but to look at him. 'What makes you think we aren't meant to be together? I said I wanted a girl who loved Whitby as much as I do and I think I've found her. There's a perfect set-up in the flat for her to work from as well, so I don't know why she wouldn't want to come here. But if she wanted to stay in York, that's cool too. So long as she visited every so often.'

'I don't want to stay in York,' replied Becky. 'Not if you're here. I feel more at home here – with you. But things don't always work out the way you plan them, do they? That's all I'm saying.'

She dropped her gaze and stared at something apparently

by their feet. Jon put his finger under her chin and lifted her face up towards him.

He was smiling. 'Do you ever stop? The glib thing, I mean.'

Becky pulled a face. 'Not really. No. It's a defence mechanism, I suppose.' Again, the nervous laugh. 'You know, don't you? I wasn't sure. But you do. You've known for ages. You with your funny coloured eyes.' She raised a finger. 'One blue, one green. That's your genetic make-up. They make you *see* everything, don't they?'

'Heterochromia,' said Jon proudly. 'Supposed to have come down from someone on my mother's side, way back when. I like them.'

'I like them too,' said Becky. 'I was always jealous of Lissy's eyes. I used to want different coloured contact lenses so I looked like her.'

Jon laughed. 'Your eyes are perfect as they are. But it's your turn to talk,' he said. 'What's your story? What happened?'

Becky shrugged. 'About five years ago, I started to realise things weren't right. I had some hearing tests and I failed them about as spectacularly as Lissy failed her maths GCSE. All they could tell me was that it was probably congenital, just like Princess Alice. And then it just kept getting worse and worse. So I guess that's my genetic flaw. It's still getting worse and my hearing will probably go altogether, but nobody can tell me when; it's my own personal time bomb. But I've got no idea where it came from. And the thing is, if it's hereditary, then it could be passed down the generations. They think it was recessive in my case – it came out of nowhere. And something like that is so hard to tell someone. I wasted too much time with Seb. Do you know, one of the last things he said to me, before he went off with Abbie, was that he would never want children with me,

272

"just in case". And then, that night at the hotel, he told me I wouldn't be able to keep doing my job and I should stay with him to guarantee I could, because he would make sure everybody knew about me and I wouldn't get any more work. Which is clearly rubbish, but it did shake me up. And I needed you to know before we, well, before we took it any further. I'm a different person from when you knew me before, and I could never find the right moment to tell you. How did you know?'

'When you put your hair behind your ears at the studio, that first day when you saw the writing slope. You always put it behind your left one and sort of fluff it up over your right one.'

'Oh!' said Becky, surprised. 'I thought it was before that.'

Her mind went back to his light touches, seemingly to get her attention when they were in the crowd of people heading to the coffee shop and the studio. Her hand went up to her right ear and touched the tiny hearing aid that had been her lifeline for the last few years. It wasn't the one she had started the day with, though. That had fallen down the chasm of the cliff when she'd been hanging over it. Bloody typical. Just as well she had a spare one in her handbag. You just never knew when you'd need it.

'I've just got the one,' she said. 'It's no good having one in the other ear; no sound gets in there to amplify any more. It was difficult that night in the hotel – I raced into your room after the sand appeared without it.' *And the battery had been going that first day as well*, she remembered. Things hadn't been as clear as she would have liked – which had made Ella calling her name and the roll of thunder she heard even more disturbing. 'You seemed to know. You were dragging me around all that first morning.'

'More glibness. I don't know; I just knew I wanted you to come with me. I've missed you, Becky Jones. And I certainly wasn't dragging you,' said Jon, laughing. 'But I wonder if that's why Ella contacted you? She knew you would understand her; you'd understand what she went through.'

Becky shivered. 'Maybe. I've had it easier than her though. It's never stopped me doing anything I want to do. Fair enough, I can't lip-read four different languages like Princess Alice, but I get by on English. I've done what I can to learn sign language, just in case. And I can't play the piano. At all. Never have done.'

'Well, that's where I come in,' replied Jon. 'I'll be a bit rusty, but I could take it up again I guess.'

'If it's that bad, I'll take the hearing aid out,' said Becky. 'And make you practise finger spelling instead.' Then she remembered something else. 'Oh! Damn. Damn, damn and double damn!'

'What?' asked Jon, surprised.

'Adam's portrait. We never got a chance to look for it at Carrick Park. Bloody Seb.'

'Hey, don't worry. It's all taken care of,' said Jon with a smile. 'I did a little research of my own when I went back for the coffees. With all the excitement, I forgot to tell you. I called the hotel and said we,' he indicated both himself and Becky, 'were working on a project and I asked if they possibly had any pictures of Adam Carrick, the guy who lived there in the 1860s. They said there was an unnamed watercolour portrait in one of the corridors on the third floor in a stairwell – just a tiny thing, but they reckon, judging by his clothes, it was dated about that time. We'll have a look when we go back later and compare it with our photo. We'll see if it matches up. That's if you want to?'

'Want to?' said Becky. 'Why would I not want to go back there with you? I feel like it's our second home now.' She laughed, embarrassed, but was gratified to feel Jon's arms come around her and hold her tightly in agreement.

'Can't wait,' said Jon. 'And do you know what, just for the record, I don't care about it being congenital. If our children were …' His attention was suddenly caught by something over Becky's shoulder.

'What is it?' she asked, turning around. A girl was sitting on a bench overlooking the sea. It wasn't just any girl, though, Becky realised. It was the blonde girl from the Goth Weekend, the one who was following the funeral procession. Becky recognised the white dress and the neatly folded hands, only this time they were folded on her lap.

'It's her!' she said, breaking away from Jon. 'And I don't have my camera. Wait here – I need to speak to her.' She ran across the grass towards the girl, hoping she wouldn't get up and leave before Becky got there.

The girl remained motionless, still staring out to sea as Becky approached, breathing heavily and cursing her lack of fitness. 'Hey! Hey, excuse me!' Becky shouted, her voice carried away by the wind on the cliffs. She ran up to the bench and stopped.

The girl turned and looked Becky directly in the eyes. Becky's stomach flipped. The girl's face was instantly recognisable from the portrait in the hotel and the photograph. Becky stared back at her, frozen. 'Ella?' she managed.

The girl smiled at her and raised her right hand. She touched her fingers gently to her chin and then moved her hand forward and down. *Thank you.*

Becky instinctively signed back, holding her hands out, palm upwards and closing her fingers twice. *You're welcome.*

The girl nodded and looked over Becky's shoulder. She smiled and her fingers fluttered. *I have told you this before. He loves you very much.*

Becky turned to look at Jon who was leaning on the

railing, his attention on the sea waiting for her. She turned back to Ella, ready to respond. But the bench was empty.

Becky stood by the bench, staring at the spot where Ella had been sitting. She stood there long enough for Jon to come wandering over, bored of the sea and probably wondering why she was alone next to an empty bench. He took her hand and squeezed it.

'Didn't you catch her?' he asked.

'No, I did catch her,' said Becky.

'And? Did she say anything interesting?'

'Quite interesting,' said Becky. Some things were best kept quiet, she thought.

'I guess she was waiting for someone. I saw a man coming up the cliff path. He looked like he was heading her way,' said Jon. 'He seemed to be looking for someone.'

'Well, I hope they found each other,' said Becky.

'Me too. But seriously, after all your searching for her, you didn't manage to get a photograph of her?' persisted Jon.

'No,' repeated Becky. 'It's so maddening!'

'Well, it's just as well I took one then,' he said.

'Excuse me?' Becky stared at him.

Jon smiled and disengaged his hand from hers. He fumbled in his pocket and produced his mobile phone. 'It might not be the best shot in the world, but I got her,' he said.

'Let me see!' Becky had to stop herself from snatching the phone off him.

'Like I say, it's not brilliant, but she's there,' he said, his fingers swiping and tapping at the screen. 'I had a quick look. I was more interested in looking at you, though.'

Jon held the phone out and Becky eagerly took it from him. Sure enough, there was a picture of Becky running across the grass and the figure of the girl sitting on the bench, as solid as any real person might be.

'Ella,' she whispered. She couldn't stop staring at the picture. 'Jon, I know you hate digital photography, but can you bring yourself to do anything with this shot?' She looked at him, silently pleading.

'Of course I can,' he said, smiling down at her. 'I'll download her, crop her down, zoom in on her – whatever you want. I'll sharpen her up, bring her into focus. You want her for your article, yes?'

'No,' said Becky, looking back at the screen. 'I want her for a different project. I want to tell her story. Hers and Adam's.' She raised her head and met Jon's eyes. 'Will you help me?' she asked. 'You're part of it as well. Words and pictures, you know.'

Jon stared at her and the colour drained ever so slightly from his face. 'That was Ella?' he asked.

'It was Ella,' she confirmed. 'And the man on the cliff path you mentioned?' She didn't need to say anything else.

Jon truly blanched that time. 'Adam,' he said.

'More than likely,' she replied. 'We have to do it, Jon, we have to let people know the truth. We owe it to them. After all,' she pressed the phone back into his hand, letting her own hand linger in his afterwards, 'it's our story as well. Sort of.'

'But I suspect we will have a happier ending,' he said, leaning down to kiss her.

'I hope so,' she said, lifting her face to meet his.

And for the last time, she heard that voice in her head. *We were always together*, it told her, *and so it will be again.*

About the Author

Kirsty Ferry is from the North East of England and lives there with her husband and son. She won the English Heritage/Belsay Hall National Creative Writing competition in 2009 and has had articles and short stories published in *The People's Friend*, *The Weekly News*, *It's Fate*, *Vintage Script*, *Ghost Voices* and *First Edition*. Her work also appears in several anthologies, incorporating such diverse themes as vampires, crime, angels and more.

Kirsty loves writing ghostly mysteries and interweaving fact and fiction. The research is almost as much fun as writing the book itself, and if she can add a wonderful setting and a dollop of history, that's even better.

Her day job involves sharing a building with an eclectic collection of ghosts, which can often prove rather interesting.

Some Veil Did Fall is Kirsty's debut novel with Choc Lit.

www.twitter.com/Kirsticupcake
www.rosethornpress.co.uk
www.facebook.com/pages/Kirsty-Ferry-Author

More from Choc Lit

If you enjoyed Kirsty's story, you'll enjoy the rest of our selection. Here's a sample:

Impossible Things
Kate Johnson

Are they Cursed as well as Chosen?

Ishtaer is a mystery. A blind slave, beaten and broken by her sadistic mistress, with no memory of a time before her enslavement.

Kael Vapensigsson is one of the elite Chosen – a Warlord whose strength comes from the gods themselves. But despite all his power and prestige, he is plagued by a prophecy that threatens to destroy everything he loves. When Kael summons Ishtaer to his room and discovers the marks of the Chosen on her body, including the revered mark of the Warrior, both Warlord and slave seem to have met their match.

But as their lives become increasingly entangled and endangered, Ishtaer is forced to test whether the Chosen ever have the ability to choose their own fate.

Visit www.choc-lit.com for more details including the first two chapters and reviews, or simply scan barcode using your mobile phone QR reader.

The Silent Touch of Shadows

Christina Courtenay

Festival of Romance

Winner of the 2012 Best Historical Read from the Festival of Romance

What will it take to put the past to rest?

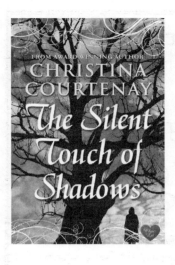

Professional genealogist Melissa Grantham receives an invitation to visit her family's ancestral home, Ashleigh Manor. From the moment she arrives, life-like dreams and visions haunt her. The spiritual connection to a medieval young woman and her forbidden lover have her questioning her sanity, but Melissa is determined to solve the mystery.

Jake Precy, owner of a nearby cottage, has disturbing dreams too, but it's not until he meets Melissa that they begin to make sense. He hires her to research his family's history, unaware their lives are already entwined. Is the mutual attraction real or the result of ghostly interference?

A haunting love story set partly in the present and partly in fifteenth century Kent.

Visit www.choc-lit.com for more details including the first two chapters and reviews, or simply scan barcode using your mobile phone QR reader.

CLAIM YOUR FREE EBOOK

of

Some Veil Did Fall

You may wish to have a choice of how you read *Some Veil Did Fall*. Perhaps you'd like a digital version for when you're out and about, so that you can read it on your ereader, iPad or even a Smartphone. For a limited period, we're including a **FREE** ebook version along with this paperback.

To claim, simply visit ebooks.choc-lit.com or scan the QR Code.

You'll need to enter the following code:

Q271408

This offer will expire October 2015. Supported ebook formats listed at www.choc-lit.com. Only one copy per paperback/customer is permitted and must be claimed on the purchase of this paperback. This promotional code is not for resale and has no cash value; it will not be replaced if lost or stolen. We withhold the right to withdraw or amend this offer at any time. Further terms listed at www.choc-lit.com.

Introducing Choc Lit

We're an independent publisher creating
a delicious selection of fiction.
Where heroes are like chocolate – irresistible!
Quality stories with a romance at the heart.
See our selection here:
www.choc-lit.com

We'd love to hear how you enjoyed *Some Veil Did Fall*.
Please visit our website and give your feedback.

Choc Lit novels are selected by genuine readers like yourself.
We only publish stories our Choc Lit Tasting Panel want to
see in print. Our reviews and awards speak for themselves.

Could you be a Star Selector and join our Tasting Panel?
Would you like to play a role in choosing which novels
we decide to publish? Do you enjoy reading romance
novels? Then you could be perfect for our Choc Lit
Tasting Panel. Visit our website for more details.

Keep in touch:
Sign up for our monthly newsletter Choc Lit Spread for
all the latest news and offers: www.spread.choc-lit.com.
Follow us on Twitter: @ChocLituk and Facebook: Choc Lit.

Or simply scan barcode using your mobile phone QR reader:

Choc Lit
Spread

Twitter

Facebook